VII
AN ADVENT

VILA
AN ADVENTURE STORY

Sarah Baylis

BRILLIANCE BOOKS

Published by Brilliance Books 1984
Copyright © Sarah Baylis 1984

BRILLIANCE BOOKS
14 CLERKENWELL GREEN
London EC1

ISBN 0 946189 90 6 (paperback)
ISBN 0 946189 95 1 (hardback)

Typeset by M.C. Typeset, Chatham, Kent
Printed and bound in Great Britain by
Nene Litho and Woolnough Bookbinding,
both of Wellingborough, Northants

CONTENTS

'When a maiden drowned – either by accident or on purpose – she became a Rusalka. This belief was common to all Slavonic peoples. But the image of this water divinity was not everywhere the same. One could say that she varied according to climate and the colour of the sky and the waters. Among the Slavs of the 'blue' Danube the Rusalka – who in this case was called Vila – was a gracious being who retained some of her maidenly charm. Among the Northern Russians the gracious, gay and charming Rusalki (plural of Rusalka) of the Danube and the Dnieper were transformed into wicked girls, of unattractive appearance, with wild, uncombed and dishevelled hair . . .'

Larousse Encyclopedia of Mythology

PART ONE

Prologue

No one in the village knew where the forest ended. Hunters had travelled many miles in all directions but when they came back they spoke only of the endless forest. They returned full of stories of danger – of mighty rivers choked by fallen timber that would crush a man and his horse if they ventured too near, of places where the ground was covered so thickly with pine needles that at first it seemed like heaven, until the horse was up to its neck in the soft stuff and both horse and man felt a surge of panic as they struggled to free themselves.

The men sat together and laughed loudly and bravely about the perils of the forest. The stories of each returning hunter were more alarming than the last, but they seemed to laugh away the fear. But sometimes at night these brave men would confide in each other about the even greater terrors of the forest, the things they had heard and seen while wrapped in their blankets beside the tiny fires that did nothing but show how endlessly black and alive were the mighty woods. These night-time terrors were spoken of in quiet voices, there was less laughter. Every man who had spent one of those nights out in the woods knew of the feeling that started with an innocent thought: 'What was that noise?' 'Did something move over there?' This feeling would grow until the whole endless night became one great fear, and men who had never been known to run from bear or wild boar would curl themselves closer and closer to the flanks of their horses in a vain attempt to remember that they were brave.

So no one knew if the forest ever ended at all. There were two other small villages further on up the river, but that was all. People just supposed that the forest went on and on until the Earth ended. And naturally, over the years, these men – as men always do – discovered or invented explanations for these terrors. Perhaps they were not alone in the great forest. Perhaps, out there, lived all sorts of strange people – spirits, gods . . . witches.

1   The Village

On the outskirts of the village stood a small wooden house. In the yard in front of the house stood a girl with a large basket of washing. On the day before Nina's fifteenth birthday, she had been sent outside to do the laundry. She was furious about it.

'It's the day before my birthday, for God's sake,' she wailed at the big broad-faced woman who was bending over a fire, stirring soap in an iron pot slung over the embers. Her mother did not answer but Nina saw her mouth become a harsh line in her face, and although she knew she was asking for trouble, she continued in her complaint: 'Mother, please let me have the day off. I've got to finish sewing that dress for tomorrow. I'll do the washing later. I'm going to be fifteen; it's important.'

'Not as important as getting those clothes washed. You can sew this evening,' was the reply. 'Now go.' Nina's mother was a heavy woman, and her voice was heavy too. She was slow in her movements, but her temper was quick, and her tongue could be sharp. 'And make sure you do it properly. Here, take this.' She handed her daughter a small pail of freshly made soap.

Nina stood staring angrily at her mother. She wanted to

say more, but she feared the consequences. Her mother glanced up at her and uttered the warning that followed the village children wherever they went: 'And be careful of the river.'

Nina fastened her long sandy hair more firmly on top of her head and wrapped the cotton shawl once more about it, tying it at the nape of her neck. Boiling with anger, she took the basket of washing and the pail of slimy soap and set off down the path that ran between the village and the beginning of the tall trees.

Her mother mopped her face and watched her go. She sighed. She could still remember feeling the same way herself – it was not so many years ago, after all – but that did not make it easier to tolerate the behaviour of her wayward girl. What use was one lazy daughter, with a husband and a houseful of grown sons to look after? Sighing again, she turned back to stir the soap.

Nina walked slowly, her anger holding her back. The path was muddy and soon her new leather shoes were covered. She knew she should have worn her wooden shoes, but she thought she might meet someone. She knew exactly whom she meant by 'someone'. A group of young men from the next village had come to help with the harvest, and for the last week Nina and her friends had been discussing ways of how to meet them. As yet they had had no luck. The men were busy with the crops, and the girls had been kept at home to thresh the corn, preserve fruit and look after the children while their mothers helped in the fields. But Nina dreamed of a chance encounter with one of these young men, and so she had been taking care to look her best.

Part of her was angry with herself for caring what anyone thought of her – she was so obviously different from the rest, more interesting, more clever; and yet part of her was desperate at the thought that she might be seen as different. She did not understand how she could feel both things at the same time.

In the last year she had swung wildy between feeling incredibly happy and desperately sad, with no halfway house between the two. When she felt happy it seemed as if somewhere in her chest was a spring of fresh water bubbling up, or that a bird had got caught inside her and was beating its wings to escape. When she felt sad everything that had looked clear and beautiful suddenly became dreary and oppressive, people who had seemed to love and appreciate her were suddenly laughing at her, thinking her stupid and ugly. When she felt like this the bird inside her went away and in its place was a leaden weight so heavy she could hardly move her feet, and instead of running around laughing and singing, all she wanted to do was lie on her bed, curled up, so she could no longer feel that dreadful weight.

Her mother called her 'moody'. 'It's your age, love,' she said, when she had time to talk. Whether she was happy or sad, Nina's father just said the same thing: 'Behave yourself, you stupid girl.' Nina's brothers too said this to her and laughed, pleased to imitate their father; they were far older than Nina – she was the youngest, and the only girl. Once, when Nina had been more moody than usual, her father had put his arm round her shoulders and said: 'Don't worry, it'll all be over soon – you'll soon be settled.' She had not known what he meant but it comforted her to feel his concern, although she could not believe that these feelings would ever subside. After this her father had walked off; he had said nothing since.

The girls in Nina's village were married early. They usually went from their father's house to their husband's by the time they had reached their seventeenth year. It had always been so. They spent their early years learning the things that women must know – the care of the house, the making of clothes and the preparing of food. Some of Nina's friends had already had matches made for them by their families. Next spring Masha, Nina's closest friend, would go along the river to the next village, two days' journey through the woods, to live with her new husband. When Nina had heard the news she had cried all afternoon. She felt that Masha was being taken away from her; it seemed so unfair that they would no longer be able to spend time together – laughing, talking and making up stories. But a part of her had been envious because she wished that it was she who could be moving to a new place. Part of her longed for people to know that she was wanted by someone.

As Nina continued along the path towards the river she looked about her at the village that was all that she had ever known. Nothing ever changed here. In winter the valley was white with snow for four months – nothing to see but columns of grey smoke rising from the roof of every house, the steamy breath of the horses as they ploughed heavily through the deep drifts. In spring the grass began to show through the snow, brilliantly green and covered with small fragile flowers; spring was time of hope, and sometimes of hunger. The villagers looked anxiously at the river when, swollen by the thaw, it began a furious escape from its broken banks.

Now, in late summer, the fields around the village were deep gold where the wheat still stood, a smudgy ochre where it had already been harvested. The gardens around the houses were full of vegetables of all sorts and the village animals grazed sleepily in the sun. It had been a good summer – enough rain and plenty of strong sunshine – the villagers were well pleased. It had been a heavy rain during the night that had turned the packed earth to mud and had threatened to flatten the crops. The river had risen a few inches and was flowing fast. Many of the younger boys had taken advantage of this and gone further up the river to where the fishing was best. They fished from the banks, taking care not to venture in. This river was their greatest fear. No villager could cross it or navigate it. It claimed lives. For as many years as could be remembered, men had merely fished from its banks, keeping a safe distance. In time the villagers had forgotten that it had ever been used to travel upon, or to play in. The only creatures that went *in* the river were the ghosts from the fairy-tales they told.

Nina soon reached Masha's house which stood close by the river – but far enough from its grassy shore to escape the spring floods. Shifting her basket from one hip to the other she looked to see if Masha was there. All she could see were a few muddy chickens scraping hopefully at the ground around the door. The house stood open, the door propped open by a heavy wooden table upon which was piled the household linen. The bedding was being aired, quilts and sheets draped over chairs standing in the sun. Glancing down at her feet, Nina noticed a small wooden bowl full of soupy green liquid – fern tea to pacify the Kikimora spirit and to keep the luck in the house. The newly polished horseshoe nailed above the doorway and the grotesque goblin doorknocker both glinted in the sun. Masha's family had taken precautions to avoid disaster.

The big hunting dog had been tied up behind the house but it had sensed Nina's approach and started to bark hoarsely. Nina could imagine the animal throwing his weight against the chain that kept him tied all day. Masha's elder brother was coming round the side of the house to see who was there. A big handsome boy of eighteen, he sauntered in the way of young men, as if his legs were somehow more loosely attached to his body than those of other people. Nina lowered her eyes and stared at her shoes.

'I suppose you're looking for Masha?' said the boy, and Nina could feel his young man's stare upon her and wondered why she did not like it. She had known Vanya all her life and yet recently she disliked him. She had begun to feel this way about almost all the young men in the village;

they were so different from the boys in the other village whom she had once seen laughing and joking and playing around. One of them had shouted something to her, she had not heard what it was, but he had waved. She hurried home, and remembered the wave and, at times, if she was lucky, caught a flash of his face behind her closed eyelids. When this happened, the bird inside her chest gave a great beat of its wings, leaving her feeling almost sick.

'Just look at your shoes,' said Vanya and laughed.

Nina's lowered face burnt with fury and embarrassment; she pulled the shawl closer about her as if to hide behind it. She stared at her muddy feet, but she did not see them.

'She's down by the river, doing washing,' the boy said, taking her blush as maidenly shame. Really, he thought, Nina's becoming quite a nice girl.

Nina murmured her thanks and turned away. Her heart thumped crossly inside her as she walked down the path and, passing under the first tall trees, she strode down the slope that led to the wide green river.

2 The Washing Platform

Nina could see Masha sitting on the small wooden platform where the women did the washing. She was pleased that there was no one else about. The sun was now high in the sky and as the strong sunlight filtered through the trees it warmed the rain-soaked earth and filled the air with the rich smell of pine. The air was loud with birds and she could hear the tentative tapping of a woodpecker coming from across the river. She loved the woodpeckers because of their shyness, the way they whisked out of sight as soon as you set eyes upon them. Once, as a very little girl, she had been given a toy woodpecker that her father had carved from a piece of oak. When she pulled a string, the little bird had tapped at its tree. She had loved it.

As her eyes searched the trees for a glimpse of the creature, a magpie flew out of the shadows and away downstream, its vivid black-and-white plumage vibrant against the green leaves and dappled water.

'One for sorrow . . .' murmured Nina automatically, and she touched her forehead. But then another magpie appeared and followed the first down the river until it too vanished amid the shadows. Nina laughed and her heart immediately lifted, all traces of irritation disappearing. She ran the rest of the way down the path, the washing basket bumping against her legs.

Masha was sitting with her red dress pulled over her knees and her brown feet dangling in the water. She had managed to finish half the washing and this had been spread over the bushes to dry in the sun. But it seemed that she had lost interest and as Nina walked up she was dangling her feet and staring across the river at the dark, tangled bank opposite. She turned as she heard Nina's footsteps, the cracking twigs sounding loud in the echoing forest.

'Oh, good, it's you,' she said, her brown eyes squinting up at Nina.

Nina put her basket on the grass and sat down beside Masha. She did not dangle her feet but, sitting cross-legged, she took off her ruined shoes and started to clean them.

If anyone had been on the opposite bank they would have seen the two girls sitting close together. Beneath them were their reflections, clear in the fast-flowing river. After the rain the water was so deep that there was no ripple to disturb its green surface.

Of the two girls, Masha seemed the more striking. Tall – too tall for her own liking – she had big, long bones, and muscles strengthened by years of the hard work involved in looking after the needs of a large demanding family. Her mother was a tiny person, not strong, and weakened by the long succession of hard deliveries of her seven children. Masha, being the eldest girl, had had to do much heavy work as a young child. Despite her size, Masha's face was delicate and unusual, with a low brow that was emphasized by the way she wore her black hair, scraped back into several beaded plaits that hung down on her shoulders. She had cast off her shawl and was letting the sun shine full upon her skin.

Nina was very different; shorter and rounder than Masha, she had a face that people tended to forget – until they remembered the way she laughed, the way her green eyes narrowed and she shouted her laughter, changing suddenly into someone both infectious and intriguing. Neither she nor Masha were at all happy with the way they looked, though each thought the other very beautiful.

'Where are the others?' asked Nina. It was unusual for the washing platform to be so empty. Washing days were an occasion for village women to gather together to talk and to exchange news.

Masha ignored Nina's question. Instead she said: 'It's your birthday tomorrow, isn't it?'

'That's right.' Nina smiled happily.

'You'll be the same age as me again.' Masha's birthday was in the middle of winter, so she was six months older than Nina.

'Mmm,' said Nina, working on her shoes.

'Guess what; there's going to be a dance tomorrow – if they finish the barley. And you'll be allowed to go 'cos you'll be fifteen. That's where everyone else is. They're cooking for tomorrow, and getting the barn ready.'

This was news indeed. Girls younger than fifteen could not attend the village dances but had to make do with gazing from the outskirts and being shooed away by the older women.

'Oh God, what'll I wear? Look at my shoes. Do you think *he*'ll be there? I'll die if he is. Is Vanya going?' Nina felt a mixture of excitement and apprehension. Although she had always been one of the loudest and most confident girls of the village in the past, she felt overwhelmed with shyness at the thought of being looked at, not as a little girl any longer, but as a young woman. Masha's news had thrown her into a panic.

'Oh, Vanya will be there all right, and, guess what, so will *he*.'

'He' meant different things to each girl. Nina had been thinking of the young man who had waved at her from the

13

barley field, but Masha meant the man whom she was to go and be wife to next year. They both fell silent. Nina was busy thinking happily about her first dance. Masha was thinking very different thoughts.

She had met her intended bridegroom only once before and had been sorely disappointed. Like Nina she had imagined that the men from the other villages were somehow different from those of her own. When her father had told her of the match, he had described a man who, ten years older than Masha, was kind, attractive, a good hunter and farmer, and a successful artist – the most highly thought of in his village. Masha's mind had taken this information and had developed for itself the image of a beautiful man, sensitive, intuitive, who would admire her for her own sensitivity, who would understand and respect her deep love of nature, the strange empathy with birds and trees that made her mind a whirl of huge ideas and beautiful pictures.

They would talk deeply about all these things, they would share these feelings, learn from each other. And, above all, he would allow her to paint her own pictures. Both of them would be artists in their own right but, loving one another, they would learn much, the work of each benefiting from the union.

The day that Masha had met Ivan she realized what she had done. Here was a man who was all that her father had said. But he was a stranger to her. And while they talked (her father keeping them in sight at all times) she had discovered that she found him rather dull. To be sure, what man could come up to the image that had evolved in her mind?

'There will be the animals to look after,' he had said, 'and the cooking, of course. But you're used to working hard, and I know you're a sensible girl.' He was obviously pleased with her, and did not seem to notice how Masha's face had fallen at the mention of cooking. (She had been too frightened to tell him of the burnt cooking pots and ruined meals that had punctuated her life, usually occasioned by her rushing outside to draw some weird and fantastic design on a piece of hide or bark.) Eventually, summoning all her courage, she had spoken to him of her love of drawing and painting and her need to express herself in pictures.

'You can teach me how to do people,' she had said, pointing to a large hanging that Ivan was in the process of completing. 'I can't draw people moving at all.' The hanging was a hunting scene, full of little figures – traditional, stylized – in truth, Masha found it rather lifeless.

'Yes, my dear,' Ivan had said, his voice kind and steady. 'You're bound to be a great help to me, you know. There's so much work to be done – more than I can cope with.'

'Oh, I want to work,' said Masha. 'We'd be a team, then there'd be more time to experiment, to find new pictures, new designs . . .' she looked at the man hopefully, but she dreaded his reply.

'Yes, a team. You can help me mix my paints, wash brushes, prepare the hides; you'll be invaluable. You can even help colour in some of my pictures,' he added generously. 'Of course, there won't be much time for you to do many pictures of your own. There's the farm work to be done as well and . . .' Ivan blushed slightly and looked down at his paint-stained hands, 'and there might soon be children.'

Masha's heart had sunk lower and lower as he spoke. She was to be his helper, to keep his home, and to encourage and praise him in his endeavours; but she was not to expect the same care from him. Why, she wondered, could he not feel that she too needed a partner who would help and encourage her. Her dream of a person who would be like a second part of her soul seemed to melt away as Ivan's kindly voice droned on. She saw herself instead as a good home-maker (she had always been that), a woman who was efficient by sheer effort and will as opposed to love of what she did. She saw the babies begin to arrive, a joy at first, but then a terrible drain on her energy. Masha knew of babies and what they demanded: eldest daughter, the care of the little ones had quickly passed from her ailing mother to her. She saw what she knew to be true: that happiness for her as Ivan's wife would come from learning to be pleased by *his* achievements, and not her own.

These were deep thoughts for a girl of fifteen. Most girls thought her lucky and envied her lot. Many of her friends – perhaps even Nina, she thought sadly – would be glad to be in her place. Why did she feel so differently?

'I wish I was a boy,' she said, breaking the silence.

Nina laughed and rolled her eyes. 'You'd be hopeless. All that hunting. You're far too dreamy.'

Masha sighed. Nina spoke the truth. Boys felt differently. Their life was one of bravery and great feats of skill and daring; the thrill of chasing creatures through the forest, the joy of the kill, the feeling of contentment as they slapped each other on the back and boasted happily of their courage. If they were not like this naturally they got teased and bullied into becoming so.

'Like poor Tomilin,' she said.

Masha's younger brother, a quiet and humorous boy, was a young man who hated the chase. But he would be made into a hunter – or suffer the scorn and contempt of the village.

'I'll wear my black dress,' decided Nina, fiddling with her sandy curls and wrinkling her nose thoughtfully. She excelled at needlework and was just finishing embroidering designs upon a dress that her mother had helped her make. She had an enormous patience with her sewing that Masha could not comprehend. Sewing made Nina feel calm and contented, as if the whole world was centred on her careful needle. This feeling of concentration had been a great comfort to her in the last turbulent year.

'I don't want to go to the dance at all,' said Masha. 'I don't want to see Ivan . . . I don't see why we have to get married anyway. Why do we have to go off and be wives to these people just when life is beginning to get interesting?'

Nina looked up, surprised at her friend's outburst. Questioning the way things were never did any good.

'You're mad!' she exclaimed. 'Ivan's nice – you said so. You're going to the other village – you're so lucky. Ivan's different; at least you don't have to marry anyone here . . . you're mad.'

She really did think Masha was mad. Nina was less in the habit of thinking things through. Her own discontents she put down to her plainness and stupidity. 'I feel the same way sometimes, but if I could meet someone different like you did, everything would be wonderful.'

'But he's not different. I thought he would be, but he's not; he's just the same.' Masha paused. She gazed at the deep green water, her eyes followed the flow of the current as it rushed south. Every now and then a large branch, even a whole tree, floated swiftly by and she watched such a one until it disappeared round the curve of the river.

'If only there was a place where people could do what they wanted. Suppose we could go somewhere we'd be free to do anything we liked . . . I could paint huge beautiful pictures and you'd make wonderful clothes for everyone that lived there.' Masha threw her arms out expansively as if to show Nina this place free from oppressive traditions, where one could follow one's own wishes.

Nina narrowed her green eyes and chuckled.

Masha sighed and kicked her feet in the water. She looked sideways at Nina and said wistfully: 'I'll miss you dreadfully. I wish you could come too. Then we could still have adventures.' She paused, and then said thoughtfully: 'I don't feel ready to be grown up.'

Nina snorted and looked at her scornfully. 'Oh, what rubbish! I wish I could go. I'm sick of being a child.'

Masha laughed and pulled her feet from the water. Leaping

17

up, she began to dance and spin on the little wooden platform. The hot sun was beating down, the birds were loud in the trees, and she seemed to be dancing out the longing for freedom that she could not find words for. Nina, howling with laughter, began to chant the words of an old ballad familiar to all the village children:

'Dance Rusalka . . . dirty hunter,
Queen of witches, man-eater,
Tree-dweller, water-walker.
Dance Rusalka, dance Rusalka . . .'

The rhythm of the words thudded in Masha's head as she spun faster and faster, her plaits flying against her face, her skirts swirling about her brown feet. She could almost feel the liberation that she longed for, the flight of a bird through the echoing blue air.

Nina, clapping her hands in admiration of her friend's wild dance, saw Masha's feet suddenly and sickeningly slip on the shiny wood. Her stomach lurched and she opened her mouth to shout a warning as Masha flew backwards through the air towards the rushing river. There was a huge splash as Masha hit the water and disappeared below its smooth green surface.

3   The River

'Masha . . . Masha . . . Masha!'

Nina was screaming at the impassive face of the water. Masha was nowhere to be seen. Nina gazed desperately down the river, scanning the water with her eyes . . . nothing. The forest around her had become deadly quiet, the birds were listening too. But Nina's ears were deafened by a roaring in her head – the sound of panic and despair.

Then suddenly, further down the river, she saw Masha's black head appear above the surface. Nina's eyes, keen with anguish, saw Masha's mouth open in a desperate attempt to breathe.

'Don't go down, don't go down,' Nina urged hoarsely – not screaming now. She saw her friend collide heavily with a huge tree stump around which she managed to throw her arms. Nina's eyes followed the black dot clinging to the stump. Then the river swept round the bend and Nina was alone.

Her heart beat sickly in her breast, her hands were clenched in the folds of her dress. She had never felt such pain as this, or such helplessness. Moaning feverishly she again scanned the bland surface of the water. A jumble of broken branches and tree stumps was floating towards her. She looked up the river, down the river, back up the slope to the village. Her body was tense and trembling. The jumble of drifting wood was coming nearer, she stared at it until she felt that her eyes would burst from her head. Then, just as the tangled mass was about to rush past, Nina took a deep breath and hurled herself into the water. Spluttering and choking, she grabbed hold of the nearest branch.

The shock of the water was dreadful. Even in the height of summer this river was never warm. But it was not the cold that Nina so dreaded, it was the actual feeling of being totally below the water – in the river – this huge, violent thing that she knew had claimed the lives of many of the village people in the past. It was an element completely foreign to her. She knew the river as one knows the wind and the snow, and yet no one who lived in the village would ever have dreamed of venturing into it. It was forbidden to do so. It was witchcraft to do so. They may fish for food from its banks, they may wash their clothes in it, and yet they must fear it as they would fear the wild animals.

Deep and wide, the river formed a fearsome boundary for the villagers – they could never cross its lethal width. Had they dared to, they would not have known how. They feared it as they feared the forest. Like the great woods it was a place of unseen terrors, inhabited by weird and deadly creatures. Most loathsome of all these river-dwellers were the dreadful Rusalki, sometimes as beautiful as the moonlight, sometimes resembling the drowned corpses that were their food and their sustenance. If a person fell into the river and was washed away the villagers knew that the Rusalki had claimed another victim for their own.

As Nina clung terrified to the jumble of wood she felt all these inherited fears wash over her. The impulse to save a loved one had, for a second, made her forget the certain victory to be claimed by the river and by its eerie inhabitants. In a moment of desperation she had made her suicidal leap and at the same time had broken the most total taboo of her childhood. For Nina to enter the river in any manner meant certain death or, worse, abduction by the fiendish water-spirits, the dead things that dwelt in green trees and green waters. As she was swept round the curve of the river she was yelping hysterically, like a small beast caught in a trap with no escape. She was certain that at any second she would feel the arms of Rusalka wrap themselves round her legs and begin to pull her down into the cold brown depths of the river. As she clung even more tightly to the branch she took great gulps of the sweet summer air, expecting every mouthful to be her last. In this fashion the girl was swept along, almost unconscious from shock and fear, while all round her the life of the forest continued as if nothing untoward had occurred within its vast expanse.

As the seconds passed the black fog of fear began to clear enough for her to see the futility of her leap from the bank. What was the use of them both dying? Why had she done it? What use would her death be? She shouldn't die, it wasn't fair; she began to cry pitifully. Her hair, smeared across her face, was getting into her mouth and it was perhaps this minor irritation, together with the basic human desire to have one's death justified in some way, that caused Nina to begin to feel that even more powerful human emotion, the determination to survive.

Minutes had passed since that fatal jump and yet she was still alive, no one had claimed her; the river, though determined to end her life, had not yet done so.

Nina cautiously shook her head to free her eyes and mouth of the lank strands of hair. Clutching the branch even more tightly she raised her head and looked around her. What she saw smote her with a feeling that she could not comprehend. On either side huge trees rose towering into the sky, great rocks formed banks that tumbled down to the water, shedding long grey reflections across its surface. The river, with a gentleness and steadiness that she would not have believed, was bearing Nina through a place that no one had seen before.

Although the trees that crowded the banks were the same as those she knew in the village, they were not the same. In the village she had known every tree, every branch, the shape each twig had made against the sky. But here she was seeing new trees, stronger, taller than those with which she had been so familiar. No man had ever come here with an axe, no path had ever been hacked through these colossal woods.

The sense of wonder that swept Nina as, wet and bedraggled, she was borne through this new land, gave her a growing feeling of strength and determination. Every second that she remained alive made her feel more confident of surviving this ordeal. As she looked about her she had time to examine the banks in great detail. Above the sound of the water she could hear the raucous sound of the birds, the rush of the wind through the trees – her eyes took in the new sights and colours as if they had never truly been seen before. On the opposite bank she saw a small deer drinking; as she was carried past the creature raised its delicate head to gaze at her with steady black eyes. She had never seen a deer so close before and the fearlessness with which it beheld her seemed to add to her own growing courage.

Feeling by this time almost brave, Nina looked ahead down the river. It had become perceptibly wider, the distance between the two banks was growing. The rocks on the banks were smaller, sometimes giving way to small beaches of shingle. Here and there where the banks were gentler and less rocky stood ancient willows, dipping the tips of their yellow branches into the water. As the river grew wider, so its progress grew less rapid, and as it began turning sharply to the right, the collection of forest debris to which Nina clung began to drift slightly nearer the bank.

More long minutes passed and Nina, still gazing ahead, saw that as the river flowed round the bend it once more became narrower and more swift; the water tumbling over the rocks up ahead was white with spray. Turning her gaze to the bank she saw that the trees had ended and on either side huge cliffs of rock towered over her. The late summer sun could no longer reach the river and the water had become grey and menacing. Then, as fear threatened once more to overwhelm her, Nina was thrown sharply over the branch to which she clung. The mass of timber had drifted closer to the bank and now was beginning to jam among the rocks. Holding on for her life, she felt her wits sharpening and before the current could move her on, she flung herself towards the bank, grabbing the nearest big rock and pulling herself over it.

She lay quite still for many minutes. The feel of the solid rock beneath her was delightful to both her mind and her body. Exhausted and aching she wept with relief, her eyes closed. But quite soon she began to feel an intense cold creeping over her in this sunless place. A wind was coming over the water and slashing through her sodden clothes. Without knowing what to do, she got up and started stumbling through the shallow water among the rocks and over the shingle at the water's edge. She continued in this dazed fashion for the best part of an hour, by which time the sun had gone and the shadows on the river were long and black.

As she staggered over the shingle, Nina's mind was a blank. She focused on each heavy step forward, mindful that if she began to think, the black fear that surged within would swiftly overwhelm her, and she would be left shrieking and helpless as the night closed in. Her wet dress hampered every step, its black folds clinging like stone about her aching feet. Her long hair clung wet and slimy about her face, but she left it there, too fearful to pause for a second in her progress.

Above the sound of the roaring rapids she could hear the first calls of an owl, hidden in the trees far above her. As night fell she had managed to get only about a quarter of a mile further down the river. Resting for a moment, she saw before her a huge tangle of fallen timber that had been thrown to the bank by the angry river as it surged through the rocks and shallows.

Making her way towards it with a vague idea of finding shelter and maybe making a fire, she glimpsed a splash of red among the branches. Without thinking she stumbled up to it and then, as she looked down, her heart began beating faster; below her, sodden and bedraggled in her red dress, lay Masha.

4 Fire and Fog

Nina had to shake Masha for several minutes before she could get her to open her eyes. She was bruised, sodden and shocked, and had swallowed a large quantity of water during her trip down the river; but she was alive, and that both girls had survived seemed, to Nina, a miracle. She was filled with purpose as she roused Masha, got her sitting up and proceeded to gather dry wood for a fire. This was the first priority, even before talking, as Masha was shaking with cold.

However, to light the fire was not such an easy task. Nina had a pouch with flint and tinder, but the tinder was wet and the grass and leaves under the trees had been soaked by the dew. As Nina desperately searched for dry material she cursed the way she had taken for granted something as basic as fire – and not just fire for heat, but for light also. It was now almost totally dark – the massive trees formed a black temple behind them, before them lay the murmuring ebony river.

At last Nina succeeded in getting a spark to catch a wisp of grass. She added more dry leaves and then some twigs. Her hands were steady as she cautiously created this tiny fire. Forcing herself to be patient, she added larger and larger twigs. At last the fire was big enough for her to add some more sizeable branches that had been rotted by the river water and then dried by the sun. The first suddenly burst into life, shedding light all about. Huge shadows towered over the cold bedraggled girls, but the area about the fire seemed to become a real haven of warmth and comfort.

Masha, rousing herself at last, staggered towards the flames, her dress, still sodden, clinging about her legs. Her voice was small and scared: 'I'm so cold, Nina, I'm so cold. How will I ever get warm?'

'We must dry our clothes,' replied Nina. 'We'll never get warm wearing these things.' She herself, having had something to do, had forgotten how chilled she was. 'Get undressed, we'll dry everything out – we can't be colder with no clothes on.'

Masha's fingers were frozen and useless. It was Nina who carefully unbuttoned her and pulled her out of her clothes. She pushed Masha closer to the fire and then, gathering a handful of leaves and grass, started to rub Masha's body vigorously, like a tired horse. She saw Masha's skin gradually turn rosy, losing the blue and ivory hue of intense cold. With Masha beginning to warm up, she stripped off her own soggy clothes and did the same to herself, cursing her long hair which, dripping and tangled, clung icily about her.

'We'll get warm and then tomorrow we'll find our way back,' she said and, indeed, the comfort of Masha's presence and the now roaring fire had filled her with optimism. She felt vital and alive . . . and hungry.

'I'm starving – we'll just have to wait till we get back. We can't catch anything. I wish I knew how to fish.'

They were soon to find out how ill-equipped they were for adventure, with inadequate clothes, no supplies or tools for hunting – and only one pair of impractical shoes between them. (Masha's wooden clogs sat, presumably, on the washing platform back at the village.) But now, as night fell finally about them, both girls were grateful for the fire, and this seemed the only thing that was important. They stretched out luxuriously in front of the leaping flames, casting shy looks at each other's body. They had never seen each other with no clothes on before. In fact, they had never really seen anyone with no clothes on – the odd criminal bound for a ducking in the river, or maybe the tiniest of the children. The villagers were modest people, and as they never used the river for bathing, what use had they for nakedness?

Gradually, as they talked, the girls began to make sense of the thing that had happened to them – the sudden wrenching away from all that they knew; the awful confrontation with fears.

'I was certain that Rusalka would get me,' confessed Masha in a hesitant voice.

'Me too!' agreed Nina. 'Right after I'd been singing about *Her* . . . I don't know why I followed you – it just seemed to happen.'

'I'm glad you did – God, to be alone here, imagine. I thought you'd summoned Rusalka – I thought she'd grabbed me.' Masha remembered the ghastly moments when, completely submerged in the river, she had screamed and screamed, only to have her mouth fill again with the sweet but deadly water. 'But then it was just the river, and not Her at all.'

'Why didn't She take us?' Nina wondered. 'What could have stopped Her?'

'I don't know – maybe She's waiting.'

'*Don't*, Masha – for God's sake!' Nina continued to try and comb out her hair with her fingers, beginning to tear at the knots with desperation. 'We mustn't get scared; there's nothing to be scared of here, not if we keep the fire going – the fire'll keep the animals away. You're not frightened, are you?' She looked over at Masha who, sitting near the flames with her arms wrapped about her, was looking at her with wide, unblinking eyes.

'N-no, not really,' Masha said softly. 'It's strange, but I'm not scared. I don't think anything's going to get us, not if we don't start to panic.'

It was strange that the girls were so unafraid. Sitting small and naked in the midst of such endless black forest, they were, in fact, totally vulnerable. But somehow the blazing of the fire, its heat and light, seemed to promise protection against anything that might come from the forest to threaten them. This spitting, roaring fire that Nina had created seemed very different from the dull, glowing hearths at home – kept small and safe for cooking and baking; this fire in the forest was a wild courageous thing – elemental, protective and dangerous. The flames leaped higher and higher, illuminating the tall trees and the silent river, and the crackling rustling woods.

'It's beautiful, isn't it?' said Nina.

'Mmm.'

They fell quiet, watching the fire the way all travellers have watched fires. Through the forest around them filtered noises, as small animals came out to claim the night. The trees rustled although there was little breeze. It was a still and gentle night, not cold now that they were freed of the clothes that Nina had placed on rocks near the fire to dry. Perhaps it was apprehension of the morrow which made the girls silent; just to gaze into the fire and watch its pictures was enough.

'We'll get back. We'll manage,' said Nina, glancing over at Masha. But there was no answer. Feeling greater fatigue than seemed possible, Nina got up and put some great logs on the fire. Then she fetched the two dresses, now warm and dry, and, huddling close to her friend, she lay down and covered them both. Her mind, already surrendering itself to slumber, tried to plan what should be done the next day, but all that her tired thoughts could summon was a sense of the great river that had brought them here – the sound of it, so close to her sleeping head, penetrated her dreams and she was borne away upon it.

Thus, too exhausted to be frightened, the two girls spent their first night away from the village. They never heard the cry of the fox, or the owl as she called to her mate, or later as she swooped down with a silent rush to kill some tiny creature by the river. Nor did they hear, towards dawn, the sound of distant laughter far down the river, or the faint splash of a heavy object being pushed through the water. Nina and Masha slept soundly, protected by their fire.

Masha woke first. She was cold and damp. She could hardly believe how every one of her joints and muscles screamed with pain as she shifted her bruised body. Opening her eyes she could see, over the shape of Nina's huddled shoulder, the wide grey river flowing silently past. It was misty – skeins of white fog hung over the water and the tops of the trees were completely hidden. She could not hear a sound. The birds, having deafeningly greeted the grey dawn, had fallen silent; only occasionally a solitary trail of sound would echo round the trees, cutting the air like a flute.

Masha lay still and made plans. They would soon be very hungry indeed and they had a long way to go before reaching the village; they did not know if they would be able to get back at all. They were barefoot and ill-clad. They had no tools or weapons with which to kill, for food or in self-defence. But they had each other and they seemed to have courage.

This was something that was new to Masha. The kind of bravery needed for living in the forest had never been asked of her before. She had never had to prove herself physically in any way – she did not count the constant hard work of washing, feeding and caring for a family; that did not take courage. Or perhaps it did. She pondered upon this until she became confused and returned her thoughts to more practical matters.

Her adventure had taken its toll in aches and pains, but she had not broken any bones, nor had Nina. In theory they should be able to make their way back. At least they were on the right side of the river. She shuddered as she contemplated the permanent exile and lingering death that would have awaited them had they been washed up on the opposite shore. Her older brothers had often spent nights out in the woods, albeit not alone, but they had had extra blankets, horses, food and spears. No woman in Masha's knowledge had ever spent time in the forest; they would be the first.

Leaving Nina to sleep on, Masha got dressed and knelt down to blow on the fire; a few embers glowed among the ashes. She added more twigs and grass, then a couple of branches. Then, barefoot, she trod gingerly over the shingle and stood at the edge of the river. Somewhere there, in the cool, grey water, hid fish – breakfast. If only she or Nina had brought hooks and line. But of course they never carried such things. She turned and walked back past the fire and then scrambled up the bank and under the first trees. Beneath the shade of the forest, the mist seemed thicker and Masha could only see a few yards ahead. But she immediately realized that this was a very different kind of woodland from that which surrounded her village.

At home the undergrowth had been cleared – the villagers used the wood from the thickets for thatching. This was real forest. Here the space between the trees was almost impenetrably dense. Brambles, bushes and piles of needles and leaves covered the ground between the trees. Progress would be painfully slow with no knives with which to hack a path. Her heart sank – they would be able to follow the uneven beach that bordered the river by the rapids, but only for a hundred yards or so; after that, she knew, the forest came right to the water's edge.

Undeterred, Masha struggled a few yards through the mass of thorns and creepers, her dress catching irritatingly at every step. Her mind was firmly set on food: if pigs could find sustenance in the woods, rooting around for acorns – so would she. But she could see nothing edible at all. Only a few berries that had not been devoured by the birds still clung to the bushes – she began to gather these. But her dress had no pockets and the berries were squashed to pulp in her hands by the time she had fought her way back to Nina. Forcing back tears of frustration, she put the messy pile of fruit on a stone and went to wash her hands. Beneath the trees on the opposite bank she could see two fat rabbits feasting on the fresh grass by the water. Gazing at them intently, she realized that she was looking at them with the eyes of a hunter – she still saw them as beautiful, and admired them for their freedom, but now she also saw them as food.

A sound behind her made her turn. Nina was sitting up and rubbing her eyes.

'Ow! Oh, the pain! I hurt everywhere.'

'Yes, I know, but it's better when you get moving,' said Masha, wishing more than anything that she had something more substantial to show Nina than the pulpy heap of berries. Nina's eyes followed hers.

'Aah, breakfast,' she said bravely.

Once Nina was dressed, both girls crouched by the fire and within seconds had devoured the scanty meal. It had only served to remind them how very hungry they were.

'We'd better get started,' said Nina. 'It'll be awful, but we can't be that far away. How far do you think we came?'

'A good few miles, that's for sure,' said Masha, wiping her hands on her dress. 'If only there was some way we could get back *on* the river, the way we came.'

'You're mad! I've had enough of that for a while,' said Nina.

'But it's so stupid,' persevered Masha. 'Fish can go

upstream, we know they can. The river's slower than yesterday, if it didn't rain it'd be easy to hang on to something and go back up . . . if it flowed the other way of course,' she finished lamely.

'We're not fish,' said Nina. 'And anyway, the current's not going to turn round, not just 'cos we want it to.' At that moment she had no desire to set foot in the river again, not even so much as to paddle. 'People can't travel on the river . . . if they could, they'd have done it. Be practical.'

'People,' said Masha, 'don't fall in and survive; but we did.' She could not help thinking of the ease with which they had come so far the day before. Why did the men of the village have to force their way through the forest to get a few miles up- or downstream? They didn't use the river to help them. Even though over the years it had cleared a path through the trees, they never used this path. Masha fiddled thoughtfully with her beaded plaits and gazed at the river.

'Surely if we could tie something together we could float back.'

'Float? Rubbish! It's going the wrong way and that's all there is to it. We'll just have to walk. Maybe the forest clears out a bit further in, we'll have to go and see; only for God's sake let's remember where the river is – otherwise we'll have had it.' Nina got up and stared towards the trees.

Masha, abandoning her hazy idea, was suddenly reluctant to leave the fire. The fog was thickening all the time and the opposite bank was no longer clearly visible; she could barely make out Nina's sturdy shape as she trudged heavily towards the trees.

'It's too foggy, Nina, we'll get lost. We can't go yet,' she called.

Nina turned and looked back.

'We've got to. Look, Masha, we can't just stay here and starve; we've got to go now. It's no use dreaming about it. Just try and keep your sense of direction, and make sure we stick together.'

Masha did not reply. She was certain that they should stay by the river. The danger of getting lost was too real. She felt sure that eventually they would find some way to get back upstream without leaving the river. Nina had now disappeared into the undergrowth and Masha could hear her tearing at the brambles to try and find a way through. She had no choice but to follow. Wearily she started after Nina. Her stomach was growling and she felt the sick feeling of hunger in her throat – a feeling that, with the run of good harvests in recent years, she had not felt for a long time.

'All right, I'm coming,' she yelled, and pushed her way among the branches.

Later that day, at the top of a tall pine tree, the owl was fluffing her feathers against the damp of the fog. From where she sat she could see the mist enveloping mile upon mile of forest. The only thing that showed her where the river flowed was, in the distance, an even deeper blanket of white fog that tumbled slowly and silently between the tall trees like a ghostly snake.

The morning was almost over, although there was no way to tell the position of the sun in the sky – the heavy fog entirely obscured any yellow rays that would have warmed her huddled little body. She shifted on her branch and then was suddenly alert. A noise had disturbed her and she looked down through the mist.

Far below she saw two shapes battling through the deep bed of needles that flowed like waves between the trunks of the ancient trees. As these shapes, one in a red dress and one in black, waded through the sea of needles, small cries of distress came floating up to her as the creatures fell forward, pitched over by treacherous hidden roots or as, thrown down unseen banks and hollows, they disappeared, half-covered by the soft and slipping sea.

'Wait! Where are you?'

'Here.'

'I can't see you.'

'I'm here.'

'Please – can't we stop?'

'No, we must get back.'

'My feet . . . I can't.'

'Come on. Here, lean on me.'

The owl raised herself to her true height, preparing to fly; she shook her rattle of a tongue in alarm. But, looking down, she soon realized that these intruders below were no threat – they were in enough danger themselves. With her owl's brain she hoped that these clumsy beings that had disturbed her rest would pass far away from her before they perished, as she knew they must. She shook herself and, huddling down, she once more shifted slightly on the branch and closed her golden eyes.

'It's no good . . . I can't go on . . . I've got to rest. Please, Nina.' Masha's voice was agonized with exhaustion, each breath burnt her lungs and tore at her throat. Although the stronger of the two, Masha had received far more of a battering the day before – for the last hour it had been Nina who led the way, willing them both on with words of encouragement that they both knew to be hollow and fearful.

'All right, we'll have a quick rest,' said Nina, her voice sounding thick and heavy in the fog. She collapsed at once, as if felled by an axe, and then crawled wearily over to Masha. Leaning against her she stooped down and rubbed her bruised and bleeding feet. The eyes of both girls were red from crying, though both had tried to hide their tears from the other in a vain attempt to keep up their spirits. They had long since forgotten the exact moment when they had discovered that they were lost.

Leaning together in an ocean of pine needles, they gasped for breath and nursed their wounded feet. The fog was thicker than ever and the forest was as dark as on a winter's afternoon. Half-buried in the soft carpet of earth and needles it was inevitable that they would soon close their eyes, and although both girls fought against it, first Masha and soon Nina were deeply asleep.

They woke together with an awful jolt. It was almost dark and the fog had cleared slightly. As their tired eyes opened in fear and surprise they saw, planted firmly apart a few yards from where they lay, a pair of legs.

'Well, well, well . . . babes in the wood!' said a pleasant voice.

5 Vila

The voice belonged to a young woman who stood looking down at them with an expression of amusement and concern. She was dressed, as far as they could see, in a man's hunting costume. Above the baggy leather trousers, which were criss-crossed with thongs, she wore a soft jacket made of deer-hide, gathered at the waist by a belt from which hung a large curved knife and an embroidered pouch. Dangling from the back of the belt by their hind legs were two fat rabbits. Across the woman's shoulders hung a knapsack to which certain cooking tools were attached – a small pot, a tin mug, a leather water-bottle.

As the girls gazed at her in disbelief, she quickly came over to them and kneeling down she swung her pack round and untied the water-bottle. She put it first to Masha's lips, gently holding her by the shoulder to support her. When Masha had drunk enough she did the same for Nina. Then she sat back on her heels and looked hard at them both.

'Hallo,' she said. 'I'm Vila.'

The girls stared stupidly back at her. After a moment, during which the woman simply smiled at them in a very friendly manner, Masha said: 'Hallo.'

Nina cleared her throat. 'Hallo,' she croaked.

'Well, at least you can talk,' said the woman. 'There's no need to be afraid of me, you know.' She smiled. 'I'm rescuing you.'

Nina and Masha continued to stare, like a pair of startled children. The woman laughed, and her laughter filled the forest, an enchanting and reassuring sound to the two girls. All three looked at one another.

Nina and Masha saw a brown face with a strong jaw and a large tender mouth. The black eyes that gazed at them were very serious, despite the laughter; they looked as though they could spark with anger as quickly as with amusement. Vila had a marvellous face – strong, confident and unafraid.

She stood up and looked about her.

'We must get back to the river before it's dark. We need more water.' She looked back at the girls. 'It's not far. Do you think you can make it?' Her dark eyes sparkled humorously. 'You have had a hard time, haven't you.'

Nina and Masha both burst into tears. Vila, looking at them, was trying hard not to laugh again. The girls had no idea what they looked like, what Vila saw was really a strange sight. Crouching together, waist–deep in pine needles, they were in a most bedraggled and ragged condition. Their clothes had been ripped apart by brambles and their limbs were covered in scratches, their hair was a tangle of leaves and needles, and they were extremely dirty. Their faces, blotched with past and present tears, were tired and grimy. Seeing the girls' sobs increase, Vila sprang into action.

'Come on,' she said, and hoisted them both to their feet. 'Just follow me, I won't go too fast.'

She set off through the forest, striding with little apparent difficulty through the thick layer of needles. Nina and Masha, their chests heaving and their noses running, stumbled after her, making progress that was almost as rapid, so determined were they not to lose sight of their rescuer. As they walked,

Vila spoke to them over her shoulder, telling them to take care, pointing out certain pitfalls, and indeed she seemed to be finding a steady path with no hidden roots or rabbit holes although, as far as the girls could see, there was no real path there at all.

'I found your fire, down by the rapids. I thought you must be here by accident, so I followed, to see who you were.' The woman's voice, strong and sure, came back to them and seemed to cheer them on and give them strength. 'It wasn't hard to see where you'd been – round in circles mainly – you don't exactly cover your tracks.' She waited for them to catch up. 'You should've swum across. There's a good path on the other side, it goes a long way in both directions: very useful, but a bit too public for my liking.'

'We should've what?' panted Masha.

'Swum.'

'Swum?'

'What's that?' Nina tried the new word a few times under her breath – it felt strange in her mouth. 'What's "swum"?'

Now Vila's laughter once more rocked through the trees. She ran her fingers through her shaggy brown hair as she turned to look at them with the eyes of a hawk.

'Oh, no. Villagers – I should've guessed.' Her laughter continued, but more to herself than at them. 'Villagers,' she murmured softly. 'Well, well.'

She shook her head as if to clear her mind of disturbing thoughts. 'I'm sorry, I shouldn't laugh. Now do hurry up, we're nearly there.' She turned and ran lightly along a fallen tree, jumped off the other end and then started to climb a steep bank. The girls followed in a slower and more clumsy fashion – by now their feet were in a terrible condition. Vila, they saw, was clad in soft fringed moccasins that encased her feet snugly right up to the ankle; neither girl had ever seen the like before.

From the top of the bank, Vila called: 'Come on, we're

there.' She turned and vanished down the other side. Gasping with fatigue, the girls made a final effort, boosting and hauling each other up the bank. Reaching the top they looked over and saw, sparkling before them in the evening sun, the broad band of the river.

Crouching on the grassy bank, Vila was gathering shreds of moss to light a fire. She looked up as the girls staggered down towards her.

'Ah, there you are. Right, food first. I expect you're hungry.'

Both girls nodded vigorously as Vila pulled a large lump of bread from her pack, also some cheese, apples and a small jar of honey. As Nina and Masha gulped down the rather dry provisions, Vila was creating a fire in a way that made Nina embarrassed, recalling her own fumbling attempts of the night before.

'You'll need something more substantial,' said Vila, and she proceeded to slit open the rabbits. 'Ugh, horrid business.' She skinned and gutted the creatures, the girls looking on, amazed at her speed and skill. When it got to the nasty bit of chopping off their heads and feet, Masha looked away.

'Poor things,' she said.

'Don't be so feeble,' said Nina, her mouth full of bread.

'I hate doing this,' said Vila. 'I don't eat much meat, but out here there are times when food is more important than scruples.'

'How did you catch them?' asked Nina.

'I shot them, of course.' From her pack she pulled a small wooden crossbow. 'Silly creatures, they don't run away fast enough.'

'I don't like meat either, much,' said Masha.

'Ooh, you liar!' exclaimed Nina. 'I love it.'

Masha shook her head and swallowed her mouthful. 'The men from our village kill everything they find – it's vile.'

Vila looked up and nodded. 'It's certainly pretty stupid to

kill things you can't eat. But then killing's done for a variety of reasons.' She went to the water and washed her bloody hands; her eyes stared sombrely at the opposite bank. 'We kill to eat,' she said, as if reciting. 'We kill to eat – and we kill to survive.'

She turned and picked up the raw, red corpses of the rabbits. 'These poor little fellows were threatening my existence,' she said, laughing softly, deep in her throat, 'so I shot 'em.'

'Well,' asserted Nina, 'I'm very glad that you did.'

While Nina and Masha rested, and while night fell softly about them, Vila created in her little cooking pot a delicious stew. From her pack she took herbs and salt and some barley. At one point she disappeared into the forest and came back, ten minutes later, with wild garlic and some strange roots that seemed to be potatoes of some kind. All this went into the pot. When the air began to turn colder, she produced a thick woven blanket and told the girls to wrap themselves up. While Vila worked, Nina examined the designs woven into the blanket.

'These are marvellous,' she said. 'I've never seen anything like this before.' The patterns were bold, almost child-like – the colours were deep and warm. 'The patterns go all over the place, there's no real design, but it works well anyway.' She was used to the formal, geometric patterns of the village, traditional designs that were handed down through the years. She remembered, as a little girl, her grandmother teaching her many of them. 'Remember, Nina,' she recalled the old woman saying: 'These are very old patterns. They have always been used in the village. You must learn them – they are powerful . . . they must not change.' And she had told her about the pictures, too, that the women wove and sewed into the cloth, each one telling a story that was based on the distant history of the villagers – heroes hunting ogres, floods that swept away naughty children, the legend of Rusalka that

Nina had just been finishing embroidering on to her new dress.

Masha, too, looked at the designs. 'They're beautiful,' she agreed. 'But they're wild and different. I don't understand them. They feel like some of the things I've tried to draw – but I could never do it properly.'

Vila looked up from stirring the stew.

'Oh, I'm sure you could . . .' She looked amused. 'But listen – I don't even know your names.'

'Nikolayevna, Maryia Natasha,' said Masha, formally using the patronym and her full name.

'I don't want to know your father's name, or what's written in the family Bible,' said Vila. 'What's your real name?'

'Masha,' said the girl, surprised.

Nina covered the slightly awkward pause: 'I'm Nina.'

'Good. Now we know.' Vila leant back. 'It's ready.'

They settled down to eat, sharing the one spoon that Vila had with her, or sopping up the savoury stew with more of the bread. A comfortable silence prevailed around the fire as, far above them in the black sky, star after star began to gleam and the full moon, which had been hidden the night before, commenced her cold mysterious flight over the trees.

When they had finished eating, Vila stood up and brushed the crumbs from her clothes. She carefully covered the remains of the stew and then stood the bowl in a shallow pool of water, propping it up with rocks. She built up the fire using thick dry logs, stacking them so that they would burn steadily through the night. Then she gathered the rest of the bread, only a few morsels, and threw it into the water.

'Here you are, fish – here's some supper,' she called across the water, then she wiped her hands on her trousers.

'Vila!' shouted both girls at once, their eyes wide with horror.

'What?' asked the woman, surprised.

41

'You musn't throw bread away.'

'Not even the tiniest bit.'

'It's dreadfully bad luck.'

They looked at each other and crossed their fingers for luck.

Vila laughed. 'What utter nonsense,' she said, unimpressed. 'Superstitious rubbish.'

'No, really,' said Nina. 'It's true.'

Masha nodded in agreement.

Vila looked at them. 'Why?'

They stared back.

'Just because,' said Nina.

'Everyone knows it,' added Masha.

'It wasn't a loaf, you know, only crumbs.'

'It's all the same,' said Nina.

Masha nodded.

Vila sat down and clasped her knees. Her black eyes glinted mischievously at them. 'Hmm. Now, let's see. Don't spill the salt, no shoes on the table, be careful not to break a mirror, don't leave a crease in the tablecloth, never kill a spider, touch wood, cross fingers . . . I suppose you even put milk out for the Leshies?'

The girls nodded.

Vila shrugged. 'I prefer to think that I make my own luck.' She yawned. 'With all due respect to the mysteries of the universe, I don't think that giving the fishes a bit of old bread will land us in such dreadful trouble.' She lay down and wrapped herself up in a corner of the blanket, rolled over and fell silent. Nina and Masha stared at each other in amazement. Who was this woman who could so confidently mock the oldest traditions?

However, fatigue soon washed the surprise from their confused minds. They lay down next to Vila, all three sharing the thick blanket. They were as tired as they had been on the previous night, but now, feeling safer and better fed, they were comforted, if made a little shy, by the sturdy presence of the woman next to them.

Sleepily, Nina asked: 'Vila, where do you come from?'

Ignoring the question, Vila sighed contentedly and turned over to sleep.

'Tomorrow we'll go down the river,' she murmured. Sighing deeply once more she fell silent.

6 Upstream or Downstream?

The morning broke fine and sunny – the sky cloudless and blue. Even while the dew lay on the ground and a few ribbons of early mist wreathed above the surface of the water, the air was getting warm. The leaves of the old willow that hung over the river shone brilliantly yellow against the sky, trembling and catching the early light.

Beneath the old willow its watery double shifted and wavered as fish began to break the river's surface to catch gnats. From time to time, one of them would throw its whole body into the air and then twist and topple back in a blaze of silver. The lovely morning was noisy with birds – liquid trills and chatters, shrieks and cries echoed through the woods. Every plant or creature that belonged to the forest was alive and fraught with purpose – the whole earth was breathing.

Vila had woken with the first of the birds. Gently she had lifted the blanket and rolled away from the sleeping girls. After splashing her face with water she had silently run along the bank, ducked under the willow, and disappeared round the curve in the river. Now, an hour later, she was returning. She moved with a strange grace – light on her feet, jumping any small obstacles, springing on to fallen trees and leaping off. Sometimes she used her strong brown hands to help her over the rocks, but she did not clamber and crawl like most two-legged creatures – rather she leapt and sprang like a monkey, or loped like a wolf.

As she approached the spot near the willow where they had spent the night, she saw Nina coming from behind a fir tree, pulling down her tattered dress.

'Er, I don't feel too good,' she said.

'Too much to eat – after too little,' smiled Vila, walking past. Nina soon caught the woman up. They walked the rest of the way together.

'Where have you been?' asked Nina as she walked along, trying to imitate Vila's flexible stride.

'I've got a friend who lives near here,' Vila replied. 'I went to see if she was home. I wanted to ask her some questions.'

'Oh.' Nina was full of questions herself, but Vila seemed preoccupied with her own thoughts. They got back to find Masha tending the fire.

'Morning,' said Nina.

'Morning,' Masha smiled up at them, her rosy face shining. She had woken to find herself alone and curiously happy in the glorious shouting forest. She no longer felt lost and frightened, pursued by fears – rather she was dazzled by a sense of liberty that was new to her. Now she was busy about the camp, trying to be useful.

They sat down around the fire, Nina and Masha looking expectantly at Vila. The older woman was looking serious.

'Now listen,' she said. 'After we've had something to eat, I'm going to take you to where I live. It's about five miles downriver from here.'

The girls looked at her. Then Nina voiced her fears: 'But we really should get back, Vila. They'll be terribly worried about us.'

Unlike Masha who was smiling happily, Nina was becoming increasingly concerned about what must have happened in the vilage since their disappearance. She could picture her mother, the hard, silent woman who loved her, albeit it in a quiet, distracted manner – she would be frantic with worry. Her brothers, whom she usually dismissed as an irritation, suddenly seemed dear to her; something in her throat pulled with a nagging pain when she thought of them.

Masha kept silent. She wanted to go on with Vila. She was ignoring those feelings that would pull her back from whence she came. She knew that these feelings were within her, but there was so much that she dreaded, waiting for her back at the village – a bleak future, not of her own choosing – that she was able to suppress them. Today she wanted to savour her new-found freedom.

Despite the warmth of the morning, Vila's next words chilled the girls: 'They think you're dead, you know.'

The words fell about the girls like stones. Unbelieving, they stared at her, and then at each other. Nina, knowing somehow that Vila spoke the truth, fought against it with anguish.

'We might just be lost. People get lost . . . if we go back now it'll be all right. We'll explain what happened . . . they'll understand.'

'Has anyone ever come back from the river? Do you remember that ever happening?' asked Vila.

Nina and Masha stared at her. Reality was like a bitter taste in their mouths. A feeling of dread further depressed their spirits as, powerless to prevent it, Vila's questioning began to unlock their darkest, most suppressed memories. The thoughts of both girls were the same. They were thinking of Saskia.

Years ago, there had been a girl who lived in the village. Her name was Saskia. Both girls remembered playing with her, though the memories were faint and hazy – made distant by time, and banished to the depths of their minds – because to remember Saskia was painful and disturbing. Saskia, with her long black pigtails snapping behind her as she laughed and ran – slanting black eyes and skinny limbs. Very shy with children that she did not trust, she had been, for those with whom she felt at ease, a brave and exciting companion. Older than Nina and Masha, she had been ten when they were only six.

She had disappeared one spring, when the river was in full spate, swollen with melted snow and jagged with great blocks of ice. Her mother, missing her, had gone to the group of children who were playing tag on the first bruised grass of spring. 'Have you seen Saskia?' she had asked. The children had gathered round. 'Yes,' a boy answered. 'She was here a minute ago – she followed the dog.' He pointed towards the river. Saskia's mother had followed the clear footprints of the little dog, and the larger footprints of her daughter. They led, as her beating heart had known they would, to the broken bank of the rushing torrent. The children, standing puzzled and curious on the grass, had seen the woman fall to her knees, and the great scream of pain that had rent the cool spring air was remembered now by Nina and Masha as they sat by the quiet sparkling water.

The villagers had given Saskia up for dead. But, two weeks later, as the village was preparing for nightfall, a small figure, clad in strange clothing, had appeared on the outskirts of the village. Nina and Masha did not remember the uproar and confusion that this little figure had occasioned, but they did remember the terrible events of the next day, even though, shocked and bewildered, they had quickly pushed the memory to the deepest corner of their childish minds. They remembered the awful sight of Saskia's mother as she fought to free herself from the hands of several strong men, and the look of dazed sorrow on the face of Saskia's father as he tried to restrain his despairing wife.

Then, as the spring dusk had swiftly fallen, they remembered seeing a blaze of torchlight, and hearing shrill, angry voices and the sound of pipes and horns that shattered the air, cruel and urgent. They remembered a savage procession, and a small figure bound to a chair, carried high above the crowd as the line of chanting people wove in and out the houses. Nina's mother had kept her inside, but Masha had gone with her family and had followed the line of people. She remembered some of the things that she had heard, although she had not understood them at the time: 'A witch! A witch!' the people had cried. 'She brought the flood to kill us all.' And then she had heard the deep voice of a neighbour cry: 'Rusalka! Send her back; she'll drink our blood and kill our crops. Give her back to the river, dirty Rusalka!'

The torchlight procession had moved on, and Masha's father had gathered his children together. His eyes had shone with a strange light, and Masha recalled the words he had muttered: '"Thou shalt not suffer a witch to live." That's what it says. If she can really walk in the river, let her try. Let her go back to the rest of her foul brood.' He had taken them inside, and Masha had heard nothing said since. Among the children, Saskia's name was never mentioned again.

Nina and Masha looked at each other.

'They threw her back in the river,' said Masha, her eyes wide and scared.

'We didn't know it was her,' said Nina, but her voice was unconvincing and flat.

Vila had been watching the two girls as they opened their memories. Her hair hung over her eyes and her face was full of sympathy and concern, her large expressive mouth was set in a strange half-smile that was both angry and sorrowful.

'Tell me what you remember,' she said.

Nina burst out: 'There was a girl . . .'

'. . . she was only small . . .'

'. . . she fell in, but she came back . . .'

'. . . they said she was a witch, they threw her back . . .'

'. . . we weren't allowed to see her . . .'

48

'. . . she was called Saskia.'

The girls fell silent, empty with sadness.

'They'll call us witches.'

'They won't have us back.'

There was silence.

Vila got up. She brushed off her trousers and ran her fingers through her hair. 'Anything may happen,' she said. 'Take one thing at a time.'

She scanned the river with her dark eyes. 'We must get going. Try and have something to eat.' She fetched the remains of the rabbit stew. She ate none of it herself, and Nina and Masha merely picked half-heartedly at it, all appetite gone. They moved together for comfort, trying to marshal their thoughts. Nina was near to tears, gripped by a sick, hollow feeling of homesickness.

'I'll get the boat,' said Vila, standing up. She quickly stripped off her jacket and trousers and stood, lean and brown, by the side of the water.

Nina and Masha looked up, wondering listlessly what was this new word: 'boat' – a silly-sounding thing. They looked at the woman as she stood poised on the bank. Why had she taken her clothes off? What was she about? They were suddenly wrenched from their feeling of indifference by the sight of Vila, her hands pointed as if in prayer, suddenly leaping strangely into the air and disappearing below the surface of the water, like a fish that had caught a fly. Their hands flew to their mouths as they gasped in surprise.

Before they had time to think, Vila's head bobbed above the water many yards off and she turned and grinned at them, her hair sleek about her bony face. She appeared to be 'walking' in the water, hands paddling up and down on either side, strangely suspended in the river although there was nothing there to keep her afloat. She did not seem to feel the sluggish tug of the current. Then, as they watched, astonished but fascinated, Vila turned and, putting her head down,

49

began moving through the water. She made swift progress, her feet kicking behind her and her arms moving up and down, scything the water one after the other – she seemed to be using the water actually to pull her body along. She was near the opposite bank when she turned and looked back at them. Seeing their dumbfounded expressions she laughed aloud and cried: '*This* is swimming. I swim, you swim – we swim, they swim – we *all* swim. But Rusalka,' she laughed louder, 'Rusalka *walks in the water*!' She threw her shining head back and flipped over like an otter; for a second the girls on the bank could see only her two small feet, pink and shining, and then Vila was suddenly standing in the shallows on the other side of the river. The water ran off her body as she shook her head and scraped back her wet hair. Then, running quickly over the shingle she vanished into the undergrowth.

Nina and Masha stood and stared. It dawned on them that they had finally seen what all children have always imagined and been told stories about: with their own eyes they had seen magic.

'Oh, my God, Nina, did you see that?' breathed Masha, her long limbs frozen in an attitude of incomprehension.

'What happened?' gasped Nina. 'What *was* it?'

'Magic!' exclaimed Masha, not frightened but exhilarated.

Vila reappeared on the other side. She was dragging a strange object that seemed to be made of leather stretched over some curved saplings. It was about ten feet long, but only a couple of feet wide, and the bottom was curved down in the shape of an arrow-head. The whole thing was hollow, with an open top. Vila pulled it to the edge of the water and pushed it in. Expecting it to sink under the surface, the girls were surprised to see that it floated buoyantly on top. Once in the water, it seemed to become very light. Vila looked up and grinned.

'This is a boat,' she called across, giving it a shove and

jumping into it. From inside she took a narrow piece of wood that was flattened out at one end.

'This is an oar, or a paddle.' She was using it to pull the boat through the water, first on one side and then on the other. 'This is rowing. Actually, this is good rowing; I'm rather an expert!' She laughed and, indeed, she did look expert to the girls, though they had never seen it done before. The little boat was finding a straight course across the river, scarcely showing that the current was tugging at its side. In no time, Vila had arrived and was pulling the boat up on to the shingle.

Masha was fighting to control her leaping thoughts. She turned exultantly to Nina and thumped her on the back.

'There. I told you! I told you there was a way of doing it. What's it called? A boat? I knew it!'

'All right. Well done,' laughed Nina grudgingly.

Vila had quickly dressed and fastened her belt. Now she gathered her belongings together, put everything in her knapsack, and started to stow it all away in the front of the boat. The remains of the fire she carefully covered. Having finished, she turned and looked at them.

'Boats are the simplest of things once you know about them,' she said. 'It beats me how you villagers do without them. And, quite honestly, if you all learned to swim you'd save yourselves a lot of trouble.'

'But how did you learn?' cried Masha.

'Who taught you?'

'Oh,' said Vila. 'Everyone knows about it where I come from.'

'But why did no one teach us?' said Nina. 'Why can't the people in our village do it? Why did no one discover it?'

Masha nodded eagerly: 'Yes, they say it's forbidden to go in the water. But how can it be? It's so simple.'

Vila laughed. 'Well, people forbid the most natural things for the strangest reasons. I suppose your villagers just got frightened of the water.'

'But it looks such fun,' said Masha. 'Will you teach us?' Her imagination had been fired by the sight of Vila's graceful watery skill. She had often silently watched the wild otters and water-rats splashing into the water from their holes in the bank, and had envied their boisterous confidence. She thought she had never seen anything as beautiful and free as Vila's swimming.

'Naturally,' said the woman. 'We haven't got time now, but once we get home there'll be lots of opportunity.'

The word 'home' reminded both girls of their worries. Vila's swimming and the appearance of the boat had caused them to forget their recent misgivings. Now Masha said: 'Where is your home?'

'It's just down there. You'll like it.'

Vila could see that the girls were once more beginning to look anxious and lost. She urged them to hurry, though they had few belongings to gather. Then, directing them to sit in the boat, one at each end, she sternly told them to keep still.

'It'll go over if you bounce around,' she said.

Once they were ready, she pushed off. In no time they were in the middle of the river. She guided the light craft skilfully, pushing sharply with her paddle to keep it straight, but mainly letting the current carry them along. Nina and Masha sat and gazed about them. Once more they were part of the river, part of its flow. But this time there was no fear of the water, no shock at its alien coldness. The smooth movement of the boat and the sight of the banks slipping steadily by entranced them. Masha, who had not felt the same excited thrill as Nina during her headlong journey from the village, began now to feel the wonder of this new form of travel.

All was peaceful and silent on the river. Only the drip of water as it fell from Vila's paddle was heard as they drifted along. The chattering of the birds had sunk to a placid twittering. From time to time, a trickle of song pierced the hot air. Once, a whole family of water-voles was heard splashing and plopping into the water, and then the little creatures were seen swimming in a line, each rapid little body leaving in its wake a shining V-shaped wash.

The river was getting wider all the time; it was now almost half a mile across. Small islands were dotted here and there between the banks, some even large enough to support a few trees. The water was becoming shallower too. Clumps of tall grasses could be seen reaching their waving heads above the water and shedding their glimmering reflections across the surface. Rushes thronged the banks and strange birds that neither girl had ever seen were stalking on tall orange legs among the whispering reeds. A huge heron flapped its stately way past them over the river to its nest of dry sticks and mud in the marsh. As they went on, the forest was set further back and the sense of space that this gave the girls made them giddy and breathless. Used to constantly towering trees, they had never before seen such a large expanse of sky. Ahead now there were no trees at all, only the shining grey of the water rising to meet the dazzling blue of the heavens.

The current had become slower and slower, and now Vila was having to paddle with deep, regular strokes. In front of them was by far the biggest island they had seen and the river had split into two broad channels to flow past the island on either side. Vila steered to the right of the tangled mass of trees and rocks and then, as they drifted by, Nina and Masha exclaimed with delight. Before them, shining in the sun, lay a large clear lake. In this way, the two girls, who had never before ventured from the shelter of the mighty forest, arrived at Vila's home.

PART TWO

1 Under the Oak-tree

Masha was sitting under a great oak-tree a few yards from the eastern shore of the lake. Her knees were drawn up and hugged by her arms, her chin resting upon them. She was gazing over the lake, her eyes absorbing the scene before her. Around her, a light rain fell, pitting the dull mirror of the lake and creating circles upon circles of widening ripples. The old oak-tree under which she sat sheltered her from the gentle rain. The roof of leaves, now beginning to turn from green to gold, formed a whispering dome above her, and the rich earth where she sat was warm and dry.

Far across the lake, among the scattering of huts and houses, there was no sign of movement. From time to time a few wet hens ventured out from under carts or cattle-troughs, but then seemed to think better of it – the rain would send up the worms, there was no hurry. The patient faces of several cows stared out from a barn – they chewed and stared, their dreamy eyes gazing vacantly at nothing in particular. From several of the dwellings thin columns of smoke rose into the sky. Everyone was inside. With the crops gathered, most of the work that needed to be done could be dealt with indoors and, indeed, after the toil of harvest, no one complained about the occasional rainy day.

Masha was wondering how long she had been here. She had soon lost count of the days. But since she and Nina had arrived with Vila, the new moon had waned and now was waxing nightly – it would soon be a month. It seemed to Masha that she had been in the village on the lake far longer. She had quickly come to feel completely at home among these strange new people, and now her life in the forest village seemed a distant memory.

She smiled, remembering the first day. The village had looked very different from the way it looked today – in the heat and bustle of the harvest, there had been activity everywhere. As Vila had steered the little boat towards the village, people had called to her in greeting, pausing to look curiously at the two unkempt and ragged girls who were staring so open-mouthed and wide-eyed about them. There had been so much to see, so much that was new and different. Strange houses dotted the shore, decorated with intricate designs and pictures, each house surrounded by a blaze of herbs and flowers. Accustomed to buildings of log and timber, these structures of clay seemed extraordinary to the newcomers.

Then there were the people. More women dressed like Vila, others wearing loose beaded jerkins that swayed above their bare brown knees, some merely with pieces of woven cloth draped about their waists. The men too were mainly clad like Vila, in leggings and jackets, but they were of bright, vivid colours – less strange to the girls than the mannish garments of the women, but different nevertheless. The hair of both women and men was twisted, beaded and braided in many different styles, or cropped short for comfort. No woman bothered to cover her head. In the heat of the sun, many of the people had discarded articles of clothing, apparently not bound by the conventions of modesty that Masha and Nina were so used to.

That day everyone had been working – storing the newly

gathered grain and straw, threshing and flailing, drying fruit and vegetables in the sun. No one seemed to be directing the proceedings, but everyone was taking part; even the smallest of the children was helping in some way. Cart after cart rolled in from the fields that stretched away over the gentle hills. The faces of the people were happy and tired. The business of gathering a good harvest, of knowing that the winter months would be a time of plenty, not a time of hunger and illness – these feelings could be well understood by the two girls. But what was new was something that had taken Masha a long time to begin to understand.

On that first day, she had not known why this village had felt so different. She had sensed the difference immediately, but she had not understood it. Now, as she sat as still as stone beneath the oak, she was thinking about these things – analysing, weighing up, comparing . . .

When they arrived, Vila had tied the boat to a platform that had stretched for many yards along the shore, jutting out into the water. Other boats of different shapes and sizes were likewise tied there; they bobbed gently up and down, each one reflected with startling clarity in the clear water below. Piled upon the jetty were shining piles of what looked like thread, loosely woven together, here and there covered with pieces of weed. These were fishing-nets, and Masha had soon learned how, around dawn, they were taken out to the middle of the lake and cast forth. There they stayed till dusk, their position marked by painted corks.

Vila had dismissed their constant questions: 'All in good time,' she had said. She led them along the shore, stopping here and there to speak to villagers and to discuss the harvest and the weather; but she did not yet bother to explain the presence of the two strangers she had brought with her. The people seemed friendly, and had smiled at the girls, who smiled shyly back. No one seemed very surprised – everyone was too busy to be curious.

They reached a cluster of about a dozen houses. Nearest to them stood a small hut outside which were tethered two small goats. A dog rushed out of the hut barking wildly and bounding up to Vila.

'Down, boy, down!'

While she was hugging the dog, a small boy tottered out on chubby legs and he too threw himself at the kneeling woman.

'Stepan!' exclaimed Vila. 'Hallo, darling. How are you?' She lifted the child high in the air and then hugged him to her and gave him a kiss on his giggling mouth.

'Vila!' A woman stood in the doorway, her floury hands on her hips. She was small and slight, with a cloud of dazzling red hair framing her freckled face. Around her body was tied a loose piece of cloth with dark, swirling patterns – Masha saw that whoever had woven Vila's blanket had made this garment too. The woman's expression was one of pleasure, though she was trying to look stern.

'Why will you never tell me when you're going to stay away? Do you have no idea how worrying it is?' Looking at Vila grinning up at her, her arms full of leaping child and dog, she laughed reluctantly. 'Thank God you're safe,' she said, and went up to embrace her.

Masha and Nina had then been introduced to the woman, Ania, and to Stepan, her little boy. They had been ushered into the hut which, tiny and chaotic, was a complete delight to them. Far too small for two women, a child and a dog (and sometimes, Ania laughed, two goats) the hut was full of beautiful and interesting objects that the girls found enchanting.

'Who made these?' Masha had gasped, staring at the odd woven pictures that hung on all four walls.

'Those are mine,' Ania had answered.

In the corner of the hut, surrounded by soft, embroidered cushions, stood a wooden carving of an owl, fully three feet high. It was crudely executed, but strangely powerful, its wings outstretched, its talons grasping the base of the tree trunk from which it was carved. From its mouth, incongruous and absurd, hung one of Stepan's woolly socks.

'The carvings are Vila's,' said Ania, and she indicated the roof of the hut. From all four corners stared more owls, each in a different position of flight, but all with huge searching eyes. 'I sometimes think she's an owl herself,' she laughed.

Looking around, the girls noticed bundles of herbs hung up to dry over the hearth. They recognized the slender branches of hare's foot and the large ragged feverfew, chervil and moonwort, rest-harrow and many others. They had been surprised to see the strings of garlic hanging alongside the onions and cooking herbs – dill, rosemary and thyme – instead of round the windows, to keep away the vampires. Also, they noticed the absence of witch-hazel, a spray of which was a common sight in their village, as it was a certain way to discourage any malicious works by witches or women suspected of the evil eye.

In another corner of the hut burned a small fire, and on the hearth sat a pot of something that smelt delicious. On the table, freshly made bread cooled in a basket. Masha and Nina, having eaten little breakfast, realized that they were once more very hungry.

While they ate, the girls had asked many of the questions that Vila had so far left unanswered. Nina had started.

'Do you live here alone?'

'Yes, we do,' Ania had replied. 'Vila built this house, and when I came to the village she asked me to live here too.'

'How wonderful!' exclaimed Masha. 'You lucky things. We'd never be allowed to live on our own.'

Vila and Ania had smiled.

'Why do you dress like a man?' Nina asked, looking at Vila.

'What do you nean?' Vila looked surprised. 'Oh, the trousers. Well, it wouldn't be too clever to tramp around the forest in a skirt.'

'Is Stepan your baby?' Masha had asked Ania, although it was easy to see the resemblance between the woman and the chubby little boy.

'Yes,' she had replied with a proud smile.

'I share him,' said Vila laughing.

The girls had asked other questions until Vila stopped them. 'Hold your horses. There'll be time for all that.'

Then she had told Ania of all that had happened since she had found the girls in the forest. Ania had listened carefully, her face solemn. Eventually, when Vila had finished, Ania turned to the girls. She seemed to be choosing her words carefully.

'Now that you've come here,' she said, 'you'll find that your story is not so unusual. In this village there are many people who have had to come and make this their home, whether they chose to or not. Some of them arrived by pure accident, like you – some of them have come for other reasons.' She paused to stroke the cheek of the little boy who, exhausted by excitement and the hot sun, had fallen asleep in her lap, his sticky thumb in his mouth.

'Not all of us, of course, come from other places. Some of us are born here. The village is growing. Stepan knows no other place – this is his real home. But before he was born I lived somewhere else. I lived in a village many miles through the woods – perhaps it is not unlike your own village.' Her eyes became sad and distant as she remembered. 'I was no older than you when I left – was forced to leave. Where I come from a girl is praised if she has many babies; but only, of course, if she has a husband. I made a mistake. It was an accident really . . .' She leant and kissed the sleeping child. 'A lovely accident, as it turned out.'

Masha and Nina looked sad. They had heard of such things happening. Vila burst out: 'It wasn't your fault. Oh, those stupid, cruel . . .'

'All people tend to be stupid and cruel if they haven't looked for another way to be. The people where I came from were frightened by anything that happened which changed the order of things. They thought that if they kept everything in order then God would smile on them and the crops would never fail. Anything new and different is frightening to these people – a new thought, a new action . . .'

'A new pattern,' said Nina.

'A new picture,' said Masha. 'Or not wanting to hunt if you're a boy, or not wanting to marry if you're a girl.'

'Exactly,' said Ania. 'And fear is very strong, you know.'

The girls nodded, remembering their fear of the river.

Nina said: 'We thought Rusalka would get us when we fell in. But she didn't. The river isn't as scary as we thought.'

Ania and Vila both laughed.

'Ah, Rusalka,' said Ania. She looked piercingly at Masha and Nina, and then asked: 'What *is* Rusalka?'

The girls looked at each other.

'She's a water-witch,' said Masha, surprised that Ania did not know.

'She lives in the water, and in green trees,' said Nina.

'She eats men, drags them into the water.'

'She sings in a beautiful voice, but she's dirty and ugly.'

'If a girl falls into the river, she becomes Rusalka.'

Ania asked: 'Did you become Rusalka?'

The girls stared.

'N-no,' they stammered.

Ania said gently: 'People clothe their fear in stories. If the people from your village could see this place, what do you think they'd say?'

The girls thought about it. They thought of the swimming, the boats, the strange laughing people, the casual nakedness, the way the work was shared between women and men.

'They'd think you were mad.'

'They'd say you were wicked . . .'

'. . . immoral . . .'

'. . . belonged to the devil.'

'To the people of your village,' Ania said, 'we're all Rusalka.'

At that moment, as Masha and Nina struggled to understand, Stepan had woken up. He began to chatter loudly, bouncing up and down on Ania's knee. All conversation had been suspended.

That afternoon, Vila showed them round the village. They had met many people and seen many things. They saw girls and boys of their age working together – fishing, binding corn, mending carts, playing with the children. They had seen a woman making great pots on a wheel, using the red clay from the lake shore. A young man was helping her, painting the half-baked pots with bright glazes. They saw a man making a vast carpet from coloured wools, the vivid pictures leapt from the fabric to meet their eyes as they watched. They saw a woman quietly fishing from the side of the lake, a baby at her breast. Everyone seemed busy at what they were good at.

Towards evening, the people had drifted away to their homes to eat. But later, in the dusk, fires had been lit and the whole village gathered. There was much talking and laughter, argument and discussion. The voices of the villagers had risen in the twilight to mingle with the glowing sparks that flew upwards from the fires. There was music and dancing, in celebration of hard work and a good harvest. To the two girls, used to the reserved and traditional gatherings of their own village, it had seemed wild and thrilling. Everyone seemed free to come and go as they pleased; free to dance and sing, or free simply to sit quietly and watch. Masha had sat and watched, observing the mingling of the people. Nina had joined in the dancing, her face flushed and her long hair tumbling down her back. At one point she had collapsed on to the seat next to Masha. Seeing her bright eyes and rosy cheeks, Masha had smiled.

'You've been to your first dance after all,' she said, and laughed.

Nina grinned and rushed off to join in another round, leaving Masha sitting and looking on, breathing in the newness of all she saw.

That had been nearly a month ago. Now Masha, clad in the clothes of the lakeside village, with new clay beads in her braids, sat under the oak-tree and turned her mind to the present.

Nina, she knew, was not as contented as she. Her friend had shared her delight in all the things that they had experienced since arriving. She had made friends, and she had become involved with village life. But it seemed she had not felt the same enduring sense of homecoming as Masha.

For Masha, these new people seemed to take for granted all the things that she had wondered about in her old life – her love of nature, her hatred of conflict, the thrill of finding new ways of creating beauty. But Nina was more practical, less concerned with these things, more interested in the simple business of village life. She had been popular and successful in the old village, though Masha knew she had not always felt so – only to Masha had Nina confided her frustrations and angers. But even then, while pouring her troubles into Masha's patient ear, she had never seemed to feel the same need to escape, the same need to be different.

And today, Nina had broken down over breakfast and poured out her homesickness. Then she had walked out.

Masha had tried to stop her, but it had been Vila who had followed. Ania had said: 'Leave her, Masha. She needs to be on her own. Vila will find her and talk to her. They're very alike, you know. They find it hard to accept things they don't like. Vila will help.'

So Masha had not followed her friend. Instead she had taken a small boat and had crossed the lake to come here, to her favourite place. In the shelter of this old oak-tree, Masha could find a solitude and a stillness that, if she waited patiently, would show a corresponding stillness and silence within herself. Her mind would clear like the water's surface when the ripples have finally disappeared, and she would feel part of the tough old tree, part of the soft leafy ground and the cold dark lake.

Now, sitting hunched and still, Masha listened to the gentle sound of the rain and waited, happy and alone, while the peace of the place slowly stole upon her.

2 The House in the Cornfield

About a mile further on through the forest, Nina was making
her way along a small well-beaten track. She had been
walking fast for the best part of an hour and had managed to
shake off the worst of her anger. What was left, aching within
her, was a dull sense of misery – a lead weight that made her
have to force one foot in front of the other, each step an
effort. She trudged along, oblivious to her surroundings, her
eyes fixed on her feet as the rain fell softly about her. At last,
at the crest of a small hill, she stopped and sat down. She
curled herself up and hugged her head with her arms. She
needed to think.

She was homesick and unhappy – embarrassed at the scene
that she had created that morning. She had not wanted to
upset her friends, but seeing them so happy had made her feel
worse. Her behaviour had made her feel furious and
miserable, and she had felt more excluded and out of place
after her outburst than before.

Unlike Masha, she had no clear idea if she wished to stay
with these people or not. One part of her knew that here she
was allowed freedoms that her own village would not have
dreamed of giving her. But another part of her felt alarmed
by these freedoms. She loved being able to come and go as

she pleased, loved not being bullied into doing things she hated: she liked all these new forms of independence, but she feared them too.

Since arriving, she had met many of the village people. At first she had been thrilled by the casual way that the villagers behaved with one another, not bound by that reserve and antagonism between the sexes that she had taken for granted in her old home. But she had also felt insecure in this new atmosphere – part of her longed for the rigid formality of the old life, the way that things had been so strictly arranged and supervised. At home, she had been able to rely on being entirely passive – any mistakes that were made she had been able to blame on others. Resistance to tradition had been useless, so she had never truly had to assert herself. Sulky and rebellious, she had been used to fighting her parents while, deep down, she had been relieved not to have to make decisions. It was safer, somehow, not to have had to think for herself.

In this new place, people made up their own minds. There was no weighty tradition to tell one how to think. It was confusing and tiring. Sitting there, cradling the heavy hurt within her, Nina remembered some of these times of doubt and uncertainty. Without realizing, she began the long task of confronting her confusions and sadness.

In the first few days, she and Masha had been busy from dawn till dusk learning to do things they would normally have never been allowed to do – swimming, using boats, fishing, even helping to build a house. Nina had tried her hand at most things – making pots, weaving – at one point she had learned how to skin a deer and treat a hide. But most of her spare time had been spent adapting some of the new pictures and designs that Masha was now at liberty to paint. (No one had leant over their shoulders and disapproved of these new creations, or forbidden the bold colours and daring abstract shapes.) It had been at these times, while quietly working, that Nina's thoughts had been drawn to her old home. It was then that she missed her family and friends, and wished that they too could share these new experiences.

She had confided these thoughts to no one at first. Masha was spending more and more time with Ania and Stepan, talking deeply with the older woman about all sorts of things that Nina could not fathom – the spirit of the forest, the difference between people, the nature of fear, and of beauty; Nina had been too wrapped up in her own tumult to listen. Although she had made many new acquaintances among the villagers, she always felt stupid and slow beside them – out of place, old fashioned; she felt that her longing for her family and friends in the forest would mark her down as a baby.

Eventually Vila had come to her one afternoon, while Nina was sitting outside the hut intently sewing a beaded belt. She could not decide whether she wanted to give the belt to Vila as a gift, or whether she wanted to keep it for herself.

'Hallo,' the woman had said. 'Still sewing?'

'Mmm,' Nina answered, wanting to be left alone. She kept at her work, not looking up.

'You don't do much else nowadays,' Vila said.

'I don't know why I bother. It's rubbish anyway.' Nina threw down her work. She felt sad and sulky.

'Hmm, doesn't look much good to me,' Vila agreed.

Nina's eyes stung with hot tears.

'I was going to give it to *you*,' she said and bit her lip to control its trembling.

'Oh, Nina, love, you are silly,' said Vila. 'You know it's lovely. You're very kind.' She paused. 'I do wish you'd tell me what's wrong.' She looked down at the girl, whose flushed cheeks showed her to be distressed.

After a second, Nina's feelings poured forth in a torrent; it was a great relief to speak.

'I don't know, Vila. I don't know why I feel so awful. I like being here . . . but I don't belong. Everyone thinks I'm stupid. I feel so clumsy . . . and fat . . . and stupid. No one understands me. I don't fit in. I miss my mother.'

Vila looked hard at Nina, her eyes black and thoughtful. She ran her fingers through her hair, making it stand wildly on end.

'Let's go for a walk,' she said. 'I know someone that you should meet.'

Nina nodded. Fighting back the tears she had risen and followed Vila.

They had walked a long way, not as Nina had expected through the village, but up and over the fields, following a dusty cart-track. On either side the banks were bright with poppies and cornflowers, and as Nina looked about her she could not help feeling a great thrill of excitement at the sight of the hills rolling away under such a broad blue sky – disappearing into the hot, hazy distance. This new breadth of vision – such a widened horizon – was something that she could never quite get over.

As they walked, Vila had spoken to Nina, reassuring her, giving her encouragement in her firm and certain way. 'You're not stupid, or fat, or clumsy. You're being absurd if you think that you are. You're not brilliant at everything yet because you've only just started. Most of the people here have been here all their lives. Things take practice, you know.'

'But this isn't my home,' cried Nina. 'I'm only here by accident.' Her voice shook. 'I have no home.' She was conscious of being melodramatic, but Vila's straightforward manner would not allow the girl to relapse into self-pity.

'What do you mean "home"? You have somewhere to live. If you want your own home, you can build it. I'll help you. Look, Nina, you belong where you decide to belong. You may not be completely grown up yet, but you're no baby – hardly!'

'I don't fit in,' persisted Nina stubbornly. 'You don't

understand.'

'God, Nina, do you really believe that I don't understand? I've been fifteen too, you know; you're not the first person. I know what agony it is. Of course, you won't believe me – but your feelings are quite common.' Vila's eyes flashed and she once more ran her fingers through her hair. 'When I was fifteen –' she laughed harshly, 'I was so angry I thought I'd just die from it. I was just like you – only worse.'

'What happened?'

Vila dismissed the question. 'We're talking about you, not me.'

'I know, I'm just "moody and difficult" – that's what my mother always said.'

'Poor woman!' laughed Vila. 'I can sympathize with her. Listen, did you ever feel these things back in the forest village? Or were you blissfully happy the whole time?'

Nina laughed grudgingly. 'No, I suppose I was the same.' Then she added: 'But I do miss them so – it hurts awfully. I hated them then, but now I want to see them so badly.'

Vila put her arms round Nina's shoulders and squeezed hard.

'Nina, I know that. I know how awful that is. Believe me, I feel for you; it's the worst feeling in the world.' Nina was surprised to hear the normally strong voice shake slightly as Vila said: 'And I won't say anything stupid like "it'll pass". It won't pass. But it will get better.'

'Oh, Vila, but they would have me back. I'm sure they would. We could explain,' said Nina urgently.

Vila had stopped. They had come far across the fields to the edge of the forest. The trees towered over the cornfield: a tall black line between the earth and the sky. Nina had never been to this place before. Near the trees stood a small round hut.

'Well, we're here,' Vila said.

They walked up to the hut. There was no one around.

Nina looked at the hut. At first glance it seemed like many of the other village dwellings. It was surrounded by a carefully tended herb garden, and bright flags of poppies swayed in the wind round the edges of the small plot of cultivated ground. Like many of the village houses, the hut was adorned with pictures painted in bright colours and vivid patterns. But something about these pictures stirred Nina's memory as she looked at them. They were not expertly done, and looked as if they had been executed by someone who needed to tell a story, rather than for pleasure or decoration.

To the left of the door over one whole portion of the clay wall was painted, with an almost childlike simplicity, a huge forest – row upon row of trees, dark and sombre. Through this forest tumbled a winding river. Painted beside this river, among the trees, was a collection of little log cabins and, standing among the crude little houses, a little girl was depicted. She was clad in a black dress upon which Nina saw the traditional decorative embroidery unique to her own village.

'It's my village!' she exclaimed, looking at Vila.

The woman nodded and pointed to the right of the door where the pictures continued. Nina looked and saw that this portion of the wall was covered with bright, savage red and orange, signifying fire. Again, in the midst, was the little girl. Around the edge of the whole picture, enclosing it like a border, were the faces of many people. Their mouths were open and shouting, their faces distorted and cruel, and their eyes were red, and filled with hate. Underneath, at the very bottom of the wall, was painted once again the winding blue of the river. And there again Nina saw the little girl, this time being swept away in the water.

As Nina had stood and looked at these strong, blazing images, a woman had been approaching. Nina turned from the hut and looked at her. She was a few years older than Nina – perhaps nineteen or twenty years old. Her long black hair was bound in plaits around her thin face, and her slanting eyes looked nervously from Vila to Nina and back again. There was silence, and then Vila spoke.

'Hallo, Saskia.'

The woman said nothing. She stood amid the poppies and twitched at a fold in her dress in agitation.

Nina's heart was pounding. Saskia! So she had survived. She looked again at the pictures on the walls of the hut, and she understood them.

'I've brought someone to see you,' Vila said gently.

The woman shifted from one foot to the other.

'Vila, you know I'm not used to company,' she said, and her voice was high and soft and trembled slightly. Saskia certainly spoke the truth. She was obviously unused to meeting people, living out here away from the others.

'I know,' said Vila. 'But Nina needs to talk to someone.'

'But . . .'

Vila broke in: 'I know it's hard, but she needs to know why she can't go back. I thought you could explain better than me.' She moved towards the door of the little hut. 'We're very thirsty,' she said.

'All right . . . you can come in.' Saskia led them inside.

The hut was dark and sparsely furnished – a simple wooden chair, a small table and a narrow bed in one corner. Inside, too, the walls were covered with paintings; as Nina looked at them, Saskia poured some fresh water from a pitcher into a wooden bowl.

After she had drunk, Vila said: 'Nina remembers about you. She comes from the same place. She came with another girl, by accident. Do you remember her, Saskia?'

The thin, nervous woman looked anxiously at Vila.

'You know I try not to remember . . . but I never stop remembering. There were many children who were my friends . . . many children . . .'

'We found her after she fell in,' explained Vila to Nina.

'She was almost dead – and so small and scared. We were out catching logs brought down by the flood. It's dangerous for us too in the spring, you know, but we managed to save her. It was a miracle that she survived – many don't. We brought her back here. But she was so unhappy and homesick. She cried and cried, poor little thing. So we took her back to the village. We hoped that because she was so young they might accept her. Tell Nina what happened, Saskia.'

There was a silence, during which Saskia looked down at her clasped hands. Then she began, her voice gaining strength as her story unfolded, her eyes seeming to see once more that terrible time.

'I went to my house. It was dark and quiet. My mother and father brought me in. They cried . . . but we were all so happy. No one asked what had happened, they were all too happy to care.' Saskia's eyes hardened, her voice became loud and angry. 'Then the Council came. All the big strong men with loud voices. They shouted and talked at my parents – it seemed to go on all night. Then they took me and put me in a dark stable. They tied me and hit me. They asked and asked about the lake people, but they shouted louder when I answered. Then they left me alone. I couldn't see in the dark . . . I was hungry . . . my mother didn't come to get me. I thought I was going to be in there for ever . . . then they came. There was fire everywhere – torches, singing. I thought it would burn me . . . they threw me back in the water – it was so black and cold . . . but it was better than the fire.'

There was silence. Then Vila spoke.

'We'd waited, of course, to see if they rejected her. We had boats tied up nearby. We saw it all happen.'

Nina was silent. She looked at Saskia who was sitting so still now, her eyes as hard as flint. Eventually she broke the silence.

'What did the Council say?'

Saskia looked at her. 'They said they knew all about the witches along the river. I told them that the people were nice and kind. They said I lied, that I was a lover of the devil.'

'Who were they?' asked Nina.

'All the bravest men: Gregor the woodcutter, Alexei Bearkiller, Piotr, Voinitsky, Vladislav . . .'

The room seemed to reel as Nina heard her father's name drop so softly from the woman's lips. She felt as if someone had slapped her.

'But my father – Vladislav – he's not cruel . . . he's *not*.'

'Oh, no,' sighed Saskia, smiling strangely. 'Not cruel.'

'But you were too young – you couldn't have told them right. You couldn't explain. If we all went back and told them . . .'

'They'd try and kill us,' said Saskia heavily. 'They just couldn't bear the thought of us.'

Vila and Nina had soon left the little hut that stood in solitude on the border between the field and the forest. They had walked back in silence.

In the next few days, Nina had tried to resign herself to the situation, and she thought that she would soon come to see that everything had happened for the best. But sometimes she was terrified by the thought that she would not be able to forget – that she would become like Saskia, that her grief would overcome her. Vila had said that Saskia had never really adjusted to the new life, that she had been too young, too scarred by her casting out. She had said that Nina would not be the same; but sometimes Nina doubted her. When she felt lonely and homesick she almost hated the village and its people, and at these times she resented Vila's advice and concern, although she had come to love the woman, and to rely upon her.

Today it had been too much. Her turbulent feelings had

got the better of her. She had left, and now she was going in the direction of her old home. All she wanted, she told herself, was to have a last look at the forest village where she had spent her life – a last look at her family. She felt that without this she would never feel at home elsewhere.

So, as the rain stopped and the sun came out, Nina sat with her head in her hands, preparing herself for the journey home.

3 The Brothers

At the same moment – deep in the forest, and miles away from the lakeside village – something stirred. The raucous birds, who had been filling the air with their songs, welcoming the sun as it appeared from behind the clouds, fell silent and listened. The rain had stopped and the sun on the wet leaves made the early autumn colours shine out bright and clean. The bracken was just beginning to turn to golden brown – everywhere green was poised to turn to red and gold; only the conifers retained their everlasting sombre foliage. A group of deer who had been grazing quietly in a small clearing lifted their pointed faces and twitched their ears, their black noses sniffing the air – something was coming. At once, the clearing was empty.

The young men stumbled wearily into the little patch of space between the trees. They threw themselves down on the wet grass of the sun-soaked glade, and waited for their burning lungs to cease heaving. They had come far, through difficult country, hacking a way for themselves with heavy knives, leaving behind them not a path, but rather a trail of bruised and trampled undergrowth. They had been obliged to travel in this slow and noisy manner, at each step being snared by brambles and whipped by branches, because there was no path of any kind that went in this direction from their village – no one ever came this way, or wanted to.

But the young men were not overly worried by the difficulties that nature was laying in their way. They were well equipped and clad in stout clothing. They were used to the forest, it was their home, and they were accustomed to its moods and fancies. When they reached the little clearing it seemed to them to be yet another whim of the great forest – cradled by massive firs, this small patch of ground seemed designed especially for weary travellers who had just fought their way through miles of impenetrable undergrowth.

Fanning his face with a frond of bracken, the younger of the two turned to the elder and said: 'How far do you think we've come?'

'About twenty miles,' said the second boy.

They were obviously brothers. Both were tall with black hair cut to the shoulder, tied back to prevent it getting caught on twigs and thorns. They both had brown eyes and a ruddy complexion. The younger had the softer face. It may just have been the five years' difference between them, but there seemed to be less harshness about him, not that the older's features were less delicate, but they were set in an expression of pleased arrogance that kept his face immobile, unable to fall into gentle or thoughtful lines.

'Let's have something to eat, Vanya,' said the younger.

'All right,' said the older boy. 'But we mustn't waste time. We said a week, and we've been out five days already.'

Tomilin and Vanya had set out from the forest village having arranged, at the insistence of their father, that if they were gone for longer than a week, a search party would be sent after them. They had been heartily discouraged from setting out at all, and it had only been the younger's persistent entreaties to his brother that had made Vanya suggest the trip. Eventually their father had relented. Their mother, having recently lost one child, had been adamant that the boys should not go; however, her weak voice had long since ceased to have any authority in the household, and her protests had been ignored. Vanya had told his father that he was only going with Tomilin in order to shut him up but, in truth, added to his irritation was a desire for some adventure. 'You can go then, son,' his father had said. 'It may do Tomilin some good after all – may toughen him up.' He had then bored his son with a long lecture on woodcraft and the dangers of the forest; Vanya had listened politely, but had considered it unnecessary – he had total faith in his own capabilities. He had gone to Tomilin and told him the news.

'They'd never let a baby like you out alone,' he said. 'So I'll have to come with you.'

'You know it'll be worth it, to find Masha,' Tomilin had said.

He knew that the reason for their expedition must be kept secret from anyone in the village. Their parents thought they were merely going on a hunting trip, to help Tomilin get over his sister's death. As far as the villagers were concerned Masha and Nina were drowned – better off drowned, too, than carried away by Rusalka. If they had known that Tomilin and Vanya were setting off to look for the girls, they would have forbidden such dangerous nonsense.

When Masha had been swept away by the river, Tomilin felt that he had lost everything – a beloved sister, a friend, and his only sympathetic listener. He had grieved and mourned with the rest of the family but had not been able to reconcile himself to his sister's death. He became convinced, not knowing why, that somewhere down the river Masha had survived. He put little faith in this conviction at first, and told himself that he was being stupid, merely trying to comfort himself pointlessly. But the feeling persevered, and Tomilin, though others called him dreamy and stupid, was not prone to idle superstitions. He was used to following his impulses and trusting his instincts – not merely accepting what others told him. He could not accept what the rest of the men said: that a person who fell in the river was better off dead. Whether Masha had perished or not, he wanted to know.

At last he had confided his thoughts to Vanya. His brother had scoffed and told him he was being absurd. But Tomilin was used to such treatment, and he continued to discuss his ideas. 'I'm sure they're somewhere out there,' he said. 'I just don't feel that they're dead. I know it sounds stupid, but they may have managed to survive. They could just be lost.'

'If a couple of girls did survive the river, they'd hardly be able to survive the forest – not for this long,' Vanya had replied.

'But maybe someone found them.'

'There's no one down there,' Vanya had snapped. 'Don't be stupid, you know there's no one there.'

'We don't know,' Tomilin persisted. 'There could be another village – how could we tell, we never go there.'

'If there's another village, it'll be a place of hags and witches. You know what it's like out there – you must be mad.'

Vanya had looked at Tomilin in disbelief – his younger brother really was out of his mind; he had always feared as much. He had no real respect for Tomilin, but he did have some affection for the boy. He was used to protecting him from the jibes and taunts of the other boys – he had taken trouble to help him become more like everyone else. It seemed that he had not succeeded.

Both brothers knew of the rumours and stories of a dreadful place downriver where dwelt all sorts of terrible people – witches, ghouls and dead things . . . Rusalka. They had heard the men whisper about such a place, though no one spoke openly of it. Vanya, although alarmed, was also curious. Perhaps it was true. Perhaps he would find it. If Masha and Nina were alive, which he doubted, and they had been captured by these creatures, perhaps he could rescue them and return a hero. He had been fond of Masha (although she was so idle and dreamy) and of Nina too. Before the accident he had thought of going to his father to ask about getting her as a wife. Although only eighteen, Vanya had put away childish things and considered himself a man. He liked the idea of going into the forest and proving himself a great hunter. Even more he was attracted by the idea of showing everyone how fearless he was.

These had been Vanya's thoughts at the time of setting off. Now, having spent five days and nights alone in the forest, both boys felt differently about the expedition. Tomilin had long since despaired of finding anyone alive – what girl could possibly live in such a wild and dangerous place? Vanya, who had had little luck with his hunting and, for all his efforts, now carried only two rather small deer-skins in his pack, had become aware that he did not feel as valiant and fearless as he had thought he would. The nights had been a misery to him – his dreams had been filled with awful visions, and at every night-time noise he had been certain that Rusalka was leaving her lofty perch in a nearby tree to come and get him. This confrontation with his own valour, or the lack of it, made Vanya angry. He was certain that other men must feel as he did, but they hid their fear beneath a show of blustering bravado. Well, so be it – that's what he would do, too: he would show weakness to no one. Thus, he deprived himself of being able to share his fears with Tomilin – to his younger brother he acted as if he actually enjoyed the dangers.

The younger boy had been scared, too – of wolves, bears and boars. At first, he had been frightened at night by the total darkness, and the strange feeling of being completely alone. He too had thought of witches and ghosts, but fearing Vanya's scorn he had said nothing. Now he had decided that these night-time fears must just be a working of his imagination. In this way, Tomilin ceased to fear the forest, while Vanya's fears grew nightly.

Now, as they sat in the sunny clearing, pulling provisions from their packs, Tomilin said: 'Do you think we're on the right track?'

Vanya looked up. He was tired and cross. He wanted to go home. Any more time they spent in the forest should be spent hunting – he'd take back trophies, if nothing else. He answered Tomilin tersely: 'We're not getting anywhere; we need more water. We'll head back for the river, and then start home. They'll be looking for us soon.'

Tomilin nodded. He would have liked to go on. Though he did not share Vanya's passion for hunting, he was enjoying himself in the forest. He had always shared Masha's love of wild things – trees, animals and birds. He liked it here, far away from the tamed land of the village.

He sat listening to the silence of the forest, then, taking from his pack a small wooden flute, he tried to imitate the liquid call of a thrush that sat in a swaying pine far above his head. The notes of the flute hung in the air and the thrush, seeming pleased to be in such good company, gave forth bubbling trails of song. Vanya, listening sullenly, munched on dry bread and smoked deer-meat and cursed Tomilin's carefree music-making.

After their meal, the boys got to their feet and shouldered their packs. Using the position of the afternoon sun as a guide, they set off westward, hacking their way through the unyielding brambles. The little clearing in the woods was empty once more.

4   Three Fires

The sun sank slowly, casting a deep golden light over the endless forest. The darkening sky was banked with clouds which tumbled fantastically above the dark line of the trees, and the horizon was a bright golden glare. The trees showed stark and black against the sunset – below them they cast deep pools of shadow. The forest was in repose. As shadows lengthened, small creatures that had been basking in the late warmth moved slightly, to catch the last slanting rays. The dusty blue of cornflowers, and the yellow of brilliant buttercups, glowed from patches of shade among the dark grass.

Nina and Vila pulled their boat up on to the shingle. They had stopped on the eastern bank, near where Nina and Masha had first come ashore – a few hundred yards downstream from the rapids. This evening the river flowed peacefully – placid and whispering between shadowy banks – the slow water black with the long reflections of trees. The evening gnats were dancing low over this ebony mirror and, from time to time, a fish would break the surface below the smudgy pillar of dancing insects, and with a splash the black mirror would break into circles of gold. Somewhere upstream a lone blackbird broke through the dusk with a shrill and echoing serenade.

'Isn't it beautiful here,' said Nina, straightening up from pulling the small boat high on to the pebbles. She stood and faced the sunset, letting her eyes rest where they would, drinking in the patterns of light and shade upon the surface of the water.

'Yes, it is.' Vila turned and looked at Nina as she stood motionless at the water's edge. The last rays of the evening sun were catching the girl's solemn face as she looked across the dark water, and her ordinary features were made rather beautiful by the fiery light. Her face had lost the sad self-conscious look that had shadowed it recently; now her expression was relaxed and open. Her body, too, reflected a new ease – she stood, hands on hips, sturdy and confident, as if the recent weeks of activity and discovery had helped loosen and strengthen every part of her.

Earlier that afternoon, when Vila had found Nina, damp and miserable, sitting on the path with her head in her hands, she had realized there was no going against the girl's determination to visit – for one last time – her old home. Nina's mouth had been set in a stubborn line and her eyes had been fixed on her feet.

'You can't stop me, Vila.'

'I know I can't,' Vila had replied.

'I'm just going back for a last look. I won't do anything stupid. I won't be in danger. I'm not a fool.'

'I know you're not.'

Nina raised her eyes to Vila's face, she was deadly serious.

'I'll be able to tell my mother I'm all right. I'll find a way. No one will know . . . only her.'

'Well then –' said Vila, with equal gravity, 'would you mind if I came too, just in case? It's safer with two.'

'As long as you don't try and stop me again,' said Nina.

'I won't. I promise.'

They had gone back to the village to fetch a boat and

84

enough supplies for several days (Nina had set out with neither food nor transport) and had found Ania alone in the little hut; Masha was with Stepan and the other children down by the lake.

'Of course you must go back, if you feel you have to,' said Ania, once Vila had explained the situation. Nina was preparing provisions and gathering some proper travelling clothes and blankets. 'You're a sensible girl, Nina, you'll be careful.' Nevertheless, the woman had smoothed her red hair away from her face with a nervous gesture, and her eyes had sought Vila's with a worried look. Vila, standing in the doorway, a solid black shape against the sunshine, had silently shrugged her shoulders.

'You're lucky to be getting away for a bit,' Ania continued. 'I haven't been out of the village for months. I'd like to go on a journey of some sort. Why don't Masha and I come too? We can meet you somewhere – tomorrow evening or the next day.'

Nina had continued to pack, fussing over the buckles of her knapsack. She wished everyone would just let her get on with it. However, since hearing the story of Saskia's return to the village, she was aware that it was a thing not lightly done. She was ashamed of the worry she was causing, but why couldn't they let her go alone? Why all the fuss?

Behind her the two women were in whispered conference.

'I'm not just going to stay here and worry,' said Ania.

'We'll be safe,' Vila muttered. 'I'll take care of her – we won't do anything dangerous.'

'Ha! You talk of going into the village – not dangerous? Vila, you mustn't go in. If someone saw you, my God!'

'Ssh, it'll be all right. We just need to talk to her mother – that's all – then come back.'

'But how do you know you can trust her?'

'From what Nina says she sounds like a sensible person, not like the father. If anything goes wrong, we'll have the

85

boat, we can get away in a hurry.'

'I'm *not* going to stay here.' Ania clasped Vila's arm and her whispers were urgent. 'You know how I worry . . . you enjoy the danger. I don't trust you to be careful. It's not right of you to leave us behind like this, Vila, you know it's not. I won't let you.'

Vila looked at Ania for a long moment – then she nodded.

'Of course, you're right. I just didn't think. We'll all go.'

So it had been arranged. Ania had gone and told Masha, and found a neighbour to care for the animals while they were away. Vila and Nina would start immediately, the others would follow with Stepan as soon as they were ready. Vila had suggested that Ania should leave the little boy behind, but Ania had been adamant. They were all to meet at an arranged point – a cluster of ancient willows a few miles above the rapids.

Nina and Vila had stopped for the night at the point where the turbulent water of the rapids evened out and became once more as smooth as a sheet of glass. Tomorrow they would have to carry the boat along the narrow path. Vila declared that the rapids were navigable, but that it wasn't worth risking the boat. Nina was relieved that they would thus also avoid risking their limbs, perhaps even their lives: her swimming had improved immensely, but she preferred not to submit her body once more to the rigours of rocks and white water.

So, as Vila made a fire and arranged their small camp, Nina stood staring across the water at the last colours of the sinking sun. She could feel the tensions of the last few days gradually draining from her; she felt relaxed and receptive. She was not thinking of the next day or the day after that, she merely looked across the river and allowed herself to observe. Behind her the little fire crackled and spat, growing brighter as the fiery sky dimmed and became the colour of slate.

★★★

Not far away, Masha and Ania had also stopped for the night. Their small camp-fire flickered through the dark as Masha added more wood. They had camped inside the forest, a hundred or so yards from the river – Stepan was already learning to swim, but he was too young to be completely safe in the water. Now he was fast asleep, wrapped in a warm blanket, exhausted from the excitement of a trip upriver.

He had kept up a constant stream of questions that Masha had patiently answered while Ania steered the boat.

'What's that?'

'It's a dead fir tree.'

'Why'd it die?'

'Oh, because it was old, probably.'

'Why?'

'Everything dies eventually, once it's very old.'

'Why?'

'Just because.'

'What's that?'

'A waterfall.'

'Why's it there?'

'It's a little stream joining the river.'

'Why?'

'I don't know, really.'

'Why not?'

And so on.

Now, with Stepan asleep, the dark forest seemed all the quieter. Occasionally a late bird chirped through the gloom and then flew off with a purr of wings. Then the call of the owl sounded across the water.

Masha was sitting cross-legged by the fire, stirring a bowl of soup and dipping a piece of bread into the thick steaming liquid. She looked over at Ania who was gently stroking the head of her sleeping son.

'Why did you want me to come, Ania?'

87

Ania looked up. They had had little chance for conversation that day. She took up her soup and began to eat. Between mouthfuls she gave her reply.

'Well, there was no way I was going to let Nina and Vila go on their own. Vila knows how dangerous it is, but she doesn't mind. She's too brave, you know, too brave for her own good. She won't let things be.'

'How do you mean?'

'She has her reasons for wanting to see your village. She's curious — always after some new kind of adventure. She spends most of her time in the forest, she takes boats out on to the river when no one else would dare to, she climbs the highest trees, goes on the farthest journeys; always taking risks — too many risks. She's always the same.'

'Is there really such terrible danger?'

'If they get caught they'll be killed. If they get seen, they'll be followed — and no one must be allowed to find our village. The thing is — Vila would quite like to fight them. Your village makes her so angry. When she comes across an idea that she can't agree with, she simply wants to fight it. The way your village is run . . . she just hates it — she can't think of any other way to change it except fighting; and if no one else is going to fight, she'll go and try on her own.'

'But can you force people to change?'

'Maybe not,' said Ania. 'But perhaps you can force them to think.'

Masha laughed. 'Not them,' she said. 'For them, freedom of thought is an act against God.'

Ania nodded in understanding. They sat in silence and watched the flames lick round the little clay pot in which the soup bubbled and steamed. The air had become much cooler — a faint breeze now came off the river and whispered towards them through the ferns and bracken. They sat quietly for many minutes. Through the trees came the haunting call of the owl as she took possession of the night.

After a while Ania got up and fetched two blankets. They wrapped themselves up and settled down to sleep.

The colours of the blankets shone through the dark, mellow and warm. The fire shifted and flared before settling into a fine bed of embers. From time to time, Stepan made tiny childlike noises, as if his dreams were invaded by strange but welcome creatures – at one point he chuckled, the high sound piercing the night air. Ania, hearing these little sounds from her son, cuddled close to him – if at any time the beings in his dreams became less than friendly, she would be near him, for immediate reassurance.

Masha lay awake listening to the forest, her thoughts chattering in her head. She focused her mind on the design of a new picture she was planning. It was a large picture of a woman who flew on the back of a huge bird that carried her far over a land of rocks and mountains. The woman's black hair streamed back and mingled with the dark swirling clouds. As Masha saw the picture against her closed lids she seemed to feel the weightless rush of the bird through the air, the tug of the wind, the dizzying scene below. She let herself be lulled and soothed by her own imagination, and she was carried down through a mass of wild images to a warm place of rest.

As Masha and Ania slept, the forest seemed to wake. All that lived within it that had sheltered from the sun now cautiously emerged to carry on their business in the cool white light of the moon.

There was one other fire in the forest that night. A couple of miles upstream, Tomilin and Vanya had camped on the bank of the river, in the shade of towering moss-covered cliffs. Their small fire cast looming shadows upon the crags, and it seemed to them to be a place of brooding menace. They, too, could hear the hoot of the owl coming faintly through the rustling night.

Tomilin raised his face to the moon and listened to the hollow cry. Shreds of cloud moved across the moon's white face, so that it seemed to the boy that the bright white circle sped across the sky as if indeed pulled by mad white horses. From time to time, the air filled with squeaking bats that came from their caves and hollows in the rock, and made their swift erratic way across the water in search of food. Tomilin followed the little spectres with his eyes, laughing softly at their ridiculous flight. 'Hooo!' he called, answering the owl. 'Hooo! Hooo!'

'Don't!' barked Vanya, his voice harsh and angry.

Tomilin turned and looked questioningly at his brother, who sat hunched against a boulder, his face illuminated by the firelight. Seeing that Vanya was afraid, Tomilin fell silent. It was not worth annoying him – he was becoming increasingly irritable and easily aggravated.

He shrugged and turned away to stare across the dark water at the reflections in the river. The moon was making a wavering white path that seemed to offer an invitation, beckoning him downstream. Tomorrow they were to turn back. Tomilin breathed deeply; the night air was fresh and cool, and seemed to him to be good and friendly. He wished he could show Vanya that there was nothing to fear. But Vanya's pride would make him savage – he had always been frightened of failure, or showing weakness – and Tomilin dreaded his older brother's brutal sarcastic outbursts.

So the boy said nothing – and while he stretched his tired legs out in front of the fire, Vanya stayed hunched and jumpy, with his back against the comforting solid mass of the boulder. When Tomilin's head began to nod and his eyes to close, Vanya remained awake, tense and trembling, starting at the slightest noise. Although his eyes were red with tiredness, he was determined not to sleep. He must remain vigilant. At any moment a black and vile vampire might flap sickeningly from one of these caves. He was certain that these small squeaking creatures were not as harmless as they looked; surely they were the impish minions of something far more deadly.

And worse, far worse to Vanya's tortured mind, was the thought of dreadful Rusalka, with her dishevelled hair full of reeds and her dirty face, her glowing ghastly eyes and her foul dead breath.

The moon continued her wild flight through the sky. More stars showed, gleaming with a pale green light. Time passed, and eventually Vanya's head fell on his chest as he surrendered himself to fitful rest. In a nearby tree the owl ruffled her feathers and clicked her tongue; she could see nothing stirring on the ground below. She spread her wings to glide silently off in search of other hunting grounds. As she swooped and sped far below the rustling black forest, she saw, far below her, the flicker of three small fires, and the tiny huddled shapes of the sleeping forest travellers.

5 Confrontations

The next day, Vanya woke at dawn with his head thick and aching, and his limbs screaming with pain. His flesh felt bruised and tender and his eyes burned with fatigue. He had managed to sleep a little, but it had been a feverish, fitful sleep, shallow and frustrating – no rest at all. His dreams had been filled with shadowy insatiable creatures who had risen from the gleaming river and had padded, cold and dripping, towards him, to lay their pale icy hands upon his brow – or to rest their vile cheeks next to his, while they licked their thin and bloodless lips. As he struggled to raise himself from the hard ground, he groaned with an anguish that came from both a soreness of body and a terrible depression of spirit.

Tomilin was still sleeping, his arms and legs flung apart, relaxed and happy. As Vanya regarded his slumbering brother, he felt a dull resentment: his baby brother, who had shunned the boar-hunt and who had cried when he saw his first bear-slaying, now seemed to be completely at ease in the heart of the great woods. Why this should be, Vanya had no idea. Tomilin did not seem to realize the dangers, did not seem to acknowledge the perils of the night – he laughed at Rusalka, and snapped his fingers at the thought of witches and wild women. If Tomilin was a coward at the chase and the kill, Vanya had to admit that the world of spirits and demons seemed to hold no especial terror for him – and this did not help the older boy: the greater Tomilin's confidence, the more Vanya was overwhelmed by a burning sense of shame.

He staggered to his feet and stumbled over to the water's edge. Kneeling, he splashed his face with water, then flung his hair back and re-tied it with a leather thong. He looked across the water and then around him at the ground, scanning the shingle and sand for tracks. He got up and found his bow, and stiffly began to walk along the edge of the river. He had set some traps further downstream, hoping to catch some otter or beaver, although by this time he had really despaired of getting much game. All he wanted now was to be at home in the village, safe among his friends and family – far away from the dreadful rustling darkness of the forest night. Once in a while, as he walked along, he glanced over his shoulder, as if suspicious of being followed. By now, Vanya was even nervous in the daylight.

The traps were empty. They had been pulled up and smashed, as if by something strong and angry – smashed, and then flung upon the bank, broken and twisted. Vanya bit his lip and felt his eyes fill with tears. His heart thumped and his throat burned with a feeling of angry failure. He turned and flung the broken traps far across the river where they disappeared with a splash. He cursed himself: 'I won't cry – I won't. Bloody bastards . . . I won't . . . acting like a girl . . . bloody things . . . I'll show them . . .'

He turned and was about to make his way back along the river when he was stopped by a sound about a hundred yards downstream – a faint splashing, followed by the crunch of a big animal on the shingle. It must be a deer at least, perhaps a boar, come down to drink. Dropping to one knee, he narrowed his eyes and scoured the shore, alert and wary, his unhappiness forgotten as all his attention focused on whatever had moved. The shame he had felt now turned to determination – nothing would evade him; not this time.

Vanya knew that whatever was there would probably be aware of his presence, therefore he had to remain completely still. And while he crouched, his eyes fixed upon the place from whence the sound had come, other noises began to filter into his aching head – the whisper of the quiet river, the sound of some early birds, the murmur of the breeze in the trees. He saw nothing: nothing moved.

Then, as if it were the most natural thing in the world, Vanya saw a young woman, dressed in a fringed tunic, emerge from the green shadows and begin to wade into the river. Soon the water was up to her knees, the soft leather fringes of her tunic floating upon its brown surface.

As Vanya watched, his heart began to pound so hard that all he could hear for a while was the thick blood beating in his ears. He felt dizzy and weak, too shocked to know whether this was fear or merely surprise. Was this woman the apparition he so dreaded? In broad daylight she seemed so very ordinary, so obviously not a fearful dead thing or a vile blood-sucker.

The woman, thinking herself unobserved, turned and looked back into the undergrowth. As she bent down to peer beneath the drooping branches, her red curls fell over her freckled face. She put her hand to her mouth and called: 'Stepan – come on, darling. Hurry up, it's quite safe.'

Her voice startled Vanya. He had half expected her to sound like the fearful maidens of his restless tortured dreams. Instead, the voice that sounded across the water was clear and sweet.

'Stepan – hurry up; they're waiting.'

The woman straightened and began to wade slowly back to the bank. As she neared the shore she opened her arms and Vanya saw, stumbling from the shadow, a chubby toddling child. The woman stayed in the water and, with her arms outstretched, she urged the little boy to step into the shallows. This he did with little hesitation, his fat legs splashing in the water and his happy face full of giggles.

'S'cold,' he said, and kicked his feet in the water, as if he thought he could warm it up by his activity. Then he tottered on, stumbled and, sitting down with a splash, began to whimper.

'Oh, come on, Stepan,' said the woman. 'It's not that bad. It'll help you wake up.' She moved quickly through the water towards him, shifting a small, curiously woven pack from one shoulder to the other, and picked up the wet child. Cradling him in her arms she turned and began to wade quickly upstream, keeping to the shallows.

Vanya had not moved since he had first seen the woman appear on the opposite bank. He was frozen where he knelt, his mouth open and his hand suspended in mid-air, halfway to fetching his bow from behind him. He did not make a move until the woman had disappeared beyond the gentle curve in the river. Once she was out of sight he sat back sharply, breathing rapidly and trying to control the trembling in his legs.

He knew what he had seen: but he did not understand it. His mind, obsessed with fear of Rusalka, was devastated by the sight of an ordinary woman holding her child. Her confidence, the natural way in which she passed through the water . . . these things seemed to Vanya to be unbelievably arrogant . . . How dare she be so unafraid, up to her thighs in the lethal river? The past few days, the frustration and fear, all combined to fill the tired young man with a feeling of outrage. What right had she to be so free and easy in the water, in the forest – so safe with her little boy, so at home?

But perhaps this really was Rusalka – urging the innocent abducted babe to his death? Could the ghostly creature possibly look so pleasant, so alive? Maybe that was her awful secret, that she looked so like a normal, ordinary woman.

Perhaps her power lay in her deceptiveness, her vile deceit? Either way, Vanya vowed not to let the creature out of his sight. He gathered up his bow and, keeping carefully to the bank, he started to walk cautiously after her.

As she waded swiftly through the cold fresh water, Ania had no idea of being followed. Although she seldom left the village, she was almost as capable and expert in the woods as Vila. She spent little time away from her comfortable house, preferring its cosy security to the forest wilderness. But she had been taught everything about the woods by Vila. So often quiet and reserved on other subjects, Vila loved to spend hours regaling Ania with tales of her exploits, explaining in detail every aspect of forest life.

She had arranged to meet Masha at a place where the cliffs towered over the river; they would then carry the boat along the path that ran beside the rapids – a matter of half a mile or so – to the place where Vila and Nina would be waiting. This morning Masha had woken with her head full of dreams and ideas for paintings – she had taken the boat and gone on alone to sort them out.

Ania had looked and listened carefully for any predators. She decided that all was clear. She was not naturally a fearful person, except when worrying about her loved ones, and Vila often told her that she was too trusting, too relaxed – about people, as well as about natural dangers. When Vila exhorted her thus, Ania would tease her, saying that she was too vigilant – like an owl, or a cat. Vila would laugh grudgingly, but would say that Ania was more right than she knew: it was safer to have the senses and cautions of an animal – to be wary, to trust one's instincts – among people, as well as in the woods.

Then Ania would fall silent. Knowing Vila's past, she understood the woman's deep reserve. She knew how long it had taken for Vila to feel safe, how long it had been before she could allow herself to trust again. Ania was simply more carefree than Vila, believing quite automatically in the basic goodness of nature and the benevolence of people.

'But then –' she had once said laughingly to Vila, 'I've never been surrounded by a pack of wolves!'

They had been sitting in front of the fire on a frozen winter's evening – Stepan, a baby still, had been at her breast. She remembered how Vila had looked up, her large mouth sullen and her black eyes hurt and angry: 'Which kind of wolf?' she had asked. 'Animal or human?'

Walking along through the shining morning, Ania rejoiced in the sight of the green and yellow leaves, showing here and there a glint of autumn crimson. It was good to be out in the woods again. Even if she had misgivings about their mission and was worried about the wisdom of going upstream to the forest village, she was determined to enjoy it if she possibly could. Anyway, anything was better than having to wait at home, never knowing if Vila would appear again, having the sick thud of anxiety and forboding knocking at the inside of her chest – making her miserable, and causing her to snap and nag at Stepan, and then curse herself for doing so. She had never told Vila the extent her adventuring distressed her – she would never try to limit Vila's freedom. She knew that to attempt to curb her wayfaring would be to change her, and Ania loved Vila for those very things that made her fearful – her bravery and independence and solitude.

Ania swung along. Her legs, splashing through the water, caused droplets to fly over Stepan, making the child shriek with laughter. The water here was shallow and swift, tumbling grey and white through the boulders. She was nearing the rapids. Masha would be waiting nearby with the boat.

As she came to the foot of a steep cliff of rock, Ania walked out of the shallows and on to the shingle. Putting Stepan down, she swung the pack from behind her and began to rummage around in it. Pulling out a small bright piece of cloth, she proceeded to dry her feet. Stepan had immediately trotted off along the shingle and settled down to play with some interesting pebbles, trying to balance one on top of another. Giving up, he began throwing them as far as he could into the river. Ania, her feet dry, put on a pair of fringed trousers and some soft beaded moccasins.

'Come on, darling. We must go now,' she called.

Stepan continued to play, absorbed in the act of throwing, fascinated by the heavy plop of the pebbles into the water. Ania got up and walked towards him. As she passed along the shore, in the shadow of the overhanging cliff, she saw, from the corner of her eye, a thin pillar of smoke issuing from a small fire. 'Ah . . .' she thought, instantly hungry, 'Masha must be making some breakfast.'

She picked her way towards the fire and then stopped dead. A young man was sitting on the shingle, a blanket round his waist, and his long hair tousled. He was yawning and rubbing his eyes, having just woken up – aroused, perhaps, by Stepan's excited chattering and the plop of the stones in the river. He scratched his head, pushed his hair from in front of his pleasant face, and caught sight of Ania. His mouth dropped open in amazement as he stared at her, and then over at Stepan, sitting by the river.

'Er . . .' He coughed and cleared his throat, blinking and rubbing his eyes again. 'Er . . . hallo.'

Ania relaxed slightly. The young man in front of her was little more than a child – and a friendly, nice-looking boy at that. Her heart stopped racing and her knees, which had begun to shake, ceased their trembling. Nevertheless, she quickly went over to Stepan, picked him up in her arms and held him protectively to her. She had noticed not one, but two packs, and another coarse grey blanket, as well as a second wooden cup and plate: there was someone with this boy – she must be careful.

, 'Hallo,' she said. 'Who are you?' Her normally soft voice was slightly shrill from alarm. Ania never carried a weapon of any kind – no one could persuade her to – and now she felt defenceless. She was also aware of the fact that it would be hard to run holding a well-grown two-year-old. Where was Masha? Why had she agreed to them separating? How stupid of her. She cursed herself for letting the girl go on ahead. There was safety with two – but alone . . . Ania felt very vulnerable.

'My name's Tomilin,' said the boy. 'I come from the village in the forest, by the river. I'm looking for my sister. She's called Masha. You haven't seen her, have you?'

Ania's mind was racing. Tomilin! Masha's brother – she had heard all about him. The one member of Masha's family that the girl really seemed to miss. A gentle imaginative boy from all accounts, unusual in many respects – a good musician, and an unwilling hunter. She smiled at him, and he smiled back. Both were naturally open, friendly people, but Ania was determined to make herself act cautiously. More than anything, she was conscious of the wriggling child in her arms: she must be doubly careful.

'Who are you travelling with?' she asked.

'Vanya, my brother. He's not here. I don't know where he's gone. I suppose he's looking at his traps.'

'Oh,' Ania paused. 'You haven't seen anyone else around?'

'No. Are you looking for someone?'

'Not really.'

Ania hoisted Stepan on to her hip and walked away from the river. She began to clamber up the sharp slope that fell down to the bank on one side of the cliff.

'I must be going. Goodbye.'

She was trying to think what had happened to Masha. Where could she be waiting? She must find her, and then they must find Vila and Nina. Afterwards, perhaps, something could be done about these brothers. She moved as rapidly as she could up the slope, wishing that Stepan was younger and lighter, or older and more mobile – instead, he was heavy, and her progress was slow. She was halfway up when she heard a harsh voice behind her.

'Stop there. Don't go any further.'

She stopped dead and turned slowly. Below her stood a second young man, older than the first. He was holding a bow, and Ania saw that it was bent, with an arrow ready at the string. The young man's face was full of anger, perhaps fear. Tomilin had leapt to his feet and now stood looking nervously from one to the other.

'What are you up to?' demanded the young man. His voice had none of the gentleness of the younger brother's, and Ania felt her spirits flare angrily at his tone of peremptory command.

'I'm trying to leave. If you put down your bow, I'll be on my way.' She raised her chin and shook the hair from her eyes. She was frightened of the weapon, but not yet of the man.

'Where's your husband?' said Vanya, and his voice came out louder than he had intended. 'What are you doing out here alone? Where's your man?'

'I have no husband,' said Ania. 'And I may ask what you are up to, but your brother's already told me. He seems less rude than you.'

'Shut up!' said Vanya, and his voice rose to a shout. He had followed this woman all the way along the river, keeping as quiet as a mouse, getting his feet wet and his face scratched, only to find his brother engaged in pleasant conversation with his quarry.

By now he had two ideas in his mind. The first was that this red-headed woman had lost her husband, and was searching for him. If this was the case, Vanya would be able to come to her rescue and find the lost man. He could already picture the little freckled face full of gratitude as she thanked him for his kindness. The second idea was that this was in fact some kind of witch, part of a tribe of dreadful creatures who lived downstream and who stole children – he had heard of them often enough during his childhood: 'If you do that the wild women will get you . . . Rusalka comes for naughty boys.' If this were the case, Vanya would rescue the child and force the witch to tell him from whence the little one had been taken.

His tired mind, muddled from lack of sleep, and confused almost to breaking point, had read the situation thus – he was capable of no other interpretation. The one thing he had not bargained for was this kind of brisk dismissal. He was ready for the woman to turn and fight, for her friendly features to distort into a mask of fury, but he was not prepared for Ania's straightforward behaviour. As his confusion grew, so did his belligerence.

'Come over here, woman. Put the child down. How do I know he belongs to you?'

Ania fought back her anger and fear. She was keeping her eyes trained on the bow and she was determined not to let go of Stepan. But by now the child, alarmed by the harsh voice of the stranger and his mother's tense replies, had begun to struggle and cry. Ania put him down and pushed him behind her. She held him tightly, making him cry louder.

'Give me the child.'

'No, Vanya,' protested Tomilin. 'Leave her alone. She's not done anything. Put down the bow.'

'Be quiet, you fool,' said Vanya, licking his dry lips. His hands were shaking on the bowstring and he began to fear that he would let fly the arrow from nerves or from fatigue. He called over to the woman: 'Bring the child here. Do it – or I promise I will shoot.'

Everything went quiet. Tomilin was rooted to the spot, unable to do anything, unable to think of a way to defuse the situation. Vanya and Ania were stock still, both of them trembling with fear and fury. Stepan continued to wriggle and whine. Behind them, the river murmured softly, tumbling among the rocks – in the distance the roar of the rapids sounded like an echo of the blood as it beat in the temples of the two people standing locked in silent confrontation.

Suddenly Vanya pitched forward. A lean dark shape had flown through the air at him and felled him with a savage kick. His bow was wrenched from his grasp and flung into the middle of the river. As he lay on his back on the shingle, Vila was sitting on his chest, her knees pinning his arms and her hands tight about his throat. Her voice was icy.

'Don't move a muscle. Don't you dare. One word and you're dead.'

6 Reunions

'No violence, Vila.'

Ania's voice was shrill as she whirled the screaming Stepan round and carried him quickly back down the slope with her. Leaving him at the water's edge, she ran over to where Vila knelt astride the prone Vanya, and quickly seized the long sharp knife that hung in a scabbard at his belt. Drawing back her arm, she was about to throw the knife into the river, when Vila cried: 'No – keep it. And make sure he's got nothing else. The other one, too.'

'Who are you? Who are you?' Tomilin had not moved. He stood and fumbled with his own knife which had become entangled in his blanket. He did not want to relinquish the weapon, but neither did he have any desire to wield it. He managed to extricate the clumsy blade and he held it in front of him, his hands shaking and his eyes wide with fright. 'Don't hurt him, please,' he cried, looking desperately at Vila. 'He was only showing off. He wouldn't have hurt them.'

'Be quiet.' Vanya's voice was small and cracked from the pressure of Vila's fingers at his throat. He was gazing at the extraordinary creature that had attacked him, her eyes black and burning and her hair wild about her head. The legs that pinned his arms with such strength were clad in leather leggings like his own, like a man's. Whatever she was, she was dangerous.

'Give her the knife, for God's sake,' he croaked, and Tomilin threw it to the ground at Ania's feet.

'Who are you?' repeated the boy. 'What do you want?'

Vila looked up at him. She grinned, showing her white teeth and looking like a wild animal. Whenever Vanya moved she pushed him back into the ground, but her hands on his throat were relaxed now. 'Who do you think we are, Tomilin?' she said over her shoulder.

'How do you know my name?' he asked, startled.

'Your sister told me. Who do you think we are?'

'Masha? Where is she? She's alive? Oh, please let me see her.' Tomilin rushed forward and fell to his knees, looking pleadingly at Vila. Ania had fetched Stepan, and soothing him with words and caresses, she joined Vila. They made a strange group, kneeling there on the shingle. Stepan, once more feeling happy and safe, began to dance round them, singing and laughing.

'Funny man!' he said, pointing at Vanya.

'Will you behave, if I let you up?' Vila asked.

The young man, red-faced with a variety of strong emotions, nodded. Vila rocked back and sprang up, releasing Vanya, who got heavily to his feet and stood looking sullenly from one person to another.

'Where's Masha?' said Tomilin. 'Is she near? Please let me see her.'

Vila ignored him. Going over to Ania, she picked up Tomilin's knife and thrust it into her belt. Then she fetched Vanya's knife from where Ania had laid it; this too she put in her belt. Keeping her gaze on Vanya, she touched Ania gently on the arm.

'You all right?'

'I'm fine.' Ania hugged Stepan. 'We both are.' She

laughed. 'To the rescue in the nick of time, Vila. You are marvellous. How did you know?'

'Masha told me. Me and Nina were waiting at the willows when Masha came rushing along in a great panic. She found their traps, so she knew there were forest people about, said they were her brothers.'

'Why didn't she say?' shouted Tomilin. 'Why didn't she wake me up?' He was jumping up and down exuberantly. He rushed over to Vanya and slapped him on the back. 'We've found her! We've done it. I knew we would. And Nina too.' He put his head back and cheered. Vila, watching him, grinned and raked back her wild hair.

'Masha's a cautious girl,' she said. 'She's learnt a lot. How was she to know there wasn't a great party of you?' She turned to Vanya. 'Is it just you two? Are you alone?'

Vanya stared at his feet. He was not inclined to answer this strange woman, who had effortlessly pinned him to the floor – him, Vanya, who had recently won a wrestling competition in the village. She'd surprised him, that's all – he'd show her.

'Are you alone?' Vila repeated her question.

It was Tomilin who replied: 'Yes, we are . . . but . . .'

'Quiet!' Vanya barked. 'Let me do the talking.'

Vila looked at him shrewdly. 'Well. Talk then.'

'We've come alone. We came to find our sister, and her friend. If you tell us where they are, we'll be able to take them home.'

Vila was looking at the young man with a curious expression, part amusement, part distaste. She glanced over at Tomilin and then spoke softly.

'If they want to return to your village, then I'm sure they will – in their own time. However, I suspect that they don't need your help, or want it.' Her black eyes bored mercilessly into Vanya, causing his gaze to waver and finally fall. 'We'll take you to where they are, but you must abide by their decisions – if you try and get away, or try and bully them, or us – I'll tie you up and dump you in the river.'

'Come on,' said Tomilin. 'They're trying to help, can't you see?' He took his brother's hand. 'Don't make trouble,' he whispered. 'Please.' Vanya nodded with bad grace. By now his tiredness was overwhelming, he was hungry too. His back hurt, where Vila's kick had landed. 'All right,' he said. 'Let's get going.'

The boys gathered their belongings and shouldered their packs. Having put out the small camp-fire, they set off, Vila making Vanya go ahead. From time to time she told him which direction to take, but for the most part they simply followed the edge of the cliff. The going was moderately easy; on their left hand the river poured and tumbled through the rapids, often as far as a hundred feet below. To their right grew an impenetrable tangle of holly, hawthorne and other scrubby bushes. Here and there, a slender sapling attempted to push its way out of this mass of thorny growth, stretching its delicate tips upwards in search of the sun. But more often than not these brave attempts were thwarted as the dark green of the ivy gently throttled the slim grey trunks. It was a harsh, unwelcoming place.

The four people had to walk slowly and carefully. Sometimes the wild tangle of the undergrowth came to within a few feet of the cliff and they had to pick their way with care, looking out for loose stones and patches of moss, made slippery by the early dew. Ania and Stepan brought up the rear of the little procession, the red-headed woman holding the child tightly. Eventually, Tomilin offered to carry him for a while.

'Thank you,' said Ania. 'He does get heavy at times.' She handed him over and Tomilin soon had him settled in the crook of his arm. He began little stories and pieces of whimsy to the little boy, and Ania smiled, recognizing the same ease with children that she saw in Masha – the ease that comes from being part of a large family and always having several smaller brothers and sisters tagging along behind.

'Masha's told me about your family. She misses the little ones,' she said.

'Yes,' Tomilin nodded. 'I like them too – better than the older ones.' He smiled ruefully, glancing forward to where Vanya was trampling heavily over the rocks. 'The rest of them treat me as if I was still a baby – all except Masha.'

'Why's that?'

'Oh,' he shrugged. 'I don't know. I'm no good at hunting. I don't like fighting. They call me a cissy.'

'The way that Masha described you didn't make you sound like that at all. She said you were a musician, that you play for the whole village, even though you're only thirteen. And you're good at farming.'

'Did she say that?' Tomilin beamed. 'I do like working on the farm – I'm good with horses. If only I didn't have to go hunting. I can't bear the noise and the blood – it's not frightening exactly, not the hunt itself. But the other hunters frighten me; they get so savage. That's what I can't bear – that and all the ritual.'

Ania smiled: 'Oh, I agree, Tomilin. I feel just the same.'

Vila, who had been listening, turned and called: 'That just makes you both cissies.' She laughed loudly. 'He's just like Masha, isn't he. Oh, we're all going to get along just fine.'

'She doesn't mean it,' said Ania. 'She's just being wicked.'

'Wicked!' echoed Stepan happily. 'Wicked Vila . . . naughty Vila.' He crowed with laughter. He was having a marvellous time – lots to see, and lots of attention.

Vanya, up ahead, nursing his wounded pride, heard the others laughing and talking. He wanted to turn round and join in the fun; he wanted to share in the laughter. But he could feel within himself a nasty, bitter voice that mumbled: 'Wicked Vila . . . I'll show you . . . just you wait . . . you witch.'

***

Masha and Nina were waiting near a collection of ancient willows that were grouped on the western bank of the river. The mighty trees were gnarled and twisted with age, whole branches had split and toppled into the water but seemed to live on, trailing their leaves in the current – yellow and green in the sun, silver-grey in the water. Here the river was much narrower, deep and slow. The different lights made it shine green where the sun fell, and, where it flowed in the shade, it was dappled a deep brown.

The girls were tending a fire. Suspended over the hottest of the ash and embers were a dozen fair-sized fish, spitted on slim willow wands. The smell that came from them was mouth-watering, and the girls were having a difficult time restraining themselves from beginning the meal; but they had promised Vila that they would wait for the others. From time to time they looked anxiously along the river.

'I hope everything's all right,' said Masha.

'Oh, I should think so,' said Nina. 'Vila would never let them get the jump on her.'

'I don't suppose Tomilin would try,' said Masha, but she looked doubtful. 'Only Vanya. He'll be a problem.'

'Why do you suppose they came?' Nina rescued a fish from becoming charred, then guiltily licked her fingers.

'Come after us . . . must have. No one else hunts in this direction. And I shouldn't think that they let anyone know they were coming this far. It's too dangerous. There's no path. We know that.'

'For our pains.'

Masha laughed and nodded: 'For our pains.'

Nina chuckled: 'Except it didn't turn out so badly after all, did it?'

'No.'

'It's probably all for the best, the way things worked out.'

'Yes.'

'We were pretty lucky, really.'

'Mmm.'

There was a pause. Both girls stared vaguely into the middle of the river.

Sitting in the dappled sunlight beneath the wild old willows, they looked very different from that day, a month ago, when they had first journeyed accidentally down the river. Then they had worn the traditional dresses of the forest village, full and heavy, then their hair had been covered by the traditional shawl.

Now, stretching her long legs luxuriantly, Masha looked down at her soft loose trousers, a present to her from one of the lake villagers.

'At least we got to wear all this.' She wriggled her toes inside her moccasins and preened the fringes of her jacket, polishing the clay beading with her cuff.

'Useful – all these pockets,' Nina agreed, rummaging around in her own and bringing out a comb with which she proceeded to tidy her long sandy hair. 'Here – tie it up for me.'

'Turn round, then.'

Masha began to untangle Nina's hair, using the fishbone comb that Nina had been given by a local carver. During their stay by the lake, both girls had been given presents of various articles of clothing. Masha's favourite was a knee-length blue tunic decorated with coloured beads that Ania had given her. Now she wore it over an ordinary costume similar to the one worn by Vila when she had discovered the girls. She had immediately taken to the lakeside mode of dress, rejoicing in the freedom it had given her. Nina had at first been unsure of wearing trousers, feeling that she looked heavy and ungainly. At first she had worn a dress, full and flowing, but decorated with the strange new patterns of the village. But then Vila had given her a pair of deerskin trousers she had made the previous winter, and Nina had felt obliged

109

to wear them. She had grown to love them, and to love the way they made her feel.

'God, there's a lot of it. However did this happen?' said Masha, struggling with a great bird's-nest of hair at the back.

'Ow! Stop!' Nina shrieked and pulled away. 'Oh, God, what a mess.' Her fingers pulled frantically at the bird's-nest.

'Hang on, you're making it worse.'

'I hate it,' Nina wailed. 'This happens every day. I wish it was short.'

Masha looked slightly prim. 'If you combed it out properly, like me, it wouldn't get like this.'

'I do.'

'Hmm. Let me plait it. Then at least it'll be out of the way.'

'No. I look dreadful like that. Oh, it's so hot.' Nina pulled the whole tangled mass away from her neck and held it on top of her head. 'Why do I have to have all this loathsome stuff anyway?'

'Let me plait it,' repeated Masha calmly. 'It's much more sensible.'

Nina turned. Her face was hot but determined. She pulled her knife from her belt and held it out to Masha.

'Do me a favour. Cut it off. I don't need it any more.'

'Nina, you're mad. I won't do it. You'll kill me later.'

'Please do it, Masha. I won't regret it. I promise. I won't kill you – I vow it by all the gods. Only do it now, or I'll lose my nerve.'

Masha looked at her friend through narrowed eyes. 'All right then, you mad thing. But don't say I didn't warn you.'

It seemed no time at all before Nina's hair lay beside her on the grass. What was left after Masha had sliced the strands from Nina's neck and temples was a great halo of tawny locks, sticking up oddly here and there, but mainly even and slightly curly all over. There was silence.

Nina turned and looked nervously at Masha. She fingered the pile of hair that lay on the bank.

She giggled. 'Well. What's it like?'

'Coo! Well, it's certainly different.'

She ruffled Nina's remaining hair and looked at her handiwork critically, her head on one side. 'It's wonderful. Have a look in the river.'

Nina peered into the water. 'I can't tell, it's too fast here – too much glare. Ooh, I do want to see.'

'Hold on, don't panic. Use this.' Masha quickly gave a rub to the bottom of a little bronze saucepan; it was pitted and dark from the fire, but it served as a mirror after a fashion. Nina squinted at herself, shaking her head and raking at it with her fingers.

'How does it feel?' Masha sat back on her heels and smiled.

Nina shook her head again and ran her fingers through her hair, making it stand up all round.

'It's so light. And it's quite curly. And it's so cool. Does it really look all right?'

Masha nodded.

Ceremoniously, Nina gathered up her fallen tresses. She looked for a moment at the shiny slippery bundle, and then she grinned at Masha. Leaping up, she flung her hair into the wide green river. Watching it drift away, she threw back her shorn head and laughed. Still laughing, she began to jump up and down on the grassy bank, shaking her head and flailing her arms like a windmill. Then she lay right down on the grass and, leaning over the water, dipped her entire head under the surface.

'Mad! Mad!' laughed Masha, as Nina brought her dripping head out of the water and shook herself like a dog, spraying her with tiny drops.

Nina's new hair dried quickly in the sun, as the girls sat by the fire and tended the fish. They gathered some herbs and made tea, then sat and talked. They talked of the forest and the lake, of parents and priests, brothers and sisters, new friends and old friends. Without realizing it they soon healed the slight gap that had seemed to come between them, as they had seen and felt things so differently in the month they had spent in the village by the lake. In this way, an hour quickly passed.

'I don't know,' Masha concluded at least. 'I can't say it in words. One day I'll paint it all in pictures.'

Laughing softly, Nina turned and gazed over the water. 'I know what you mean, Masha,' she said.

Then they were serious. Across the river, at the summit of the steep cliff, they saw a group of people begin to descend the rocky incline. From where they sat they could just distinguish Vanya, his pack slung over his shoulder, clambering slowly down the slope. Behind him came Vila, lighter on her feet, and swifter, having to wait now and then for Vanya to make some progress. Further back, and walking together with Stepan in between them, each holding a fat hand, came Ania and Tomilin.

'Well,' said Nina finally, after they had watched for a while in silence. 'Here they come. Trust Vanya to barge in.' She scratched her nose thoughtfully. 'Typical.'

Masha looked sad. 'I know he's awful,' she said. 'But I can't help feeling sorry for him. You never know, he might be sensible – I know Tomilin will.'

'Huh! We'll see.' Nina was sceptical. 'God knows what we can do – can't exactly march home in triumph – rescued. Don't they see that?'

On the other side of the river Vila, her hands cupped to her mouth, was shouting something. The girls strained to hear above the liquid thunder of the rapids.

'Hey, you two, bring the boat over.' Her voice, though faint, seemed full of merriment, anticipating the reaction about to be caused.

'Here we go,' said Nina, jumping up to untie the small boat that she and Vila had been using. They had risen early that morning and quickly carried the boat and provisions along the cliff-track. Ania and Masha's boat was still downriver, hidden among the rocks. Nina got into the bows and picked up a paddle. Masha pushed off and jumped in; they made swift progress.

The commotion this caused on the other side was just what Vila and Ania had expected. Stepan, clapping his hands together, called happily to the two girls and danced around, while Tomilin and Vanya stood motionless and stared open-mouthed. At last, as the boat neared the shore, Vanya backed away.

'What sorcery is this?' he croaked, his face ashen, and his hands trembling by his sides.

'What is it?' echoed Tomilin, transfixed by the sight.

Masha, seeing their consternation, and remembering her own, quickly called out to them, trying to explain what would at first, she knew, be inexplicable.

'Don't worry. It's quite all right. It's a boat. It's quite safe. It's fun . . . wait until you try.'

Tomilin, hearing his sister's voice, was filled with a feeling of love and relief so great that it pushed to one side his fear and astonishment. He saw Masha, dressed in a strange blue jerkin covered in beads and fringes. On her long legs were soft trousers, in her hair new coloured beads. She looked different, and yet the same. As she smiled and laughed at him, her eyes shining, he saw his sister.

'Masha!' he cried. 'Masha!'

Vanya, unable to comprehend the scene that he was witnessing, continued to back slowly away from the bank. At length he stopped and stood, limbs rigid, staring intently at the curious sight. He saw two girls, who certainly looked like his sister and her friend. But they were both dressed in the same ugly, ridiculous garments as the women who had captured him. They moved with a strange unwomanly gait as they directed their diabolic craft across the water, defying God's law by floating on its surface. And, instead of seeing what was before his eyes, Vanya recalled the whispered conversations around the fire, when the men were gathered after hunting – rumours of these strange creatures who lived high in the trees, who hunted in the water, dressing in the clothes of men whom they had lured to their death. He remembered the song of his childhood, sung to him by his mother, part lullaby, part warning:

'Sing, Rusalka . . . float on water;
Use your magic, shriek with laughter,
Come to get me, show no mercy.
Sing, Rusalka, sing, Rusalka.'

This may be his sister. But she was no longer the quiet docile girl he remembered. This may be Nina, her friend, but there was a new awful arrogance about her, and where was all that shining hair that had been her only beauty? Whatever had happened to these two maids in the depths of the forest, it had changed them in a dreadful way. He saw that Vila had already exerted her terrible influence over them. These were women of his village no longer, they were dangerous outcasts; he must beware.

7   The Mati

For two hours they had marched along through the forest in single file, making good progress. Vila and Tomilin had gone in front, using the knives to hack a path when it was necessary. However, with Vila in the lead, it had only to be done occasionally – she seemed to know ways to get through seemingly impenetrable undergrowth, and she was familiar with her surroundings, unlike the others.

It was past noon now, as they came to a place where the woodland thinned and the undergrowth lessened. Great banks of moss rose from the thick carpet of needles; the ground underfoot felt soft, covered with mould and rotting leaves. The warm midday air hung full of the sweet pungent smell of bruised, rotten wood and stagnant, rain-filled pools. The going was easy now and the travellers ceased to pant and gasp with the effort of every step. They each relaxed, eased up, and had time to look about. The journey took on the air of an afternoon stroll as they wandered through the balmy glades, gazing at the magnificent beeches and oaks, the castles of holly, and the ivy-clad trunks of spruce.

Nina, who had been walking along with Ania and the sullen Vanya, jogged forward and joined Vila.

'How far now?' she asked.

'Not far.'

Vila was being most mysterious about their destination. When they had set off, she had merely said: 'We'll go and see the Mati.' Who or what was the Mati, Nina had no idea. She had asked Masha, but her friend shrugged and shook her head: 'No,' she didn't know either. They had set off, plunging after Vila, straight into the forest, moving steadily north-east, leaving the river glinting and whispering behind them.

Now, as Nina walked along, a few steps behind Vila, she watched Masha and Tomilin as they meandered along on their long legs, arm in arm, heads together, discussing all that had happened since they had last been together. Nina recalled the joyful reunion earlier that day.

'You look wonderful. What are you wearing? What happened?' Tomilin had danced round his sister, rather like Stepan. Brother and sister had looked very similar, with their flushed cheeks and tousled black hair. 'Hallo, Nina. We thought you were both dead – it was awful. But I *knew* I'd find you.'

Masha had hugged her brother again – her baby brother, whom she had always looked after; her eyes had shone with tears. Nina had stood beside them, grinning and embarrassed – then she had sidled over to stand with Vila and Ania.

'What have you done?' Vila grinned broadly and rumpled Nina's new wild hair. 'It's wonderful – you look like a lion.'

'Do you like it?' asked Nina apprehensively. 'Really?'

'Really.' Vila and Ania spoke together, emphatically. Ania added: 'You were never going to look after it properly. You're the wrong kind of person for long hair.'

'Ha!' Vila had laughed in agreement. 'Far too lazy.'

They had stood and watched the others. Then Vila had whispered in her ear: 'Go and be nice to Vanya – someone's got to.'

Ania joined in: 'Poor thing, he looks so lonely. I'm sure he wants to be nice. He's just feeling left out. You should understand that, Nina.'

Nina felt unwilling. Nevertheless, she felt sorry for Vanya as he stood apart, looking so exhausted and confused. She had walked casually over to him. Vanya turned and regarded her with red-rimmed eyes. On his face was an expression that Nina could only take for fear and dismay.

'Hallo, Vanya.' She had smiled. 'It's all right, you know. We're quite real. Not ghosts or anything.'

She looked him straight in the eye and tried to seem friendly. To her surprise it was Vanya's gaze that broke, and the young man shifted on his feet and looked squarely at the ground. She had kept trying for several minutes, but had got no response. All Vanya did was to grunt his non-committal answers and attempt to edge away from her. Nina could not understand this behaviour from a boy who had always been so brash and confident, so fearless and so opinionated; it was very unlike him. Only when they had prepared to cross the river by taking turns in the boat, had Vanya opened his mouth: 'No! I'm not going in that. No!'

'Come on, Vanya,' Masha had urged. 'It's all right – it won't sink.'

'Not me,' Vanya had said, shaking his head. 'You can just leave me here.'

'But breakfast is over there – lots of food,' Nina had said. She tried to remember whether she had felt similar fear, but she knew that she and Masha had soon been eager to try this new thing when Vila had shown them. Why was Vanya so different?

Vila had settled it. She had quickly crossed the river alone and brought the hot fish back with her. Everyone had eaten the meal with much enjoyment; even Vanya had shared it, his hunger getting the better of him, although he regarded everything that was passed to him with the greatest suspicion.

After they had finished eating, Vila had called for silence.

'Well, now, we must decide what we do. Masha and Nina – do we go on, or go back?'

There was silence. Nina and Masha looked at each other. Then Ania had spoken: 'Vanya – why did you come out into the forest? Did you really believe that you'd find the girls?'

Vanya had looked over at Ania, sitting with Stepan in her lap, her small face kind but serious. He shrugged and said nothing.

'It was my idea,' Tomilin said. 'I persuaded Vanya to come with me. It was he who got Father's permission. But they think we're just on a hunting trip.' He paused. 'They'll be coming after us if we don't get back soon.'

'What?' said Vila. 'They're coming after you? When?'

'If we're not back . . . tomorrow, I think, or today.' Tomilin ignored Vanya who was glaring at him. 'It's all right, they'll be pleased to see that we've found them.'

'Will they?' said Vila grimly, and Tomilin looked at her, puzzled. Vila continued: 'Will they really be pleased? What would your father have said if he'd known what you were doing?'

Tomilin, looking nervously at the ground, was tearing apart a long blade of grass, shredding it into smaller and smaller pieces.

'He would have been angry, I suppose. He was cross that I kept on about Masha . . . kept telling me to forget her – that's what he told Mother, too.' He looked at his sister and his brown eyes were scared. 'But they'll be all right when they see you.'

Masha got up and went over to him. She sat down beside him and took his hand.

'Think about it, Tomi,' she said. 'Think what they might do if they see us like this.' She gestured at the circle made by herself, Nina and the two older women, as they sat relaxed on the grass, bare-headed and dressed as wayfarers. Tomilin looked at them desperately. He clasped his hands and tried to steady his voice, but it still came out high and shaky.

'They might be nice . . . they might understand. You're not dangerous, are you? You're just ordinary. They couldn't say you were wicked.'

It was then that Vanya had spoken up. He had been sitting apart, fighting sleep and watching the others from beneath tired, drooping lids.

'I don't know what you're all so frightened of.' His voice was soft, but with a hard edge to it, like the glint of a knife. 'No one will say that you're anything you're not.' He laughed, but nastily, more like a sob: 'They'll only see you for what you are.'

They all looked at him. Nina had felt her spine tingle as she watched his twisted face. He scared her.

'We must go.' Vila stood up and began to collect things together. 'We'll hide the boat. We'll go and see the Mati – we'll find out what to do.' She raked her wild hair with her hands. 'We must be careful, and move fast. Come on.'

Now Vila slowed down. They had been going gradually downhill, down a long gentle slope of short springy turf and soft pine-needles. Here and there a twisted root threaded its way over the ground, while, to either side, great banks of golden leaves lay in drifts. With each soft gust of wind a thousand more leaves swirled into the air, catching the light as they spun and fell; and yet the trees were still fully clothed – these were the very earliest of the leaves to be blown away. Slowly and imperceptibly all around, summer was turning to autumn.

As Vila came to a halt, Nina could see below at the bottom of the slope a small brook that flowed swiftly and noisily between steep banks of clay. Immediately, she felt thirsty and hurried forward. Reaching the bank she lay on her stomach, and, leaning down, she could just get her hands into the clear rushing water. She drank deeply and splashed her face – it was delightfully cool, and tasted as sharp and as clean as wine.

The others did the same. The day was hot and sultry, and the long march had made them sweat. They had all taken off their jackets and wore only small woven vests that left their arms bare and brown in the sun. Nina knew that Tomilin and Vanya had been shocked by this – in the forest village it was frowned on for even forearms to be shown, let alone shoulders. How much more embarrassed were the boys now as Vila, sitting on the bank, tugged off her moccasins, threw off her vest and, leaping into the water, began to paddle up and down, splashing herself and wetting her hair.

Nina turned and looked at Masha. They giggled. Nina wished that she could do the same, but she couldn't – not in front of the boys. Ania quickly took every piece of clothing from the wriggling Stepan and handed him down to Vila. The little boy gurgled and laughed as he ran up and down the stream, splashing Vila and anyone else who came near.

'Are we nearly there?' Nina called.

Vila, looking up from her water fight with Stepan, smiled and looked at Ania. The two women laughed.

'Oh, we're here,' she said, and grinned, her hair sleek and black.

Nina looked about her. What she saw was a large glade through which the stream ran swiftly, disappearing eventually into an overhanging tangle of holly. What Nina had supposed to be a natural clearing was, on second glance, a perfect circle of partially cleared land. The trees on the edge of this circle were tall beeches, their foliage shining deep golden brown in the sun, their trunks smooth and silver. In between were small holly trees, hazel and juniper. Behind the ring of beeches that stood four or five deep was another circle of trees, conifers, far older than the others. These were yews.

Soaring into the sky, they formed a complete circle, dark and mysterious, seeming to enclose the clearing protectively; they must have been many hundreds of years old.

Looking through the beech-trees at this towering green wall, Nina felt a strange constriction in her chest. This was a special place, protected by special trees. She listened, cocking her head to one side, and sniffed the sultry air, as she had seen Vila do many times. What was different? Although the sounds she heard were the usual forest noises – the birds, a slight breeze passing through the trees, the splashing of the stream – there seemed to be, below these surface sounds, a strange brooding hush: a sense of waiting.

'This is a strange place,' Masha's voice came from behind her. The two girls leant against each other and looked around.

'Look.' Nina pointed back towards the spot where they had entered the clearing. They had not noticed, but they had come through a natural arch formed by two huge beeches that leant their branches together to form a trembling golden doorway. On either side were planted two sturdy bay-trees, wild and uncut.

'It's a door,' Masha exclaimed. 'How strange – and look . . .' She pointed to the far side of the clearing, over the stream. All round the massive buttresses of the beeches grew every sort of herb and wild flower that the girls could imagine. Even at this late stage of summer, the plants bloomed in a blaze of dazzling colours. There were ragged robin, foxgloves, yarrow and camomile; lavender, tansy and loosestrife. Further back, in the dappled shade beneath the trees, were clumps of hemlock, henbane and agrimony, nodding poppies and tall triumphant angelica. Around the trunk and lower branches of a slender elm clung a cascade of brilliant honeysuckle, and beneath the burdened tree were clusters of wild strawberries and forget-me-not, enchanter's nightshade and the scarlet pimpernel. The whole place shimmered with colour, and the drone of many bees hung in the air as the diligent creatures swung, lazy and over-fed, from one bright clump to the next.

'It's a garden,' breathed Masha.

'It can't be,' replied Nina, 'it's so untidy.'

'But beautiful,' murmured Masha. 'So beautiful. Let's go and look.'

The girls took off their shoes and waded across the stream. Vila and Stepan had collapsed in a heap. Ania sat talking quietly with Tomilin. Vanya sat alone, propped against the bole of a tree. The hot sun and the soft moss, the sound of the stream and the hollow call of the wood-pigeons, the buzz of the bees and the heavy scent of the flowers, all combined to produce in the tired boy a sense of stillness. Vanya could fight his fatigue no longer, and soon fell asleep.

The water cooled the girls' hot feet. The bed of the stream was sand and pebbles, with ribbons of green weed floating in the flow of the clear water. The grassy banks were starred with flowers. Here and there stood bushes and brambles, weighted down with fruit. The girls spent a long dreamy time wandering round, plucking berries and gathering fruit, bruising the leaves of various herbs to release their fragrance. From time to time they called softly to each other, pointing out something unusual, exclaiming over some new discovery; and when they spoke, they lowered their voices and spoke gently, almost in whispers, as if they were in church.

Eventually Nina went and threw herself down on the grass beside Vila, who was lying with her arms behind her head, staring dreamily at the cloudless sky.

'What a wonderful place.'

'Mmm.' Vila nodded and smiled, lazily scratching at a bite on her shoulder.

Masha joined them. 'I thought we were going to see someone. There's no one here.'

'Just relax for a while,' said Vila, and closed her eyes.

Nina persisted: 'But who lives here? I can't see anything.'

'Wait and see. What's the rush? We're quite safe here.' Vila scratched some more and stretched sleepily.

'You're the one who was in a hurry.'

Vila opened her eyes and squinted at Nina, outlined against the sun. She smiled. 'All right, then. Let's see if anyone's in.'

Masha laughed softly: 'In where?' She looked round. 'You're teasing us.'

'Not at all.' Vila got to her feet. 'Come on.'

Moving swiftly on her bare brown feet, she trotted over to the far edge of the clearing, directly opposite the arched entrance where they had come in.

Here, amid the flowers and herbs, grew the largest beech-tree. Up and up it stretched into the sky, its whispering golden leaves waving like pennants against the bright blue air. The huge trunk was almost totally covered in ivy. Higher up, several of the major branches too had succumbed to the dark green of its tendrilled embrace.

Vila stood at the foot of the tree and looked up. She seemed to be listening. Then she laughed. Nina and Masha walked up and stood next to her. They too looked up. All they could see was a tangle of ivy, then, spread above them like a mighty fan, the burnished foliage of the tree.

As they watched, far above, something moved. The dense mass of ivy around the trunk seemed to vibrate and quiver. A few twigs and leaves drifted down about the bemused girls. The rustling overhead increased, and suddenly a voice said: 'Who's there? What do you want? I'm busy.'

The girls stepped back in amazement, then forward again, to peer more closely into the tree. Someone was up there. Who could it be?

Vila called up: 'It's me, Vila, as you very well know.'

There was a pause, then the voice said: 'Again? So soon? Vila, my dear, I'm honoured.' There was a biting edge of sarcasm in the voice. It was an old voice – creaky and irritable and proud.

'Don't be like that, Mati, dear. Please come down.' Vila was smiling broadly. She did not seem at all dismayed by her reception.

The voice spoke again: 'Let's see. Shall I come down and see my Vila? She doesn't come and see me.'

'You know how busy we've been,' Vila retaliated. 'You know what it's like at harvest. You've not been neglected.' She laughed. 'Don't be so cross.'

The rustling in the branches increased once more. Then, from out of the tangle of ivy and beech leaves, a small rope-ladder bounced and tumbled. Down it fell, and then hung swaying from side to side. Down this ladder, moving as nimbly as a teenager, came the oldest and thinnest person Nina and Masha had ever seen. It was a matter of seconds before the old woman stood before them.

The girls stared. As they watched, they saw Vila embrace the tiny creature, hugging her so fiercely that she lifted her clear off the ground. She gave the wrinkled brown face two big kisses, and then threw back her head and laughed. The old woman looked up at Vila with such love and amusement in her face that, for all its multitude of lines and creases, it seemed younger and more alive than any old face had the right to be.

The woman called the Mati stood before the girls. Having gazed for a long moment at Vila, she turned and stared coolly at the others. Her eyes too were very old, the brown of the irises beginning to turn faintly milky, the white of the corneas traced with brown; and yet they snapped and sparkled – there was none of that resignation or sad vacancy that the girls were accustomed to seeing in people of such a very great age.

She was dressed in a strange garment of green, brown and yellow, which shrouded her tiny face in great folds that swayed and swung as she moved, and yet did not seem to impede her movements. Her wiry sticks of legs were clad in russet leggings, criss-crossed with bright embroidered ribbon. Around her face a halo of crinkled snowy hair of great softness glinted brilliantly in the sun. Stuck jauntily in this cloudy cascade of hair was a single sprig of pennyroyal, its tiny flowers purple against the white.

Having studied the faces of the two girls, and been content for them to study hers, the Mati turned back to Vila and took her hand.

'Well met, Vila, my darling. It's good to see you.' She smiled, showing few teeth and many gaps. 'But why do you bring so many people? What's up? What crisis do you bring for me to solve? Who are these friends? Not lake people, certainly.'

'A month ago, when I last came here, I told you about the two girls I'd found. They'd been washed away from the forest village. Do you remember? These are they: Nina and Masha.'

Nina, stepping forward to shake the little shrunken hand, remembered how, on that first morning after being rescued, Vila had said that she had been to see a friend.

'Of course I remember,' the Mati was saying. 'Do you think my mind's going? Although . . .' She scratched her snowy head, 'a lot of dust and cobwebs up there these days . . . tcha! So old and fuddled . . .'

'Oh, ssh! You old fraud!' Vila slapped the tiny arm with infinite gentleness. 'You don't improve, Mati. Can you never be serious?'

'Oh, most serious,' the old woman assured her. She kept hold of Nina's hand and gazed deep into her eyes. The Mati's scrutiny did not embarrass her in any way; it seemed totally natural, completely kind.

'Very serious,' the woman repeated. She sighed, 'So this is Nina. I like your hair. I hope you're feeling better, my dear. You certainly seem to have learnt a lot – I hope you realize that. I'd swear you'd grown a couple of inches, but it may just be the clothes . . . much more suitable for the forest, you know, than those silly frocks. Frocks are for dancing. You never did manage to get to your first dance, did you?'

'No,' said Nina. 'Not at home.' She smiled into the kind old face. How did the Mati know all this? She spoke as if they were old friends. How did she know? 'But I've done much more than just dance. I've learnt all sorts of things. Yes, I do feel much better, thank you. Only, I get a bit sad about not being able to go home.'

'Yes, well – we'll talk about that a bit later. We'll have a good long talk, indeed we will.' She patted Nina's hand and turned to Masha.

'Hallo, Masha. You look very well, too – what pretty beads.' She smiled and looked thoughtful. 'How you enjoy being able to do all that drawing! Remember, your life is just like one of your pictures . . . something that's blank until you make a design; it doesn't exist without that first idea, does it? It's very simple really. Keep looking for beauty, my dear, so you can show it to others.'

'I will,' said Masha, beaming at the old woman and feeling, like Nina, that she had known the Mati all her life – had felt her silent guidance in the background in some strange and magical fashion.

The Mati released the two girls from her gaze. Cocking her head on one side like a bird, she looked round the clearing. Then she walked over to the sprawling beds of herbs and flowers and, wandering among them, plucked a leaf here, a petal there, secreting them away in a pocket beneath one of the many folds of her extraordinary robe. The others, led by Vila, followed her and waited patiently for her to speak. Eventually she turned and came back to them.

'So you've brought Ania to see me. Good. And little Stepan. He's twice the size already – they grow so quickly when you're old – it takes no time at all.' Her voice creaked and shrilled, piercing the heavy murmuring air, curiously comforting. 'But these two young men. Who are they? Perhaps they have been out hunting in the great forest? Hunting deer? Or hunting sisters? Well, well, I'm sure they didn't mean to take pot-shots at poor old women . . . probably a mistake . . . still, dangerous toys, these bows and arrows, eh, Vila, my huntress?'

'Has he been shooting at you, Mati?' said Vila, her face suddenly cloudy and ferocious.

'No, no. Shooting at deer, almost certainly. Old women can resemble deer – in a poor light. Don't get cross now, Vila. Really, my dear, still so young and angry? I thought Ania was beginning to make you see reason.'

'Huh!' Vila crossed her arms and sulked, then laughed. She ran quickly over to the stream and the girls heard her call softly: 'Ania. Look who's here.'

Ania and Tomilin had stopped talking and had been sitting quietly, staring at the little stream. Stepan was fast asleep, sprawled over Tomilin, his dirty face still wearing its delighted smile. Ania turned at the sound of Vila's voice. Seeing the Mati, her face broke into a joyous grin and she jumped up and ran towards them. 'Oh, Mati! It's good to see you. It's been far too long.'

'Not my fault, I'm sure,' the Mati pouted. Then, holding out both arms, she said: 'Ania, my little one. How are you, my precious robin?' The two women embraced, Ania laying her shining red curls against the white head of the old woman.

'I'm fine, just fine. All the better for seeing you again. I've brought you a present.'

'Presents later, my sweetheart,' said the Mati. 'Now I want to talk to you and Vila.' She turned to the girls. 'You two must go and wait with the others. Go and explain to Tomilin. Don't wake Vanya, he needs the rest. They'll come and fetch you when we've finished.'

The old woman turned and, going back to the mighty beech, she swung herself up the ladder and disappeared. Ania and Vila looked at each other with shining eyes.

'We'll see you later,' said Vila.

'I'm sure you'll be allowed in the tree in a while,' said Ania. 'Oh, it's such fun. Look after Stepan.' She turned and followed Vila. In a moment the two girls were alone on the ground. They stared at each other.

'Well, well,' said Nina. 'Life is certainly full of surprises.'

Masha laughed and laughed. 'It certainly is,' she said. 'It certainly is.'

8 The Treehouse

They walked back to where Tomilin sat, trapped beneath the slumbering Stepan. His flute was in his hand, and he had managed to play the child to sleep with tunes. Smiling ruefully at them, he tried to shift without waking the sleeping boy.

'What's going on?' he asked. 'Who was that old woman?'

'That's the Mati,' said Masha. 'She's wonderful.'

'She's strange,' added Nina.

'She's talking to Vila and Ania. We're to wait here.'

They sat down beside Tomilin. There was silence for a while, then the boy said: 'Go on, then – tell me more about the lake village.'

For the next hour they told of all their experiences. Tomilin asked question after question. What were the houses like? Why did they paint the outsides? Did everyone own a boat? Could girls really go fishing? How many men in the hunting party? Who was the head of the Council?

Nina and Masha took turns in answering. Yes, girls went fishing too, even children – people even took their babies with them. Yes, almost everyone seemed to have their own boat, they're easy to make when you know how. No, they didn't have a hunting party. If anyone went hunting, they just went – no party – anyway, there was no need for much hunting to be done.

'No hunting parties? What a good idea,' Tomilin's voice was exuberant. The more he heard of this place the greater his feeling of anticipation. He wanted to go there and see for himself.

'But the Council,' he repeated. 'How does it work?'

The girls looked at each other and thought.

'There isn't one really,' said Masha.

'Not a proper one,' agreed Nina.

'If something needs to be decided by everyone, then they all get together and talk.'

'And argue!'

'And listen.'

'Then they decide.'

'But there must be a chief,' Tomilin insisted.

They looked at each other again.

'Not really,' said Nina.

'There are some people who seem to be leaders, but only in a way; they don't do much leading – they just get asked. Like Vila. She's very important in the village, and Ania – people are always asking them things.'

Tomilin burst out: 'But they're women!'

The girls laughed loudly, rolling about on the soft grass, weak with hilarity.

'Shut up, you tadpole! So are we!'

'What a cheek! Really!'

'I'm sorry,' said the boy, looking embarrassed. 'But it's hard to get used to. It's a good idea, of course.' Blushing, he fell silent.

The talk went on in this fashion. The girls could not resist teasing Tomilin about his reactions to what they told him. He responded with good humour and more questions. There was much laughter. The three of them felt close and happy, safe in this clearing in the forest – it seemed a haven from the confusion of the past and the uncertainty of the future.

Vanya was still asleep when Vila and Ania came down from the tree. Stepan, hearing his mother's voice, woke up and immediately clamoured to see the Mati – somehow the news had filtered into his sleeping mind.

'Mati! Mati! Show me the tree!' he cried.

'Ssh, darling. In a while,' Ania said.

Vila surveyed them all where they sat. She raked her hair back and narrowed her eyes.

'You're all to go on up.' Her voice was firm. 'Now I want you to behave sensibly. Not too much noise, or too many questions. The Mati pretends she's only a girl, but she's not. She must be almost a hundred now, and she does get tired.'

'Of course, Vila,' Masha assured her. 'But what about Vanya?'

'Leave him where he is. Rest is the best thing for him right now. Mati says he won't wake up till he feels better, and she's almost always right. Now go along.'

They walked over to the tree. As they reached the vast buttress, they heard the Mati's voice lilting down from far above. 'Come on up. I hope none of you are terribly heavy. Be careful now, it's a long way to fall.'

'Me first,' said Nina, and grabbing hold of the ladder she swung herself up.

It was a lot harder than she had reckoned. The ladder crashed continually into the trunk of the tree, squashing her fingers and banging her knees and elbows. It was also far higher than she had expected. Swinging wildly from side to side, she eventually reached a point, at least fifty feet off the ground, where the trunk split in two. Up one of the forks, crude footholds had been hacked in the wood. It was perilous, but now, completely surrounded by swaying foliage that blocked her view of the ground, Nina felt herself to be more secure.

She climbed further up, holding on to the shallow

footholds with her fingers. Then, above her, she saw perched between three of the main branches a large wooden platform. On top of this platform stood a small wooden house.

All around the sides of the house were painted wild designs, like the lakeside dwellings – prancing deer, horses, wolves, a swooping owl, a leaping fish, and above the door flared a huge red sun. To one side of the little house a woollen hammock swung between two stout branches. Here and there, baskets of flowers were attached to the swaying grey boughs. Hearing a delicate tinkling noise, Nina looked up and saw a wind-harp chiming softly in the breeze. Next to the harp, nailed to a slim branch, was a carved wooden owl, beak open and wings outstretched. 'Like Vila's,' thought Nina, '– only more fierce.'

'Hallo,' she said softly, and poked her head inside the door.

'Hallo, my dear.'

Inside, the Mati was sitting on a pile of bright cushions, her ancient face wreathed in a welcoming smile.

Nina straightened up and gazed around her. Her first impression of the tiny treehouse was one of incredible clutter. Not one inch of space was wasted. Every wall was lined with shelves, each one carved cunningly from strips of dark polished wood. On these shelves stood hundreds of carvings – every imaginable bird and animal was there, all of varying sizes, and each showing the same extraordinary energy. Apart from the carvings, the shelves were thronged with all sorts of objects – pots and crocks, wooden bowls, dolls, sculptures made from river clay, corn dollies, a massive stone pestle and mortar. One entire corner of the room was given over to rows and rows of green and blue glass bottles, ranging in size from huge luminous flagons to the tiniest inch-high phials. Each bottle had a label that bore a mysterious legend: 'Digitalis Purpurea', 'Atropa Belladonna', 'Mentha Pulegium'.

Another section was devoted to bulky leather-bound

books, musty and ancient. These Nina regarded with an especial awe; in her own home there had been only the old black Bible – books were for priests, the knowledge between their covers was a closely guarded secret.

Nina heard a noise behind her. Turning, she saw Masha's head appear above the bottom of the platform. They grinned at each other.

'Ooh, Nina, it's a long way down,' said Masha nervously.

'Don't look,' said Nina, and she turned back into the little room. 'Look at this . . .' Words failed her as she gestured here and there.

Masha stepped in. 'Hallo, Mati,' she said politely. As she looked about her an expression of delight spread across her rosy face and her eyes shone with pleasure.

'Look.' Masha took Nina's hand and pointed up at the roof. Although the little house was so low, there was room for countless bundles of dried and drying herbs. The girls breathed deeply – a whole range of different aromas greeted their nostrils: there were dusty smells, sharp and tart smells, sweet smells, and some that were dangerous and bitter. The Mati, muttering to herself, plucked some green leaves from a small bunch hanging in one corner and tossed them into a kettle. Immediately the room was filled with a clean, tangy scent, mouth-watering and fresh.

'Balm tea – most refreshing,' said the old woman, and she proceeded to fill three small pottery bowls with the fragrant liquid.

Then Tomilin appeared. With all three now inside, the little room had become extremely crowded. Masha and Nina, deciding that the only way to avoid breaking anything was to sit down, threw themselves on to the pile of cushions. Tomilin remained standing, looking around; then he too squeezed down beside them.

They passed around the tea while the Mati, perched on a tiny three-legged stool, looked at them with interest.

'Well,' she said eventually, 'Let's begin.'

Later on, neither Nina nor Masha could remember exactly how the old woman had started. Nor could they quite recall how long they had listened – many hours surely, for when they wearily climbed back down the lurching rope-ladder, it was completely dark. Long afterwards each remembered different parts of the Mati's story, her words staying with them in the days that followed.

The whole long afternoon had been spent listening as she told strange stories and recited odd rhymes and poems, showing them maps and opening huge dusty books to reveal pictures that made their heads spin with their beauty and colour.

Question after question she had answered as the afternoon sun turned the tree to gold, and the forest birds clamoured in the surrounding treetops; and always, above any other sound, the fragile jangling of the wind-harp came to them, as it was stirred by even the faintest breeze.

And how could any of them ever forget how, as the last light faded, a great eagle owl had flown through the open door and landed with a thump on a gnarled and shining wooden perch in the shadowy corner of the room. How the great bird had blinked at them indignantly with her yellow eyes, turning her head upon her neck to peer in annoyance at each of the three intruders.

'Don't worry about her,' the Mati had said, as she lit candles and placed them at various points around the room. 'She's a cross old bird, like me. Now, off with you all. I've talked enough for today.'

They got up to go, their legs numb from sitting still so long. Suddenly they all felt sleepy and stupid, dizzy with tiredness. They longed to be curled up somewhere comfortable, wrapped in warm blankets and soothed to sleep by the murmuring stream.

'Before you go . . .' The Mati was searching around on one of the most crowded of the shelves. 'Now, let's see . . . goodness, what a mess . . . ah, yes, here we are. Presents.'

Turning back towards them, she motioned for Tomilin to come forward. Suppressing a yawn, he stumbled over to her. Only thirteen, he already towered over the person before him. The Mati had in her hand a small carving of a dog, made from dark, polished wood. Tomilin exclaimed with delight. The dog was thin and rangy, sitting back and lazily scratching an ear with its foot. Every hair had been separately etched into the gleaming surface of the wood.

'What would we do without these creatures?' mused the old woman as she handed the carving over to the boy. 'Such faithfulness, such a courageous guardian.' Her eyes twinkled. 'Be brave, little one.'

She turned next to Nina. In her hand she held another carving of the same dark wood. This time it was a perfect image of a river pebble, smooth and round, washed over the years to a silky finish; even the faint grain of the wood seemed to suggest the whorls and patterns of a wet stone. Resting for a moment on the surface of the pebble, their wings outstretched in an imaginary sun, were three bees. Nina gasped as she saw the exquisite detail in the carving of the tiny bodies, and felt the smoothness of the wood as she cradled the carving in her hand.

'Beautiful busy things,' said the old woman, looking at the carving. 'So industrious and useful – making music, making honey. Such wealth of spirit. Think of bees, Nina, think of bees.'

Nina stepped back, murmuring her thanks, and Masha stepped forward. In her hand the old woman placed a carved water-lily. Life sized, it fitted perfectly into Masha's cupped palm, and she felt a thrill run through her as she saw each individually carved petal radiating out from the centre like a miniature sunburst. On the outermost petal was poised, as if for a fraction of a second, a butterfly, with wings open to show the perfect symmetry of its design.

'Oh, Mati!' breathed Masha, her heart beating fast as she gently squeezed the old hand that had given her such a beautiful and delicate gift.

The old woman smiled up at the girl.

'A creature of the light, my dear, reborn to give joy to all who see it. A good present for you, I think. I'm glad the river brought you to us.'

Suddenly, she looked very tired. She seemed to grow even smaller as she turned away and began fussing with the stove. The others turned towards the door – Nina first, then Tomilin, Masha last. They whispered their goodnights and started down the ladder.

At the foot of the tree, Vila and Ania had set some blankets and some bowls of soup. They were sleeping over on the other side of the clearing, near Vanya – a faint flicker showed their small fire.

They drank the soup in silence. Then, throwing off their clothes, they all crawled under the blankets, and were asleep the instant their heads touched the ground. Above them, the Mati's candlelit home twinkled in the dark like a star.

9 Capture

The next day dawned grey and misty. They piled the fire with leaves that soon filled the clearing with a smoky autumnal smell. Vanya woke at last. He felt calm and refreshed, and spent the morning gathering wood for the fire and fixing various things that had broken during the course of the previous day's hike – Tomilin's boot, Ania's pack. He even offered to take Stepan for a walk, but Vila, discreetly hiding the real reason, was not yet ready to trust the young man. No, she said, they should all stay together, inside the clearing.

The morning mist soon cleared and the day promised to be scorching. The sun rose through a searing white sky and huge clouds piled up, eventually blocking the sun, but seeming to keep its heat trapped beneath them. Not a whisper of wind came through the still trees to relieve the hot travellers. They sat around by the stream, talking in low voices of unimportant subjects.

There was no sign of the Mati. No one mentioned her, or the conversations of the previous afternoon. As if by common consent they all agreed that today was a day of rest, a day to be resting; no trill of music descended through the stuffy air. Only the droning of the bees in the rambling

137

garden of herbs could be heard through the stillness.

Once the sun had passed the zenith it became clear that they were in for a storm. Murmurs of thunder could be heard far away, booming and rolling towards them, lazy and unhurried. The lowering sky darkened and the heat became intense.

'It's going to be a big one,' said Vila, and she grinned delightedly.

'Oh, you're so fearless, it's all right for you,' said Ania, leaning over to give her a shove. 'Think of others for a change.'

'I'm not scared,' said Tomilin with bravado.

'Well, you're mad then,' said Vanya. 'And you'll probably be burnt to a crisp by the lightning.'

They laughed, and cast apprehensive looks at the sky and at the vast thunderclouds that were now rolling, grey-black, towards them. A blackbird nearby gave a jagged call of alarm, and the sound trailed away through the heavy atmosphere.

Although no one was especially hungry, they got some food from their packs and munched half-heartedly on bread and honey. Earlier, Nina had discovered a small orchard of apples and cherries in a glade adjacent to the larger clearing. Although she had felt unwilling to venture from the shady ring of ancient yew-trees, she had told herself she was being foolish, and she had quickly gone and gathered and filled her pockets with the fruit from their wild branches. Now she was glad that she had bothered. The fruit was juicy and delicious – as refreshing as rain water and as sweet as honey.

As they ate, they talked about what they would do the following day. They decided not to travel at all that day. No one had any desire to leave the clearing, and they had no idea when the storm would break, or how long it would last.

'What did the Mati say we should do?' asked Nina at one point.

Vila smiled.

'The Mati never tells you what to do. Rather, she helps you see how you are to do it.'

Nina was puzzled. 'But I thought . . .'

Masha spoke: 'I think I understand.' She frowned thoughtfully. 'Well, I think that we have to go on. We have to finish this thing.'

Nina looked at the ground for an instant, then nodded her agreement.

Eventually they all agreed. They would go back to the forest village. Once they arrived, Nina and Masha would attempt to reach Nina's mother. The boys would stay with Vila and Ania until the girls came back.

There was a depressed silence after the arrangements had been finalized. Nina was thinking of her meeting with her mother. She now dreaded the pain that it was bound to cause. Masha was thinking along much the same lines – she too longed for a chance to explain to her family all that had happened.

Tomilin was sitting, his arms hugging his knees, longing for the lakeside village, certain that it was there that all his happiness lay.

Vanya, sitting apart, did not take part in the discussions. He did not know what he felt. At times he caught himself smiling and laughing with these strange women; even Vila, who had bested him – he found it hard not to admire her. But then, just as often, he would feel such powerful resentment that he had to turn away to hide his face. His feelings towards his sister and her friend were just as confused; the remnants of love survived, but they were drowned by a fierce jealousy, as if he had been beaten in some game, or had lost a contest to another boy – how dare Masha have a better adventure than him?

But it was his feelings towards Ania that most puzzled the young man. The red-headed woman still appalled him in some ways, but then sometimes, when he looked at her, he felt a strange tugging in his chest, his blood raced, and he wanted more than anything to touch her red hair and have her smile at him. It was aggravating and embarrassing; he was angry at himself for all this weakness and confusion.

'Oh, I do wish it would rain,' sighed Ania, conscious of the young man's eyes upon her. She tried to calm Stepan. Hot and bored, he had begun to whine and fret.

As she spoke a deafening clap of thunder boomed in the hot sky above their heads. The sky was darkening by the second, and lightning had begun to flash above the trees, casting momentary white light all around the glade. As they huddled together, the first fat drops of rain began to fall, splashing down on the hot ground.

'Better get under cover,' said Vila. 'Under the beech-tree, and cover yourselves with blankets.'

Within seconds the rain was coming down in torrents, and they were drenched before they had sprinted across to the shelter of the Mati's tree. They clustered round the trunk, holding blankets over their heads, more for comfort than anything else, as the tree above them provided almost perfect protection from the downpour. As they looked out at the silver sheets of water that were sweeping across the clearing, crash upon crash of thunder rent the heavy air and lightning seared the sky.

'Well, well, my toadstools; what a terrible tempest, to be sure.' The Mati's shrill voice cut through the din, and, looking up, they saw her swinging to and fro above their heads on the ladder, about twenty feet off the ground. Vanya jumped in amazement and Stepan immediately began shouting out to the old woman: 'Hallo, Mati, hallo!'

The Mati quickly descended and jumped off the ladder. She held out her arms for Stepan and as she hugged the giggling child she looked round at the others as they clustered together, draped in Ania's woven blankets. She smiled at each of them and let her gaze rest upon Vanya, who stood open-mouthed, looking as if he would like to bolt at the first opportunity.

'No need to fear an old woman, my fine lad,' she said, looking at him shrewdly. 'Forgot to give you your present, didn't I? We haven't been properly introduced yet, but I think you should take it now, just in case I forget. Now, where did I put it?' She began to rummage about in the folds of her robe, continuing to talk at great speed as she did so.

'Vila, my dear, you must take these young people away immediately, storm or no storm. It's not safe here any more. Go to the river as quickly as you can – there's danger here. Thank you for my present, Ania, dear.' She fingered a bright piece of weaving that was tied round her neck. 'Take care of yourself.' She pulled a small package from her sleeve, something wrapped in deer-skin and tied with a thong. 'Ah, here it is.'

Just as the Mati held out her hand towards Vanya, a loud noise came to them through the hissing rain, from the other side of the clearing. Turning, they saw, blurred and indistinct through the driving downpour, the shape of a man standing beneath the arched entrance of the circle. Water poured down his face and dripped from his beard, and his clothes hung sodden about him. He raised his arm and again they heard him shout. Immediately there were three more men behind him.

'Run!' The Mati's voice was sharp and urgent. She pushed Vila, trying to get her to move from under the tree. 'Vila! Take them to the river. Go!'

'No!' Vila shouted and shook the old woman's hands from her. 'We won't leave you.'

The Mati turned. Before anyone could stop her she had darted out into the very centre of the clearing. For a moment she was still, staring at the men who stood beneath the swaying beech-trees. Then she turned, and began to run to one side, fleeting across the grass like a child playing tag. She was nearly at the edge of the clearing when she fell, dropping to the wet earth as weightlessly as a leaf, cut down by the arrow that had passed through her bright new scarf and into her throat.

'No!' The people standing beneath the Mati's tree cried out as one. Vila gave a howl and, ignoring Ania's hand upon her arm, she ran towards the small bundle that lay so still upon the ground. They saw her crouch over the tiny form, touching it gently, tugging at a fold in the brown and yellow robes. The rain poured relentlessly from the sky and beat upon Vila as she knelt there, her head bent, her hair plastered across her face as the water streamed down.

'Vila, run!' Nina thought her throat would burst as she shouted. Already she could see two of the men running to where Vila knelt motionless by the dead Mati. The other two had seen them and had begun to run across, their bows already bent.

But Vila did not move. She did not struggle as the men reached her and pulled her roughly to her feet; she did not take her eyes from the small wet bundle on the ground, not even when her arms were pulled back and tied behind her.

Nina turned and looked at the others. They seemed frozen where they stood. She began to punch and shove them, shouting desperately at them to run. First Masha, then Tomilin swung round and ran from the clearing. Ania remained as if rooted to the ground; in her arms, Stepan had begun to scream.

'Vila?' Ania spoke the name in a strange questioning tone. She took a step forward, dazed and wooden. 'Vila?'

The men had nearly reached them.

'No!' Nina bellowed, and she gave Ania a great shove in the chest, causing Stepan's screams to become a thin wail of panic. 'No!' She grabbed hold of Ania and pulled the woman and child along behind her as she whirled round and broke from the cover of the great beech-tree. Hauling them behind her, she managed to reach the little orchard where she had gathered fruit earlier that day. Without daring to look behind her she ducked under the twisted boughs. 'Run, run!' she said, over and over – to herself as much as to Ania.

An arrow whistled past her head. Another thudded into the trunk of a tree up ahead. Her breath came in great aching gasps and she felt herself slowing down. Then, just as she began to stumble and fall, she felt Ania's hand upon her arm. This time it was she who was being pulled. Now Ania's eyes burned with anger, her mouth was set in a thin hard line, and her hair flamed wildly about her face.

'Come,' she said, and her voice was like steel. 'They shan't get us. Not yet.'

Wheeling round, she flung Stepan over her shoulder and sprang away. Nina, seeing the slender woman sprinting between the trees, felt filled once more with energy and strength. Taking a deep breath, she leapt forward, her fear making her faster than she could have believed. Springing over a fallen tree, she followed Ania, and together they disappeared into the brooding shelter of the forest.

PART THREE

1 The Hunters

'Speak, woman. It will be better for you if you talk.'

The big man spoke angrily. He shook the sullen captive by the shoulders, as if to bring answers from her by force; but the woman's head continued to hang down and her sorrowful mouth remained closed.

'Talk, witch!' Another voice, rich and mellow, self-important. A handsome man with black hair and a long black beard came forward. 'My sons.– where did they go? What have you done with them?'

Vila stayed silent. Her eyes were on the ground but she saw nothing. The voices were loud sounds in her head, they had no meaning.

'Come now, you sweet thing – you can do better than that.' A third man spoke. He was short and stocky, and his pale eyes were fixed on Vila's downcast face. Getting no response, he guffawed and turned away, shrugging his shoulders. He leant against a tree and proceeded to scratch his chest through his wet clothing. After a second, he spat on the ground and said to the big man holding her: 'She'll talk later – we'll make sure of that. Let's get going.'

The big man looked displeased. Alexei Bearkiller was not used to being told what to do. However, he let it pass and nodded, beginning to assemble their belongings, keeping an eye on the captive who stood, with statue-like stillness, beneath the dripping trees.

The hunters gathered their paraphernalia. The carcass of a bear was slung beneath a pole that had been hurriedly thrown to the ground; around it were scattered traps, spears, bows, a quiver of arrows. Now Voinitsky, the pale-eyed man, picked up one end of the pole.

'Here, grab the other end, Nikolai.'

The black-bearded man walked over and together they shouldered the bear. Alexei followed, pushing the dazed prisoner before him.

'What do we do with that?' said Nikolai, pointing across the clearing at the little heap of yellow-brown robes.

'Leave it,' answered Voinitsky. 'The mad old hag. Good riddance. Let her feed the wolves.' He looked up at the trees. 'Too many of these filthy harridans about as it is.'

The rain had fallen to a steady drizzle as the group made its way across the sodden grass. As they neared the far side, whence the other women had fled, two more men approached. They were panting with exertion, red-faced and sweating.

'They've gone,' cried the first, a thin, grizzled man with curly black hair that clung sparsely to his balding head. He coughed and spat, leaning his hands on his knees and breathing deeply. The other man, younger and fitter, was obviously his son, having the same distinctive bony face; he regained his composure and said to the others: 'They disappeared into thin air! We followed for half a mile, but they moved fast. One was carrying a child – it was screaming.' He paused to wipe his face with his sleeve. 'Then they just vanished, and the screaming stopped. We searched, but there was no sign.'

'That's right,' nodded the other man. 'Just like magic.'

'Show us where, Gregor,' said Alexei.

They started off again, They went through the dripping orchard and into the forest. The tracks were clearly visible where first Masha and Tomilin, then Ania and Nina had fled, followed by their pursuers. But then the way was barred by a shallow stream, made swift and full by the rain. It was only a few feet wide, but there all tracks stopped.

'We had them in sight – the last two were just in front. Then they went down the stream, through those bushes, then – pff! – gone.' Gregor held open his hands.

For the first time, Vila raised her head. There was no expression on her face as she looked around. Having studied the stream and the forest around her, she dropped her head back down.

They marched on. The rain stopped completely and a faint sun came out to shine on the dripping trees. The ground underfoot was sodden and muddy, the going heavy. On and on they went, moving north. From time to time they had to stop and hack a way through, grumbling and swearing. Eventually, towards dark, they stopped and tied Vila to a tree, and proceeded to search for dry firewood.

'I'll be glad to get home,' grumbled Gregor, as he struggled with an armload of kindling. 'This cursed forest seems set against us.'

Voinitsky was busy skinning the bear. He turned to Gregor, his hands red with blood. 'Here, give me a hand with this.' He turned back to work. 'If only we'd been nearer we could have seen who those others were, the ones that got away. I'm betting they all come from the village downriver. We've all heard speak of it – a great warren of hags and witches.'

'From where I stood, I could have sworn that one of them was Vanya,' said Gregor. 'But the others moved too fast, and then he'd gone. I couldn't be sure.' He lowered his voice. 'The one you shot, Voinitsky, the old one who came out of the tree, she certainly looked like a witch to me. And this one –' he jerked his thumb in Vila's direction 'well, she's no ordinary woman, that's for sure.'

'It was a meeting place. They were gathering for the sabbat. That's why they had the child – for a sacrifice,' said Voinitsky, and his pale eyes gleamed in the faint light.

Alexei came up. Across his massive shoulders he carried a bundle of sticks and branches. He threw them on the ground and, getting out a tinder-box, he quickly made a fire. Anton, Gregor's son, could be heard in the distance. With a great crashing of twigs he walked up, leading three small horses. Close behind was another young man, tall and blond, leading three more ponies.

'There you are,' said Alexei, looking up from the fire. 'Is everything all right, Sergei? Did you see anything?'

'Nothing,' replied the blond boy. 'I – er . . .' he hesitated. 'I thought I felt something watching me – early this morning, but there was nothing there.'

Voinitsky sniggered: 'That was Rusalka, up in her tree, waiting to grab you.'

Anton and Sergei tied up the horses near Vila. With the fire now a fair size, all six men sat down and began to roast slabs of bear-meat over the flames. There was talking and laughter as they discussed the day's events, then Alexei called for silence. 'We must decide one thing: whether we go forward in search of Nikolai's boys, or whether we go back to the village. Either way, we must decide tonight, we all have much work to do at home – we can't afford to be away too long.'

'Ask the woman,' said Voinitsky. 'She can tell us if they have Nikolai's boys.'

'Yes,' agreed Gregor. 'Ask the woman.'

Alexei nodded. He told Anton to untie Vila and bring her forward. When she stood before the group of men, her face sullen and closed in the red light of the fire, Alexei stood up and put his hands behind his back.

'Now, woman,' he said, his deep voice loud and commanding. 'We must have some answers. I hope you will be more
forthcoming than previously.' Vila raised her head and looked at him steadily. 'Tell me now,' he continued. 'Where do you come from?'

'I come from downriver – my own village,' replied Vila. 'If you let me go, I shall return there and cause you no more trouble.' Her voice shook slightly, and behind her back her bound hands were tightly clenched to prevent their trembling. A gust of laughter greeted her words.

'What village is that?'

'Ha! Do they all look like you?'

'Why do you wear men's clothes?'

'I wear travelling clothes – like you,' came the reply.

'Who were your companions?'

'Where did they go?'

'Why did they disappear like that?'

'I don't know where they went. They were my friends.'

'What about my boys?' asked Nikolai, getting to his feet. 'What have you done to them?'

'They are safe,' said Vila, her voice now clear and steady.

'But where are they? Tell me. My sons!'

Just then a sound from beneath the trees caused the men to look around. It was dark now, and the shadows cast by the fire played upon the ground and flickered on the trunks of the surrounding firs. Outside the circle, shifting from foot to foot and looking somewhat embarrassed, stood Vanya.

'Hallo, Father,' he said.

Vanya looked round the firelit circle. He saw his father on his feet in front of Vila, looking at his son with an expression part relief and part annoyance. Alexei Bearkiller stood next to him, seeming even bigger and more impressive in the glow of the flames, with his vast shadow stretching behind him over the muddy ground. The big man began to laugh, throwing his head back and clapping his hands with amusement.

Others joined in the laughter. As Vanya looked round he saw Sergei and Anton sitting together, grinning broadly – he raised his hand in greeting and grinned back at them. Lastly, Vanya saw, sitting in the shadows next to Gregor, smirking and picking at his fingernails, the pale-eyed Voinitsky.

Vanya was tired. He had been tracking them all afternoon, waiting for the right opportunity to declare himself. Now the smell of roasting meat had forced him to enter the circle of light. He was hungry and wanted company.

'Vanya!' His father was coming forward to embrace him. Over his father's shoulder Vanya could see Vila's face; her black eyes were wide, her hair stuck up wildly, and she was smudged and grimy with mud.

'What happened? What have you been up to?' Alexei came and slapped him on the back. 'Where's the other young scoundrel? You've had us worried, you know.'

Anton and Sergei got up and clustered round, asking questions: 'Where've you been? Who were those people? How was the hunting? Did you get captured?' Vanya blushed and mumbled. He glowed with pleasure at this reception, pleased to see his friends, and he noticed the look of curiosity in their eyes. Having at first felt slightly foolish, he began to feel brave and adventurous – a returning hero, valiant and bold. They weren't to know that the only reason he had followed them was because he had put his foot in a rabbit-hole, fallen into a holly-bush, and lost sight of Nina and Ania. They weren't to know that he had wanted to go with the women, had been as frightened as they of the shouts and arrows of the hunters. Now he opened his mouth to explain, to tell them the good news – that Tomilin was safe, that the girls had been found. But instead, to his surprise, he heard: 'I escaped. They've got Tomilin. They captured Masha and Nina.'

There was uproar. All the men started talking at once. Vanya's head was swimming as he realized what he was doing. Vila's face was in front of his eyes, with its look of sorrow and disgust. Through the confusion, he heard the one whispered word as it fell from her lips: 'Traitor.'

Alexei called for order. He told them all to sit down.

'Now, Vanya, I want you to start from the beginning.'

They sat down round the fire, with Vila once more bound to a tree. As Vanya's story unfolded, he saw a look of interest upon Voinitsky's broad face; he saw too admiration in the eyes of his friends – Sergei, tall and handsome, the best horseman of the village, and Anton, champion bowman, who had teased Vanya mercilessly until he had proved himself in the wrestling contest. He noticed the look of pride on his father's face as he told of his exploits. The only person whose face he did not see was Vila's; he made sure not to look in her direction.

'We went far further south than this,' he said. 'We got to a place where the river flows as swift as a galloping horse, where there are huge cliffs and mighty boulders. That's where I found the first woman. She had a little child with her and she spoke in a strange proud manner. I asked her where her husband was and she replied that she had none – she had no shame. She wore a man's hunting costume, and her head was bare; so were her legs.' His story was interrupted by sniggers from Sergei and Anton, and then by Voinitsky, who asked: 'Where did she come from? Did she come from the water?'

Vanya remembered his first astonished glimpse of Ania. He remembered the way she had swung through the water – so at home in the river – and the way the silver drops had splashed about her bare knees. As he looked round the circle of expectant faces he did not feel that he was a liar – rather he was a storyteller; it was all right to embellish a little, for the sake of a good tale.

'She came out of the water, she had hair like a flame. She had hidden the child in some rushes. She fetched him, and then she went upstream, and I followed her until she came to our camp. Tomilin was asleep. I fought them – but she was joined by . . . by that one – and I was overwhelmed. She must have used magic to quell me. Then they forced us to march over a high cliff until we came to a place where there were many old willows; and it was there that I saw them.' Vanya paused, savouring the dramatic impact that his words were having. 'There, on the other side of the river, were Masha and Nina.'

Once again, there was uproar. Nikolai exclaimed and looked worried and distressed. The others plied Vanya with questions, not waiting for answers. At last there was silence, and Alexei told him to continue.

'At first I didn't believe it was Masha – I couldn't believe she was alive. But they seemed to be real, Nina too. But they were horribly changed – they wore strange clothes, and Nina's hair had been shorn. And then they . . . I thought I was dreaming, or bewitched . . . they got into a strange thing, it was shaped like a shoe, it floated on the river.'

There was a stunned silence. The older men looked at Vanya, then at each other in disbelief. Then, one by one, they began to cast furtive looks behind them at the shifting shadows, and then at Vila as she sat slumped at the foot of a slender pine.

Gregor spoke first.

'A boat! But that's forbidden.'

'They're from that place . . . we must beware.' Alexei's voice was shaking.

'My little girl, they've taken her. She would have been better off dead.'

'Witchcraft!'

'Sorcery!'

Voinitsky's voice cut softly through the dark: 'So, now we know. We all feared it would be this way. We all feared Rusalka. Now we know.' He laughed quickly, a brutal laugh.

Vanya was confused. Suddenly he was no longer the centre of attention. The older men had moved together and were talking among themselves. Alexei was saying loudly that they should not be hasty, that they must think things over. But Gregor and Voinitsky were calling for action, saying they must fetch more men, go to the witches' village, clear it out for good. Nikolai sat in silence; at last he said: 'They've got my little boy.'

The others looked at him. Then Alexei laid a hand on his arm. 'It's too late, my friend. He's gone over to them.'

'No!' Nikolai cried. Then he turned to Vanya. 'Finish your story, my son.'

Vanya felt awful. He was scared. It had all misfired. They were taking it all too seriously. He stammered out the rest of his adventure – he no longer cared to exaggerate, to boast of his bravado, he merely told the truth.

'They took us to that place in the forest – the clearing with the tree. I was so tired. I slept when I got there . . . I don't know what happened.'

'Did Tomilin talk to them?' His father's voice was urgent.

'Yes, they were nice to him. They left me out.'

Vanya suddenly felt tearful. He swallowed hard and looked at the ground. He continued to look down as around him the talk swelled and roared. Alexei and Voinitsky were arguing.

'We must get rid of the woman,' insisted Voinitsky. 'We'll all have our throats cut otherwise. There'll be more of them about, mark my words; the place is infested with them.'

'We will take her home to stand trial. I won't be party to cold-blooded murder,' answered Alexei, but his voice was nervous, lacking any of its usual robust authority. 'You've already killed one woman today, Voinitsky. Aren't you satisfied?'

'Satisfied? With a plague of witches in the forest? Come now, these are weak words for the head of Council. Would you not crush a snake with your heel? We must wipe them out, before they infect us all with their unnatural ways – before they get to our wives and daughters. Do you not see the danger, you fools?' Voinitsky stared furiously at the others. Gregor was nodding his head in accord, while Nikolai stared morosely at the fire. Alexei leapt up and stood towering over him.

'Do you dare to call me a coward?' he blustered. 'Do you dare?'

Voinitsky cringed. He answered in a silky voice: 'I didn't say that, Alexei. No one could possibly doubt your courage . . . or your wisdom.'

The talking continued. Vanya wished he could close his ears to its ugly sound. At last Alexei called for silence.

'It's decided. We return to the village tomorrow. We'll gather the Council. You must bide your time, Voinitsky. The witch won't escape. Tonight we must stand guard. They may come to rescue her. I'll take the first shift. Voinitsky, you take the second watch. Nikolai and Gregor, third and fourth. You young ones, go to sleep; but keep your knives beside you.'

They piled wood on the fire and got blankets from their packs. Above the forest, the full moon was sailing through dark clouds. The men glanced at it anxiously, shivering as they heard, far away through the velvet nights, a lone wolf raise its sad, hungry voice to the light in the sky.

As Vanya prepared to sleep, he caught sight of Vila, a dark shape at the base of the tree. Getting up, he looked around and found an extra blanket. Taking it over, he placed it round her hunched shoulders. He thought she was asleep, but at his touch Vila raised her head. She looked startled and angry.

'Well, Vanya,' she said, her voice jagged with bitterness. 'Are you pleased? Do you see what you've done?' Her question hung in the air between them, and Vanya could not answer. 'They will hunt us, now,' continued the captive. 'They will make me talk . . . I haven't the strength to . . . they will hunt us.' She spoke as if to herself, her words hardly audible above the whispers of the trees. Vanya, utterly wretched, had no words to say.

Vila was struggling with her bound hands, trying to get something from her pocket. Vanya wanted to help her, but he did not dare. At last, she managed to take something with one bound hand. It was the small parcel, wrapped in a morsel of soft deerskin, that the old woman from the tree had tried to hand him, before she was killed.

'Here, this is for you.'

Vila dropped the package to the ground by his feet and Vanya bent to pick it up. Without meeting the woman's eyes he walked back to his place and lay down. Propped on one elbow, he slowly unwrapped the little parcel. Inside was a small dark carving. As he looked at it, Vanya felt a wave of misery sweep over him. Sitting on the palm of his hand, looking at him with needle-sharp eyes, and coiled, as if ready to strike, was a small but vicious snake.

2 Paths through the Forest

Nina woke early, as the first blue light appeared, showing where the sky ended and the trees began. As she lay and watched, she prayed that day would not come; that the soft silent night would continue. She knew that waking would bring pain, would bring the need for her to be strong and responsible – and so she wanted to stayed curled in her soft blanket, like a baby. She listened to the sweet silence – nothing stirred – the whole world seemed to be waiting for the first bird to call . . . and there it was: the liquid warble of a thrush. Within minutes the forest rang with birds, and the eastern sky was washed with light.

She sighed and rolled from her blanket into the cool dewy morning. While she made the fire, she allowed herself to think once more of the dreadful events of the previous day. The Mati was dead. Her heart gave a dull lurch as she remembered the little body falling so lightly to the ground. And Vila was captured. Nina's throat constricted, but she had no more tears left to shed. 'It's my fault . . . all my fault!' The words thudded in her brain. 'It wouldn't have happened if . . .' She put more wood on the fire, moving quietly so as not to disturb the others. Thank God, there was dry wood; at least they could eat properly. She filled a kettle with water from the little stream; she would wake the others with some herb tea – it was the least she could do. As she looked through her pack (most of their stuff had been left back in the clearing, but luckily she and Tomilin had been carrying theirs) her hand came across the Mati's carving. She pulled it out and looked at it, the wood comforting her with its smoothness. She could almost imagine the shining pebble resting in the shallows of a great river. She looked at the three bees, as they paused for an instant before resuming their search among the flowers. 'Think of bees, Nina.' She heard once more the old woman's words: 'Think of bees. Such wealth of spirit.' She sighed. She had none of the skill or valour of those tiny creatures, whose only weapon was their own death-stroke, who seemed so self-contained among the flowers, who worked so ceaselessly and so selflessly together in their castles of wax. But as she sighed, she remembered the Mati laying a gentle hand upon her arm: 'It was very brave, you know, to follow Masha into the river.' Nina recalled her reply: 'Oh, but Mati, I didn't think! I just jumped.' The Mati had looked at her quizzically. 'Does that make you a coward, Nina?'

A noise behind her roused Nina from her reverie. Masha walked up. They smiled bravely, and clasped hands.

'How do you feel?' asked Masha.

'Better.'

Nina had been beside herself with grief the day before. They had all been dazed and shocked, but Nina had not been able to halt the flood of tears.

When she and Ania had fled from their pursuers, they had seemed to run wildly, without direction. Masha and Tomilin were already out of sight, Vanya was nowhere to be seen. They had run on through the trees, gradually putting a little more distance between them and the men behind. Then, as they splashed desperately across a small stream, Nina had heard a faint cry coming from somewhere below her. As she paused for a fraction of a second, she was grabbed roughly from behind and pulled forcibly down what seemed to be a large muddy rabbit-hole. A deep voice close to her ear had ordered her to be quiet: 'Not a sound –' it had said, 'or we're lost.' A hand smelling strongly of wet earth and foxes had been clamped firmly over her mouth. Despite this malodorous hand on her face, Nina had been able to look about, her heart pounding. She could just make out, opposite her, the faces of Masha and Tomilin. Between them, with a firm hand upon the shoulder of each, sat someone the like of whom Nina had never seen before.

It was a person of such wildness and strangeness that at first she had trouble making out if it was a man or a woman. It had long tangled hair that fell about its shoulders, and here and there a twig or leaf had become terribly caught up in it and seemed destined to stay there for ever. The face below this tangled mass was very dark and very dirty. As this extraordinary person raised its head to peer up the narrow tunnel through which they had entered, Nina saw from the line of the jaw that this was a woman, quite a young woman. She wore loose garments of a coarsely woven cloth – dyed in great bands of yellow, brown and green – tied at the ankles and wrists with criss-crosses of leather thong.

The hand upon her mouth was slowly removed. Nina made no sound and kept rigidly still. Then the hand was taken completely away. Nina turned and looked at whatever had grabbed her. Her eyes met those of a person very similar to the one sitting between Masha and Tomilin. Again it was at first hard to establish the sex. Only when Nina discerned a faint trace of beard on the person's chin did she decide that it must be a man. Other than that it looked much the same as its companion – long-haired and dirty, dressed in the same coarse clothes, and giving off a smell that could only be described as disagreeable. Looking beyond him, Nina was relieved to see Ania, crouched in a corner of the burrow, her hand over Stepan's mouth as she tried to soothe him with almost silent words of reassurance. There was no sign of Vanya.

As her heart gradually began to beat more evenly, Nina made out, overhead, a muffled exchange of shouts and yells: 'Where did they go?' 'Did you see them?' There were sounds of searching – heavy footsteps above their heads, twigs and branches snapping and the sound of swearing: 'Blasted woods . . . Hell's teeth, what's the use? . . . Bitching weather . . .' Then, after several long minutes, the voices and the footsteps receded.

She and Masha had looked at each other. The same question was in their eyes: 'Who are these people? Are they safe?'

They had never found out. Once the two strange creatures had decided that the coast was clear, they had sprung up the muddy tunnel, and disappeared from sight, leaving their captives to stare at one another in astonishment. They had stayed in the burrow for a good hour. More men came and searched, then went away. When all was quiet once more, there had been an outburst of tears, anger and self-recrimination. Stepan had wailed as if he would never stop.

Nina had blamed herself for the whole thing, especially for running away and leaving Vila, although Ania, from the depths of her silent grief, assured her that it was the only thing she could have done. Eventually, Masha ventured out to have a look around. She had come back and told them it seemed safe enough. She had got them moving, urged them on, forced them to walk further up the little stream until they were right away from the Mati's clearing. Then, in the shelter of a steep bank, they had built a small fire, dried their clothes, and slept.

Now, sitting together in the grey dawn, Nina and Masha quietly began discussing what they must do.

'We should follow them,' said Nina. 'We've got to get Vila back.'

'Of course,' agreed Masha. 'But we'll need help. We can't do it on our own.'

They woke Ania and Tomilin. As they drank the steaming tea and ate the morsels of bread and cheese from Nina's pack, they argued over who should return to the lake for help. Tomilin was eager to go, but he did not know the way, nor could he handle a boat. Ania was determined to follow Vila's captors, but Nina said that it would perhaps be better for her to take Stepan home and muster the villagers. When she said this, Ania's face froze: No, she would not leave Vila to the mercy of those men – not again.

At last it was settled. Masha and Tomilin would go back. They would take Stepan and leave him at the village, and return with help. Nina and Ania were to follow the men on foot.

But where could they meet? The three from the forest village discussed it, while Ania sat, cradling Stepan and staring sadly into the distance.

'What about the hollow tree, by the pool?'

'No – too public; the children use it.'

'What about the old barn? No one goes there.'

'It's still too open; not enough cover.'

'I know,' said Tomilin at last. 'Kupala's shrine.'

'Perfect!' declared Nina.

'Of course!' Masha nodded in agreement.

Kupala's shrine was a small overgrown clearing about half a mile outside the village. There was no real shrine there any more, just a clearing full of bracken and wild flowers. People kept away from it, and children were forbidden to go near on pain of a severe beating. Masha and Nina had discovered it one day while exploring. When Masha had asked her mother about it, the little woman had become agitated: 'Kupala's shrine? Stay away from there, girl, stay away.'

Now, as Masha thought about it, she suddenly remembered the map that the Mati had shown them, stained and brown with age, tattered round the edges. The old woman had unrolled it, weighing down the corners with four small carvings. Masha remembered how they had pored over it, exclaiming and delighting in its exquisitely drafted drawings of trees, streams and villages.

'Look! Here we are,' Tomilin had said, pointing to a large elaborate tree.

'Here's the lake village. Oh, and my oak-tree,' Masha had cried.

'But look, more villages,' said Masha.

And sure enough, apart from the three villages by the river, they saw many more clusters of dwellings, some scattered through the forest, some further along the lake shore, further than the girls had ever been.

'So many people,' Masha breathed. 'Is it true?'

'Of course,' replied the old woman, chuckling.

'But why do we never meet?'

The Mati folded her hands and stared into the distance, as if remembering.

'Many years ago, before even I was born, the villages were joined by broad paths that had been cut through the woods by the people of the olden days. These paths were broad and straight. Where the roads crossed, the people put shrines to the Ancient Ones – to Yurilo, the Laughing Lord of the Corn, to Kupala, the Fern-Mother, the watery one. You've heard these names?'

'Yes.' The three listeners nodded. They knew them from wonderful stories, from whispered oaths and pledges, from strange secret celebrations that still took place in the village, in defiance of the priests and the Council.

'The Old Knowledge,' Masha said. 'That's what our mothers call it. Ania talks about it too – she uses it in her weaving.'

'I dare say.' The Mati's eyes had twinkled.

'Masha?' Nina's voice broke through her thoughts, bringing her back from the treehouse to the chilly forest morning. 'We must get going. We've lost enough time.'

They gathered up their few belongings and began to make their way back to where they had last seen the men who had captured Vila. As they walked, they made last-minute arrangements; they made each other promise to take the utmost care; each dreaded the moment when they would have o part. At length they came to the place where they had been hidden in the strange burrow underground. They had trouble finding it, so cleverly was it concealed behind ferns and brambles, in the shadow of the bank. There was no sign of their wild rescuers, no trace of where they had gone.

'Who were they?' Masha asked, and she looked towards Ania where she stood, cradling her child and murmuring words of love into the softness of his hair. The woman glanced up and the girls saw that her eyes were once more bright and brave.

'Forest people – wild and dangerous . . . but we can trust them.' She said no more, and Masha and Nina kept their peace.

At last Nina said reluctantly: 'I suppose we'll have to go back through the clearing.' She had no desire to return to the place where such dreadful things had happened; she dreaded the sight of the Mati's little body lying alone on the ground. The same thought was on everyone's mind.

'No.' Ania was down on one knee examining the ground. 'Not us, Nina. They've gone north. This way.' She pointed through the trees – a faint trail of bruised grass showed where the men had passed.

'It's all right.' Masha spoke up bravely. 'We'll go back to the river through the clearing. We have to. I think I can remember the way. We'll . . .' she hesitated, '. . . we'll look after her.' She had decided that she would bury the little body; she dreaded it, but she could not bear the thought of it lying there untended and unmourned, until the forest

164

reclaimed it.

Ania came up and hugged her. Masha held tight to the slender body, trying to extract some of Ania's strength, trying to give Ania some of her own. The red-haired woman looked up at the girl.

'Thank you, Masha. Be careful.' She stepped back.

'Yes, I will. Goodbye, Ania.'

Nina came forward and the friends embraced.

After the farewells, after Ania had finally steeled herself to hand Stepan over into Masha's arms, the two groups drifted apart. Ania and Nina started to follow the trail of crushed grass and broken twigs. Masha and Tomilin took the laughing child and turned and crossed the little stream. As Masha ducked under a bent and ancient hawthorn, she turned and glanced back over her shoulder. She saw Nina in the distance disappearing into the shadow of the huge trees. Before she vanished the girl looked around, and Masha could imagine Nina's brave infectious smile, and she saw her raise her hand in a final, determined salute.

3   The Fire on the River

'What have they done with her? What's happened?' Masha cried, as she scanned the empty clearing. There was no sign of the Mati's body.

'Perhaps they buried her,' Tomilin suggested. He wandered over to the great beech-tree and gazed up into its waving golden leaves. There was no sign of the rope-ladder. 'Look,' he said.

There at the foot of the tree was Masha's travelling pack, also the packs belonging to Ania and Vila. Tomilin picked them up.

'Here, I'll carry mine.' Masha came over and shouldered her pack. She reached inside and found the carving of the flower, rejoicing that it had not been taken. Some of her misery lifted as she stroked the dark wood. 'We'll leave the others,' she said. 'They won't be of any use.'

'Where's Mati?' asked Stepan, as he craned his neck to look up into the tree.

Masha softly stroked the little boy's hair: 'She's gone away,' she said.

'Where to?' Stepan asked, looking at her crossly. 'Bring her back.'

'I can't.' Masha could feel a lump come to her throat. The

little boy's lower lip was sticking out in a sulk. He was cross and tired. He pulled at Masha's trousers.

'Where's Vila?' he demanded. 'Where's Ania?' Seeing Masha look worried, Stepan immediately became fretful. 'Ania!' he whimpered, and his protruding lip began to tremble.

Tomilin, seeing the danger signals, tried to distract the child. He pulled faces and stood on his hands, but to no avail. Stepan now realized that he had been separated from his mother, and he felt betrayed and frightened. As he opened his mouth to wail, and as Masha and Tomilin looked at each other in despair, a loud commotion from above caused all three to gaze up into the golden halo of the beech-tree. Masha froze. Could it be? Perhaps . . . Her first thought was that the Mati was magically alive again. She tried to banish the idea from her mind. What was she? A child, to think such nonsense. She fumbled for her knife.

Up above, the noise swelled. Whatever was up there seemed to be thrashing about, oblivious to the three listeners below. Masha and Tomilin stepped away from the tree, pulling Stepan back, ignoring his protests. 'Mati!' he cried, looking up. 'Mati!'

While they watched in apprehension, the lower branches began to sway. There was a final burst of shaking and rustling and then, to their astonishment, they saw a dark figure jump out of the tree. It dropped lightly to the ground, like a cat, landing on all fours and looking about before it straightened up. As it crouched, sniffing the air like an animal, Masha and Tomilin recognized the strange dirty creature that had pulled them down the rabbit-hole, saving them from capture. She was looking at them steadily with eyes that were of the palest green – almost yellow – like an eagle's, and thickly fringed with black lashes that served to accentuate their colour. She raked her long tangled hair back from her face, a gesture reminiscent of Vila.

'Hallo.' Masha took a step forward, holding out her hand in greeting, as one would with a wild animal. 'Thank you for helping us. You saved our lives.'

The thin dark face creased into a smile as the strange woman grinned, showing sharp white teeth. She cleared her throat, and said in a voice that was husky from lack of use: 'Who try to kill you? Who are these killers? They shot the Mati. Perhaps I will kill them. I will decide.'

'The Mati, where is she – the body? It's gone.' Masha pointed to the middle of the clearing where the old woman had fallen.

'We take her,' said the wild woman. 'Not leave her for crows.'

'Where?'

'To the river . . . for burning,' said the woman, seeming surprised at their ignorance. 'Back to the river at last, for the Mati. Come! You come too. Bring the child.'

'Who are you?' But Masha's words hung in the air. The woman had turned, and, loping across the clearing, she disappeared through the arched entrance, moving like a deer, swift and silent. Tomilin grabbed Masha's sleeve.

'Do we go? What do you think?'

'I think she's a friend. We'll follow – we're going to the river anyway. Maybe she can help.' Masha hoisted Stepan on to her shoulder. The little boy had been so fascinated by the odd dirty woman that he had forgotten that he had been about to cry. Instead, he gave a gleeful cry as Masha began running as fast as she could in pursuit of the green-and-yellow-clad stranger.

They had to run fast to keep up with her. She seemed to assume that they were as swift as she. Darting through the trees, she covered the ground faster and more silently than they would have believed possible; fleeter and more agile even than Vila. In comparison with her, their progress was both loud and clumsy. On and on she ran, until both Masha and Tomilin felt that their hearts would burst. They took it in turns to carry the giggling child – he seemed to become heavier with every step, and they were already laden with their back-packs. Just as Masha thought she could go no further she saw before her, glinting in the sun, the broad green sweep of the river. They must have run at least two miles with no rest.

'Oh, thank God!' she gasped, as she saw the figure ahead slow down and stop. She dropped Stepan and collapsed on to the ground, her lungs burning and her legs shaking uncontrollably. Tomilin dropped down beside her, coughing and spluttering with exhaustion. They leant against each other and waited for their hearts to stop racing. The woman turned and called back to them: 'I went too fast?' Hearing their gasps, she showed her teeth in a grin.

Masha and Tomilin got up and staggered through the last of the trees and out into the open. Looking around, Masha tried to remember which part of the river this was. It looked familiar – tall trees crowded to the very edge of the water. Surely they were not too far from the forest village. The woman had led them north, away from their boats. Masha groaned. Why hadn't she thought of this? Now they had wasted all this time. They had to get back to the lake, to fetch help.

She was about to voice these thoughts when something bobbing at the edge of the water caught her eye. It was a heavy wooden raft, made from tree trunks that had been lashed together, and lying on this platform was a small bundle of yellow-green robes. It was the Mati's body. The old woman looked happy and peaceful, as if she was having a short nap. Heaped about her were piles of ferns and flowers, and at each corner of the raft great sprays of rushes had been fastened, freshly gathered from the river, dripping and gleaming in the faint sun. Kneeling beside the raft, the woman was fastening to the front a small carving of a swooping owl, which she had taken from somewhere among her dirty robes. It was obviously to fetch this little creature that she had gone back to the clearing.

By now it was well after noon, though the sun was obscured behind dark banks of cloud, rarely showing its face. The storm of the previous day had done little to clear the air – it was still humid and overcast. Masha felt terribly oppressed as she went over to the raft and looked down at the old dead woman. It was not just her body that was tired – she felt as if every ounce of energy and will had been sucked from her. The dead person in the raft was no longer the vital woman of the treehouse: she was merely broken and hollow. How could Masha summon the determination to get them back to the boats, and then to the village? All she wanted was to curl up under a tree and sleep for days. She slumped down on the river bank and put her head into her arms, closing her eyes.

'Ah, here's Fox.'

Masha looked up at the sound of the woman's husky voice. Emerging from a tangle of rushes and reeds, up to his thighs in the river, came the other wild creature. Upon his back was a huge pile of kindling. He threw it on the grass and flung himself down beside it, wiping his face with his yellow sleeve. He looked at Masha, then over at Tomilin and Stepan. When he saw the child his grimy face broke into a grin, as sharp and as white as the woman's. He held out his hands to Stepan: 'Here,' he beckoned. 'Come, little one.'

Stepan trotted over, not in the slightest apprehensive of this wild-looking man. He flopped down next to the stranger and looked at him with round eyes. Then, taking a deep breath, he looked back at Masha. 'Pooh! Smelly!' he said, pointing at the man and holding his nose.

'Stepan!' Masha and Tomilin exclaimed in unison at the child's frankness; but the man laughed, leaning over to poke Stepan gently in the ribs, and making the odd gurgling noises one would make to a baby or a puppy. He sniffed at himself and nodded at the child. 'Fox,' he said, by way of introduction – or explanation. Then, turning, he looked back along the river. Throwing his head back, he gave a shrill barking cry, over and over, piercing the muggy air. But as he did so, Stepan caught sight of the raft and gave a joyous shout: 'Mati!' he laughed, and started across to the boat.

'Oh, no!' Masha leapt to her feet. 'Stepan! Mati's asleep. Leave her, darling.'

But the man Fox reached the child before her. He scooped the little boy into his arms and carried him over to the raft. He talked to Stepan so gently that Masha could barely hear the words: 'Look. The Mati's dead now . . . deep, deep sleep . . . has to go on a long journey down the river. Ssh, quiet . . . mustn't wake her, little one. Say goodbye now . . . goodbye . . . goodbye.'

Masha bit her lip as she saw Stepan wave his small hand at the figure in the swaying raft. But the child seemed satisfied by the man's words and stayed cradled happily in Fox's arms. Then he gave a shriek and pointed along the bank. Coming towards them, lifting its feet delicately, its tail waving behind it like a banner, was a real fox. It trotted towards them and then stopped and looked over at the man as if to ask if these new people were safe.

For the next hour Fox kept Stepan amused. They went up and down the river bank, playing with the fox and splashing in the shallows. This gave Masha and Tomilin time to speak with the woman. They asked many questions, which she answered slowly and deliberately. She too asked questions, and they eventually told her all that had befallen them since they had left the lakeside village. It turned out that she knew a great deal of what had happened, in the same way that the Mati had seemed aware of things that she had yet to be told.

'How do you know about the hunters?' Tomilin had asked at one point.

The woman had turned and looked up into the canopy of

green leaves overhead. She pointed up into the treetops. 'We watch,' she said simply, as if that made it clear.

'How?' asked Masha, bewildered, but the woman stayed silent.

Tomilin said: 'If you knew about the hunters, why didn't you stop them? Couldn't you keep them away? Why didn't you help us then? We could have rescued Vila.'

The woman looked solemn. She laid her small hard hand on the boy's shoulder and looked into his eyes. 'We did not know they would find the clearing. That was unlucky. We were far away, me and Fox, seeking . . .' She sighed deeply, and her yellow eyes were grim. 'We were not vigilant. We did not watch. We have paid.' She fell silent.

'What's your name?' Masha asked at last.

Then the woman laughed, and her laughter was like a bird's – strange and rare. 'Watch,' she said, and she put her fingers to her lips and gave a long shrill whistle. The sound sang over the river, causing Fox to look up from his play and smile. At first nothing happened. Masha and Tomilin looked up into the sky, but the grey air was empty. Then soaring towards them, with large wings slicing the still air, came a great bird. The woman reached into her clothes and, pulling out a thick leather glove, slipped it on to her left hand. Masha and Tomilin stepped back as the bird swooped down to land on the woman's wrist, with a rush of air and a beating of wings. The woman stroked the fierce, panting creature and turned to them, smiling.

'Hawk,' she said, and nodded her head in greeting.

Hours later, towards dawn, the travellers and their dishevelled guides were moving swiftly down the river towards the lake. The moon had set, and now only the still silhouettes of the trees and banks could be seen. The sky was a deep purple-blue, not quite black, and pricked here and there by a glinting star.

The people in the long boat were silent. Hawk and Fox knelt fore and aft, propelling the light craft with deep strong pulls of their paddles. The only sound to be heard was the drip of water from the blades of these plunging paddles, and the occasional call of a night bird among the rushes.

The boat was unlike those of the lake village. It was far bigger, easily twenty feet long, made from bark rather than hide, rendered waterproof with a kind of gum. The outside was painted in green and yellow bands, like the clothes of Fox and Hawk. On the front were drawn two hawkish eyes, and from the stern waved a red fox's tail. There was plenty of room inside for Masha, Tomilin and Stepan – and their belongings; Fox and Hawk seemed to travel with nothing at all, whatever they needed they pulled from the folds of their clothing. Their animals had vanished – they obviously travelled separately.

Late in the afternoon, as the light had started to fade, Fox had produced this boat from where it was hidden in a clump of tall reeds. Masha had been desperate to get away. 'We must hurry,' she had said to Hawk again and again. But the woman would not be rushed, and when Masha finally decided that she and Tomilin would go alone to find their boat, Hawk had flashed angry green eyes at her: 'Stay. Wait for dark. The Mati's farewell must not be hurried.' But she and Fox had brought out this boat, and had managed to put Masha's mind at rest. 'We have time enough,' they had assured her. 'Hunters travel slow – over ground.'

So Masha had forced herself to be resigned. Indeed – she had longed to forfeit her dreadful responsibility, and now she was being made to do so. These people were obviously safe; they were in some strange way like the Mati. Not only did they wear the same odd clothes, but they had a wildness and a loneness that reminded Masha of the old woman. Seeing her worried look, Fox had come to her and gently stroked her hand. 'We take you back,' he said. 'We help you move fast. Show you how. Don't fret.'

They had made a meal with a pigeon caught by the hawk, and with wild vegetables found by Fox and Stepan. Then Masha and Tomilin had watched as Fox and Hawk had made the final adjustments to the Mati's funeral pyre. Carefully and lovingly, they heaped it with wild flowers and herbs, then they piled on more kindling. Afterwards, they had sat on the bank, motioning the others to be quiet. For almost an hour the two people had sat and watched. Mainly they were silent, but from time to time they sang, in a language that seemed more animal than human. It had no words, but it expressed a sadness which needed no words. Then, as the light died about them, they told Masha and Tomilin to take their places in the long boat. Once they were settled, and the sleeping Stepan had been wrapped in blankets and set in the bows, Hawk had unfastened both the raft and the bark canoe. Leaping aboard, she and Fox began to tow the heavy raft out on to the river. All about them, the light was fading fast, and the moon sailed high in the sky, shedding its pale light upon the surface of the silent water.

What happened next, Masha would never forget. When the raft was in the centre of the river, Fox turned and with a slash of his knife, severed the rope that joined the two craft. Then he deftly struck flint on flint and at once had a small flaming brand. This he tossed into the very heart of the kindling that heaped the wooden craft. A second later, Hawk had steered the canoe a distance off, letting it drift in the current while they all turned and watched.

The raft burst into a pillar of flame. The fire made a noise like a roaring wind, and the spit and crackle of the burning wood was almost deafening. But above these sounds rose another even stranger – the song of the two wild people as they said their final farewell to the old woman who had been their friend. But then, as the flames reached their height,

Masha saw sliding from the shadows, like graceful apparitions, a score or more of long canoes like their own. In each gliding craft sat creatures like Hawk and Fox – wild, savage people, with long hair and ragged robes. Each held in their hand a flaming brand, and the glow of these torches shone upon the black mirror of the water like the spectral flickering of souls. And the song that came to Masha across the river was at once joyous and tragic, filled with great tenderness and with great violence. Up and up it soared into the sparkling night, rising with the flames like a wordless requiem.

Once the flames had begun to die slightly, Hawk turned the boat, and with Fox started to speed the craft through the water away from the burning pyre. They thrust the paddles into the water as if they were one person, and they never looked back. Soon the Mati's raft was far behind.

Masha turned and gazed behind her. Somewhere, an owl called mournfully across the water, and in the distance she could see the warm orange glow of the raft as it burned amid a world of silver and black. She turned once more and stared forward into the darkness. They would be at the lake by morning. Lying back in the rushing canoe, she closed her eyes and fell asleep.

4 Dunya

In the warm, sweet-smelling darkness of the cowshed, Vila eased her sore hands – still tied behind her – and settled back into a soft pile of straw. Although the shed was empty now, as all the cows had been hastily led away for fear of her laying some hex or enchantment upon them, they had left behind the sweet smell of their breath, and a sense of their gentle slowness. Vila wished they were still in the shed with her – any creature, in fact, to help dispel the terrible feeling of loneliness that was engulfing her. Although accustomed to spending weeks in her own company, this deserted shed seemed the most desolate place she had ever known. Sitting there, she recalled some of Saskia's words to Nina – they seemed to come from long ago: 'I couldn't see in the dark . . . I was hungry . . . my mother didn't come to get me. It seemed like I was going to be in there for ever . . .'

She closed her eyes to block out what little light filtered through the cracks in the bolted door, and tried to imagine that the shed was full of slow, heavy cows, gently chewing the cud and shifting on their feet in the deep straw. If she could summon them up, perhaps she would not feel so desperate. As the picture inside her head began to form, a soft shove on the back of her raised knees made her jump and open her eyes. In the dim light, she could make out a ginger cat that had come from out of the gloom to wind himself about her legs in a friendly fashion.

'Hallo, puss,' she said. Unable to stroke him with her hands, she put her face down and buried her nose in his fur, as if to breathe in some of his friendliness, and she heard the deep rumble of his purr, and felt his claws gently digging into her thighs as he tried to settle on her lap.

'I know someone with hair just that colour,' she told him. But the thought of Ania brought to the surface those tears which had threatened to come the moment she had been flung into this shed. Vila, who had yet to flinch from the most brutal jeering and insults, put her head down on her knees and sobbed. Her tears drove the cat away. He stalked off into the corner, and though she called he would not come back.

She had been put into the cowshed by the elders of the village. After a day's march through the forest, hindered rather than helped by the presence of the horses, the hunters had made a triumphant entrance into the village. Their progress had been more rapid than Vila had anticipated, and they had arrived early that morning. Crowds had gathered to see their return and word soon spread that they had captured a woman from another village. As the news travelled, it was quickly embellished by teller and listener alike, and by now the captive was thought to be a fierce and deadly witch, who had enchanted Tomilin and bewitched or murdered Nina and Masha. Vanya's name was on everybody's lips – he had managed to break the spell put upon him and had escaped to warn the others of their peril, bringing useful information of the enemy.

Vila had not been surprised by the violence of her reception. She was no stranger to the way that ordinary people could be transformed into a shrieking mob. As she had been jostled through the dusty village square she had heard their cries: 'Witch!' 'Sorceress!' Even the little children had joined in, aping their elders, wildly excited by the commotion. And yet Vila was sure that, before their appearance, the village had been peacefully carrying on its day-to-day activities, with no thought of hurting a single soul. What was it that changed people thus? Ania would say that it was the fear of something they misunderstood, but Vila suspected that it was instead just what it seemed – a desire to hurt and bully, and an opportunity to do so.

What had Vila felt as she had been brought into this small cluster of dwellings that seemed to crouch or cower between the mighty flanks of the forest and the broad swathe of the river? What had been her thoughts as she had passed the low wooden houses with their curtains of fine lace at the windows, their tidy yards and gardens – all so achingly familiar, so much a part of that misty undercurrent of her mind that she called her memory?

As she was marched through the narrow streets, she had gazed about her hungrily, despite her fear; for it was from here that Vila had come. This was the village that had been her home for almost fourteen years. This was the place from where she had been hounded when, as a young girl, she had finally declared herself free from its authority – independent and unrepentant. Grimly, Vila smiled in the shadowy cowshed, as she recalled the dreadful circumstances of her leaving.

She had been so very different then. Thin and timid, always in the background: a stammering unhappy child with long untidy hair and a sad, pinched face. Her mother and father had died when she was small – scarcely five – and she remembered them dimly, but with little affection. They had been as poor as it is possible to be and yet remain alive, living hand to mouth, constantly in debt, constantly hungry. They had been carried off one winter by a fever that they would have survived had they been warm and well fed; and they left behind a sad little girl and a baby, who ceased to breathe a few minutes after it was found by a kindly neighbour.

The neighbour had taken Vila in, saying that she would treat her as one of her own. Perhaps she had tried to; but Vila, remembering the slaps and the shouting, the coldness and indifference, knew that she had been unable to do so. They had disliked each other almost immediately, and Vila had become the drudge of the family – their servant. The other children, taking their cue from their mother, treated her as they would have treated an unlucky animal; no one thought to mention to them that the girl might have feelings, just as they.

When she was thirteen, she had been given in marriage to a man who made his living buying and selling goods in the three villages that bordered the river. He was a pedlar, plying his trade back and forth along the banks of the river, selling pots and pans, cloth and ribbons; anything that the villagers wanted he managed to get from somewhere. He was old, angry and often savage. He stank, and got habitually drunk on the cheap alcohol that he made and sold. Vila spent a year with him – a year of such horror and misery that even now she had difficulty believing it had ever taken place.

Eventually, something had hardened within her and, determined to take no more of his blows and curses, she had run to the family who had raised her and asked them to have her back. She had no desire to return to them, but where else could she go? But they had turned her smartly round and told her to go back – it was her duty. She had appealed, told of her treatment at the pedlar's hands, gone from door to door pleading for somewhere to stay, but no one had helped her. The women had turned from their doors, wiping their hands on their aprons. Some of them had seemed sorry, but none of them was willing to bring trouble to their home – it did not do to get between a husband and wife, even if the wife was a pinched and starved-looking child.

Only one woman had shown any kindness: the woman Dunya, who lived with her husband Vladislav and a houseful of growing boys on the outskirts of the village. She had seen Vila's desperate flight from one house to another, and had taken pity on her and hidden her in the stable behind the house, so that the drunken pedlar would not find her and take her back.

But she had been found. After only a day, the pedlar came to reclaim his property. Along with him came a horde of children and young men, one of whom had decided that it must have been some spell cast by this recalcitrant girl that had laid low his father's prize cow. This vicious accusation needed no substantiation – the villagers wanted little encouragement to pull the girl from the stable, to declare her a wicked, meddling woman and a practitioner of the black arts. What they would have done, had Dunya not managed to slip the bar from the shed in which the villagers had put the frightened girl, did not bear thinking about. She told her to run away, far away from the village. 'Follow the curve of the river. Go right into the forest. It's your only hope. Good luck. God keep you.' Dunya had thrust a bundle of food and warm clothes into the arms of the bewildered girl and had accompanied her to the edge of the village, to the eerie clearing in the woods known as Kupala's shrine.

Thus had Vila left her village. Now, as she sat still as stone on the pile of sweet straw, she seemed to see again the broad friendly face of the woman who had helped her escape; who had stood with her newborn daughter in her arms, watching her run through the first of the massive trees – to perish, or to survive.

Vila had survived. But in doing so she had determined that the memories she kept of the forest village should trouble her no more. In the years that had followed, she had forced herself to forget the faces that had never shown her kindness – as they would surely forget her. She was not the first to have been driven into the forest, and she would not be the last.

Now, returning to the village, she recognized none of her captors or her tormentors, and no one seemed to make any connection between this strong, wild-looking woman and the sad, undernourished girl who had so mysteriously disappeared so many years ago. Only one face had seemed to shine out from the crowd of mockers and cat-callers that had greeted Vila's arrival – that of a broad-faced woman, stout and strong, who had come to the door of her house at the end of the village, and had stared in a puzzled fashion at the woman who was being so proudly paraded through the streets. Their eyes had met and Vila's heart had given a lurch. Could it be . . .? At once, all those banished memories had begun to tumble back into Vila's bruised mind.

It had been Dunya. She had been brought to her door by a loud commotion outside, and her heart had sunk as she had seen the gathering crowd, the wild looks and the screaming faces. 'Oh, no,' she murmured to herself as she moved slowly through the dusty yard to take a closer look. 'Please God, don't let it happen again.'

She moved nearer and began to follow the crowd into the village. She saw the proud-faced woman being pulled along, and she – as did all the villagers – had marvelled at the strange, mannish garments and the short, wild hair. Could it be one of those women from that place of which they never spoke? Then she heard something which made her stop dead in her tracks. A woman, whom she recognized as the woodcutter's wife, could be heard saying to her neighbour: 'They say she captured those two girls – you know, Dunya's girl, Nina, and her friend . . . carried them away to her village.' The neighbour nodded: 'Yes, so I heard. So this woman must be a sorceress of some kind, Rusalka even.'

A child nearby heard these words, and soon the cry resounded through the village square where the villagers were standing around, gossiping and speculating. 'Rusalka!

They caught a Rusalka!'

The captive turned at the sound of the word that was echoing through the air, made shrill by the childish voice. As she did so, Dunya met her gaze and saw in her dazed black eyes a look both of fear and of sorrow.

'Vila!' Dunya breathed the name silently to herself. The small, frightened girl had been brought back at last. She had become a woman, and she knew of Nina – Vila had seen her daughter. Dunya turned and strode back to her house. She would bide her time. She would wait for dark, then she would find out what had happened. It was time for Vila to help the woman who had once helped her.

5   The Assembly

By now, the meeting hall by the lake was almost full. More villagers arrived each minute. They were ushered in and brought up to date by those who had been the first to hear. They stood about in groups, talking in low voices, wondering what could have happened to distress Masha so. Where were the others? Who was this new boy? What were the two wild forest folk doing here? They seldom came to the village, preferring the solitude of the woods.

They had all been asleep when, at the first light of dawn, the long boat had drifted into the village. Masha and Tomilin had leapt out and had lost no time in rushing from one dwelling to another, rousing the sleeping villagers and telling them to hurry, get up, there must be an assembly. Yawning and rubbing their eyes, they came through the misty morning to gather in the tall building that doubled as meeting place and grain depository.

These formal gatherings were rare. Not even the oldest of the villagers could remember any serious threat to the safety of the village. They were too isolated. The people of the forest villages kept their distance – they knew nothing of the lake people; or they knew, but kept away. So the village was peaceful. Perhaps it was a peace founded upon fear and superstition, but for many years now they had been left alone. They were content to be thought of as witches and demons – if that meant that they could continue to live without conflict. The only strangers to come here in the last hundred years had been outcasts and refugees. They had posed no threat – indeed, they had even helped strengthen the bonds that held the lake-dwellers together, reinforcing as they did the sense that this was a place of refuge, a haven from ignorance and antipathy. As the villagers gathered, they had little sense of danger.

The assembly room was really a barn – used for dancing and celebration when the weather was poor. It was here that many of the villagers kept their supplies – flour that they had no space for in their own out-houses, the seed for the next year's sowing. As they stood about, or sat in small groups talking, the sides of the massive wooden storage-bins cast unreal shadows upon their faces, and the soft mountains of grain glowed strangely in the early light. At one end of the hall, ploughs and scythes lay next to upturned boats and broken harnesses. Against the end-wall stood huge lengths of unseasoned timber, stacked together and towering over the people below, dwarfing them and making them seem oddly puny. The wood gave off the dry, papery smell of sawdust, and this mingled with the fishy smell of the boats and the dusty, pungent smell of the grain. Mounted on the other walls, like a great arbitrary patchwork, were a multitude of objects: cartwheels and horse-collars, horseshoes and plough-shares, broken cross-bows and broken cradles. From a cobwebbed rafter overhead hung a quantity of fishing-net that tumbled to the dusty floor, looking in the luminous light like a rippling black waterfall.

Masha stood in the middle of the room. Her hands were in her pockets and her head was bent, her gaze resting on the scuttling progress of a small iridescent beetle that was making its way towards its home beneath an upturned bucket. Beside her stood Zikov and Sonia, neighbours of Vila and Ania, in whose care the dog and the goats had been placed. They were big, jolly people, both of them, and their solid presence beside her did much to make Masha less nervous as she felt upon her the expectant, worried eyes of the villagers. As silence fell at last, Masha cleared her throat and prepared to speak.

'Something terrible has happened.' She paused and looked round the room. All around she saw the faces of the villagers, these people who had taken her in, who had welcomed her and supported her, showing her a degree of trust and affection that had been quite new and totally unexpected. How could she tell them? Already she could feel the heavy weight of blame falling upon her, as relentless and as final as a shroud.

'Vila has been captured – by men from my village. It's all our fault. We shouldn't have tried to go back. You all warned us, but we didn't listen. It's all our fault. We brought this on you, this trouble . . . we shouldn't have come.'

She felt a broad hand upon her shoulder as Zikov brushed past her to stand in front of the listening villagers. His very breadth and presence seemed to lull the murmur of anxious voices that had sprung up at Masha's news. He stood before them, his brown beard thrust out and his eyes solemn and serious.

'Masha will want to take all the blame for this unhappy event,' he said. 'But we all know that Vila puts herself in danger every time she goes into the forest. She is an adventurer – we all know that.' Turning, he said to Masha in a low voice: 'Tell what happened. You can't do that if you're blaming yourself. There is no time for recriminations.'

Masha looked at him gratefully, but could summon no smile. Again she cleared her throat and prepared to speak.

'I – we . . .' Her voice, sounding bleak and hollow in her own ears, trailed off. In her pocket she could feel the polished smoothness of the Mati's carving – the perfect symmetry of the petals and the fragile wings of the butterfly. As her hand caressed it, she heard again the old woman's words: 'A creature of light, my dear, reborn to give joy . . .' And as she remembered, the dark guilt seemed to lift slightly, and she found that her voice was once more brave and steady.

'They killed the Mati – these men from my village. They shot her with an arrow, and she died straightaway. She died saving us. We escaped, all of us except Vila. The Mati is dead: but she was well mourned.'

At her words a great wave of shock and sorrow rocked the room. There was no wailing or screaming, merely a gust of sighs that swept through the crowd of still people and was followed by a silence that seemed to throb with sadness.

But then, as eyes met in grief, the mood changed and the lofty building became charged with a desperate anger, wild and electric.

'We have little time,' continued Masha, raising her voice above the loud but wordless noise. 'We must go back to the forest. We must rescue Vila, and help Ania and Nina. We have the advantage – we have boats. But there's little time. I feel that they will act swiftly.'

Now voices called out, harsh and shouting, from all sides.

'Damn them! Why do they kill?'

'They force our hand. We must act now.'

'We have greater strength than they. We can take her back –'

'– and show them not to come near us with their filthy murderous minds.'

'I'll go.'

'I too!'

Voice after voice cried out in rage and fury. The mood was one of puzzlement, but underneath lay a blood-red vengeance.

Masha stared about her. She clenched her fists at her sides

and felt the anger swirl about her like a river. Part of her knew that she too longed to pick up a bow or a spear and rush headlong from the village, carried along by a tide of emotion that was both unfamiliar and yet strangely real – as if it had always been there, threatening to overwhelm.

'No!' Sonia's voice sounded shrill above the cries of the villagers. She thrust her way into the centre of the throng that had begun to mill around, as if anger would no longer allow these people to stay still. She held her arms above her head and motioned for silence. One by one the voices dropped, as the people turned to listen.

'Will we act like them? Will we allow our hurt and pain to make us like them? Listen to yourselves. What do you sound like?' Silence fell like a stone as her words echoed through the room. 'Do you want vengeance, then? Vengeance? For whom? For the Mati? Do you forget her so easily? Would she have called for blood?'

'But what shall we do? Let them kill us? Capture us? Without resisting?' A voice came from the back.

'No.' It was Tomilin. He came forward, shy and frightened. He hardly hoped that his timid voice would be able to raise itself above the sound of the crowd. But there was something within him that would not allow him to stand behind the others and listen to this wrathful storm.

'No,' he cried. 'We won't let them kill us. But neither will we let them turn us into mad hunters.' His voice cracked as all eyes turned towards him. At his sides, his hands could be seen shaking – making gestures as if to try and clothe his thoughts.

'Stranger!'

'What does he know?'

'He's only a child.'

'He's one of them. How do we know we can trust him?'

'Send him away!'

More and more voices were coming from the crowd –

aggressive, sorrowful voices, loud with hurt.

'Quiet!' Zikov's command roared through the hubbub. He pushed his bulk forward and stood with Tomilin. 'Let him speak.'

Tomilin stared at the ground. He knew that if he was heckled further, he would cry, like he had at the bear-slaying. He wished he was anywhere else – away from this madness. He cursed himself for a coward. But then, as had his sister, he felt in his pocket the carving that had been given to him beneath the arching dome of the beech tree: 'Be brave, little one.' As the words went through his mind, Tomilin raised his face to the crowd.

'I *am* a stranger. You do not have to take my words. But I want to say that I have longed for this place ever since Masha told me about it; perhaps I longed for it even before she told me – it seems that way. But now I find that there's not that much difference after all. If you want to form a hunting pack, then we can't stop you. But I won't go along. I will never go hunting. I am no hunter.'

His body shook with nerves, his lips were dry and the blood roared in his ears. But somehow his mind felt suddenly lighter, as if these words – unspoken till now – had always been a terrible burden to him, and the speaking of them had in some way set him free. He felt as he did when he played his flute – played a tune that had evaded him for many days, but had at last come out and been sent into the air to linger and fade. Masha moved across and squeezed his trembling hand.

This time the silence lasted. People muttered and murmured, but no more shouts were heard. The mood changed to one of determination. The anger ebbed away, leaving in its place a feeling of urgency, of desperate haste.

For more than two hours the lake villagers discussed their plans. Without realizing, Masha and Tomilin found themselves at the very centre of the preparations – questioned, consulted and advised as equals; no longer were they strangers. Their initial courage had bred greater courage, and now they spoke with a confidence neither would have thought they possessed. Fox and Hawk came in from where they had been waiting – lounging by the canoe, which they had tethered to the jetty by the lake. They seemed strangely out of place and ill-at-ease in this high building, taken from their native home in the woods.

It was decided that only five of the villagers should go with Masha and Tomilin. They would set off immediately by boat; travelling swiftly they should reach the forest village the next day. They would meet up with Ania and Nina – they would find a way to liberate Vila.

Zikov and Sonia were both to go. Stepan, their own children and all the animals were put into the care of an old man who lived nearby. Among the other villagers who were to accompany them were two women named Irena and Daria, both of whom Masha knew well. They were close friends of Vila and Ania, and had been deeply distraught at the news of Vila's capture. Also among those who gathered by the boats were Elizabieta, the potter, and her son, Ilyich, both of them as renowned for their skill with a bow as for their skill in moulding the red clay of the lake shore. Boris, tall and thin, was also well known to Masha – she had spent many happy hours in his company, as he read his long fantastic poems to her, delighted to find such an eager listener.

These were the people who silently and grimly gathered their belongings and met down by the water, where the slender boats bobbed by the jetty. The mood was one of sadness and determination, and as Masha watched the preparations she felt reassured by the strength and courage of these people who would leave the village they loved, and go with her up the river to the place from whence she came, and from whence, also, had come the hunters who threatened their peaceful life. Now, with the first heat of their anger abated, they did not long for confrontation with the forest men – they dreaded it, but knew it had to be.

As she sat on the jetty, watching the final preparations, a voice at Masha's shoulder caused her to turn. There was Hawk, her hair hanging long over her yellow eyes. 'We must go now. There is not much time.'

Masha and Tomilin had chosen to travel in the long canoe with Hawk and Fox. As they settled down for the journey upstream, they both turned and looked at the lakeside village with its brightly painted dwellings, its barns and out-houses, the thin drifting smoke that rose from the chimneys into the misty autumn air.

'I didn't really see anything,' said Tomilin wistfully.

'Oh, you will. We'll be back.'

But as Masha spoke she knew that she was afraid. She felt no excitement, no thrill of adventure. She knew now what Ania meant when she refused to follow Vila into the forest, refused to forsake the security of her cosy hut and follow her friend into the brooding darkness of the woods: there is adventure enough in just staying at home.

Masha shook her head to clear her mind of these thoughts. Stretching her long legs before her in the speeding canoe, she sighed and turned her face forward. Upriver . . . Whatever happened in the next hours and days would decide whether or not she would be able to return to this peaceful place by the gleaming lake.

6 Women Talking

'Psst!'

'What?'

'Get down. I heard something.'

'Where?'

'Shhh!'

Nina motioned for Ania to get down. She smiled grimly to herself as she saw her companion's red head sticking out from a clump of undergrowth, as eye-catching as a squirrel. She held her breath and listened. Birds . . . a faint rustling a few yards off. She listened for a few seconds more, then breathed again – these were just ordinary forest noises.

They were less than a mile outside the village and Nina, conscious of this closeness, felt her senses to be sharper than ever before. Almost certainly there would be no one about – the villagers did not venture into the forest in this direction – but they couldn't be too sure.

'It's all right.'

She stood up and made her way through the golden bracken to where Ania crouched. They stood and looked about them as Nina decided upon a course, and then they set off once more through the tangled mass of the forest floor.

They had tracked the hunters for the whole of the previous

day. It had not been hard. The men had cut a swathe through the forest, leaving behind them a trail of bruised foliage, chopped and damaged trees; at one point they had even found a den of young bears – these the hunters had clubbed and left behind, as too heavy to carry; Nina had been alarmed at the extent of Ania's disgust and fury.

But this morning the men had veered off and entered the village from the west, and Nina and Ania had gone as close as they dared, but then they had headed east, to find the clearing where they had arranged to meet the others. Nina was familiar with the woods around Kupala's shrine. They would wait until dark before moving into the village to find out what had happened

'I'm sure we're nearly there.'

Nina surveyed the forest. It was as dense as ever. But something told her that the little clearing was not far off. And, sure enough, after pushing their way through more lush greenery and brambles, and climbing over mossy trunks that were halfway to becoming part of the rich mulch of the earth, they stumbled, tired and surprised, into a small sunlit glade.

In the centre of this little clearing was an ancient, ruined well, built obviously on the site of a small spring, for the ground around was wet and marshy. Only a few of the stones still stood – the rest had fallen down and lay scattered on the grass, covered by tendrils of creeping vine and tiny forest flowers. The two travellers threw themselves down on the carpet of grass and moss, rejoicing in its softness after the rigours of a day and a half's battle with the relentless tangle of the forest. They threw off their jackets and shoes, breathing in the sweetness of the air, and letting the weak sun shine on their upturned faces.

Eventually, Ania propped herself up on one elbow and looked about. Her face showed clearly the strain that she was under – separation from the two people she loved most in the world was taking its toll – there were deep lines beneath her eyes and her brow was wrinkled with anxiety. Yet she looked about her with interest, a curious smile on her lips.

'So, this is Kupala's shrine. It still has a magic feel, even though it has been neglected so long. How strange that the trees have decided not to grow in this circle.'

'Do you know about Kupala?' Nina had little of Masha's interest in ancient mysteries, but now, while they waited for dusk, she wished to encourage Ania to talk, to take her mind from her sorrows.

'Oh, yes.' Ania smiled. She crossed her legs and gazed into the distance. 'She is the spirit of fresh water, of springs and streams. Her festival is at midsummer. The women build holy fires and bathe in the springs. They make a statue of Kupala to throw in the water; or else they burn it in the fires.' She got to her feet and walked round the clearing, examining the trees and the ground beneath them.

'Look, here are some of her flowers.' She bent and plucked a long purple weed from where it was growing in the damp soil near the well. 'Loosestrife.' She held it up for Nina to see. 'They used to call it "tear-weed" – they said it tamed demons . . . who knows. Mati used to say it was good for stopping nosebleeds, and heavy periods.' Stooping, she plucked some small green leaves from a cranny in the broken well wall. 'And look: "The herb that breaks." It was meant to break metal: but Mati called it spleen-wort. She used it for bladder complaints.' Ania laughed, remembering the old woman's scorn of superstitions.

'So the Mati didn't believe in all that old stuff?' asked Nina, putting her arms behind her head and staring at the clouds.

'Oh, Nina, there's a difference between believing all those things that are obviously nonsense, and believing that midsummer is an important time, and worth celebrating. There will always be symbols.'

'Hmm. I don't know. It all seems the same to me.'

'Huh! You're just like Vila.' Ania's face became shadowed with pain at the thought of her friend. She passed her hand over her tired eyes and slumped down on the little broken wall.

Nina jumped up and began to fetch what little food they had with them. She must try and keep Ania's thoughts away from Vila and Stepan. 'Here, let's eat something. I'm hungry. You must be too, by now.'

They ate and talked as the sun moved slowly through the sky and the light faded. Tall birch-trees encircled the clearing, and as evening fell the luminous silver of their bark glowed from the shadows. They decided that they should try and reach Nina's mother; although they could not be sure of her help, it was almost certainly safer than going into the village with no clear idea of where Vila was held.

And so, an hour later, in the still of the twilight the two shadowy figures left the little clearing in the woods and set out towards the village, moving as silently and as stealthily as cats.

At the same moment, on the outskirts of the forest village, Dunya was softly closing the door behind her; she had told her husband that she had an errand on the other side of the village. She made her way past the quiet houses, keeping to the edge of the forest and making sure that she stayed in the shadows. Only once was she spotted – by a woman who had come out to tend a sick cow with a bowl of warm mash.

'Good evening, Dunya. Where are you off to?'

Dunya cursed softly. 'I'm taking this to old Katya,' she said, indicating the basket of food she held beneath her arm. 'She's not been well. It must be the change in the weather.'

The woman nodded sympathetically. 'Poor old thing. And no one to care for her. Give her my best wishes.' She put down the bowl of mash and gave Dunya a conspiratorial look. 'Have you heard? They say they'll try the witch tomorrow. The Council's meeting now – and me left with all the work.' She snorted and raised her eyes aloft. 'Men!'

Dunya summoned a laugh. 'Hmm! Typical.' She began to edge away, not wanting to prolong what could easily become an exchange of gossip and scandal. She knew this woman – a tiresome, meddling creature, with no interest in anything that did not concern others.

The woman went back indoors. As she walked away, Dunya took greater care not to meet another soul who might express interest in her destination. But the village was curiously deserted – the menfolk were at the meeting of the Council and the children had been kept indoors. It was unusual to see no youths loafing in the square, or any children playing tag between the houses while their mothers gathered at the well to talk. The empty streets filled Dunya with a sense of dread, and she hurried on, anxious to get to Alexei's cowshed where Vila was held.

There was no one standing guard. Whoever had been placed there to make sure the witch did not magically escape had wandered off. Dunya could not believe her luck. They would be back, she was sure, but at least there was time for some words with the captive. She went to the back of the shed, having first made sure that the huge doors were well secured with ropes and chains – no hope of slipping the bar this time.

She found what she sought in the fading light – a small knothole in the wood of the shed wall. Putting her lips close to this tiny opening, the big woman leant and whispered into the dark interior of the cowshed.

'Vila! Vila! Can you hear me?'

Inside, Vila lay curled upon the straw. As dark had filled the shed she had fought a rising tide of panic within her but, forcing herself to be calm, she had managed to drift into a fitful sleep – until now, as into her tangled dreams came the sound of her own name.

'Who's there?' She struggled to sit up, unable to rub her eyes with bound hands, longing to be able to stretch her aching limbs.

'It's Dunya . . . Do you remember? From long ago . . . I helped you once.' The slow solid voice that came through the wooden partition was so real that Vila soon realized this was not a dream.

'Is it really you?' she asked, trying to hear from whence came these comforting words.

'Yes.' There was a pause, then again the voice spoke. 'You've seen Nina, my little girl? Where is she? Is she . . .'

Vila smiled at the description. 'Yes. She's safe . . . I think. They didn't catch her. I don't know what happened. Can you get me out? What are they going to do with me?'

'The door is locked – and guarded. There's nothing I can do. Did they hurt you?'

'Not much.'

But Vila winced as she remembered the cuffs and blows, the shouted questions and accusations that had accompanied her through the village. She remembered the face of a bearded youth who had managed to get close enough to spit in her face. Worse than this, she remembered how, in the forest at dead of night, the pale-eyed Voinitsky had lurched towards her, breathing foul breath and fouler words upon her, and how she had bitten with all her power upon the hairy hand that had fumbled at her neck.

'Can you get to where I am?' Dunya's voice guided Vila to the tiny knothole. On her knees in the straw, she managed to put her lips near the wall.

'Here?'

'Yes.'

Vila sobbed. The proximity of a sympathetic being made her long for release even more painfully. She shook her head to clear her thoughts.

'They'll come to rescue me. How much time do we have?'

'The trial's tomorrow.'

'Oh, God . . . can they hurry?' She spoke the words to herself.

'I've brought you this. But take care. They mustn't find it.'

Vila heard something pass through the hole and drop softly upon the straw. Clumsily she turned and searched with her tied hands. Soon they felt beneath them a slim shaft of metal – a slender knife, unsheathed and deadly sharp. She clasped it gratefully. If she never had the chance to use it, still it would make her feel less helpless, less powerless, in the midst of her persecutors.

'I must go. Someone's coming.'

'No!' The thought of being once more alone in the stuffy blackness of the cowshed filled her with despair. But already she could hear the sound of Dunya's footsteps as she quietly walked away. Then came the sound of voices, and she strained her ears to hear.

'Hey, woman, what are you doing here?' A man's voice, loud and imperious.

'I've brought some food – for the prisoner. She may be hungry.' Dunya's voice, caught off guard, and trying to hide it.

'Witches don't need food. If she wants something she can conjure it up. Be off with you, and don't waste your sympathy. No one's to come round here. Come back tomorrow – that's when all the fun begins.'

Inside the shed, Vila slumped to the ground. Many hours passed before she fell once more into a fitful, shivering sleep, curled up like a child upon the fragrant floor.

Outside, Dunya was walking back to her home, her heart thumping angrily. How could she have been so stupid as to have let herself be seen? Pray God that the man hadn't recognized her. She strode on, strong and heavy beneath the light of the stars and the waning moon.

197

As she neared her own house, she saw that lamps had been lit and the door stood open. A path of warm yellow light poured from inside, welcoming her home, ushering her in. But somehow she did not feel welcomed. She did not feel a sense of belonging – her home was no longer a place of security and permanence. Her sons would soon leave and her daughter was gone; her husband at this very moment was helping to plan the death of a witch. What comfort could she find in her home? She lingered, looking at the house that she had come to as a girl. She had thought she had been happy . . . now she stood and wondered.

A noise behind her startled her from her reverie.

'Mother?'

Dunya turned, puzzled. What was that . . . her imagination?

'Mother?'

Dunya turned. Before her in the dim light stood a young woman. Tall and sturdy and strong – yet at the same time graceful and assured – with hair that glinted in a halo about her head. It was Nina: the same pleasant features; the face that could so easily change from a sulk to a smile. She wore strange clothes, and her hair had been shorn, but it was her little girl. She had come back – strangely grown.

'Nina . . . my baby.'

Rarely demonstrative, the big woman stumbled forward and pulled towards her the daughter whom she had never thought to see again. 'You're safe . . . you're safe.' Dunya blinked, and suddenly she wept.

Nina's arms tightened around the broad shoulders. She had never seen her mother cry. Dunya had always been a strong woman, of few words, scoffing at moods and sentiment, shrugging off any attempts to get close. Now, as Nina comforted and reassured her, she saw how slender is that line that separates the role of mother and daughter.

'Ssh, don't cry. It's going to be all right. Ssh, mama,

ssh . . .' She rocked and rocked the crying woman, feeling strong emotions that have no name. Then she dropped her arms. 'But we must talk. Can you come with us?'

Dunya raised her wet eyes and saw, behind her daughter, another woman, a slender red-headed woman, who was watching them with great gentleness. This woman stepped forward and held out her hand in greeting: 'I'm Ania. We have come to fetch Vila . . . and to see you. Please, you must help us.'

'Wait.' Dunya turned and entered the path of light that shone from her house. Pausing for an instant to wipe her face on the hem of her dress, she walked slowly up to the door and went inside.

Her two youngest sons sat at the table. They had eaten the stew that Dunya had left on the fire, and now they sat talking in low voices. They glanced up as their mother came in, then returned to their conversation.

'I have to go out,' she told them, as she cleared the plates from the table. 'Old Katya – she needs tending.' Dunya prayed that old Katya was indeed poorly, the old woman scarcely ever ventured out – her excuse would almost certainly be believed.

The boys nodded. Had they looked up, they would have been surprised at the look of tenderness upon their mother's face. But they merely grunted again, as Dunya picked up a shawl and hurried out of the door. In the shadows the two figures waited for her.

They led her away from the village and into the woods. Walking quickly and quietly, they soon reached a small clearing that lay in the midst of dense undergrowth. The darkness was intense, and yet these two women found their way with little difficulty. Dunya marvelled at her daughter's new ease of movement, her lack of clumsiness, her speed and purpose.

Once in the clearing, Ania lit a fire. They sat round it and talked softly, Ania keeping watch in case they had been followed. Nina quickly related all that had befallen her and Masha since the day they had disappeared from the village. Dunya kept silent, listening to her daughter's words with wonder. At last Nina fell silent; and then it was that Ania, unable to restrain herself any longer, asked for news of Vila.

'Have you seen her? Do you know if she is safe?'

'I have seen her – this evening. They have her under guard. They will try her tomorrow. She . . . she shall be found guilty.'

A cry of fear escaped from Ania's lips. She leapt up and seemed about to rush back to the village in a desperate bid to free her loved one. But Dunya managed to calm her. Using all her skill from many years of mothering, she was able to make Ania see the folly of any impetuous attempt at liberation: what good would it do if she, too, were captured?

Then the big woman told them of the way in which she and Vila's histories were so strangely interwoven. She told them of the frightened girl that she had set free so many years before; and Nina, listening to her mother's words, could scarcely believe her ears. So Vila, too, had come from this village. She, too, had been unable to return – forced out and kept out by a wall of fear and superstition.

'I watched her leave,' said Dunya in conclusion. 'But I never knew what became of her. I thought she would die. But better to die in the woods than to die at their hands.'

Now Ania spoke. In her quiet voice she added what she knew of Vila's past. Vila – the woman that they loved; held prisoner now by men that they had never asked to hate. She told of all that had befallen Vila when she had stumbled, almost dead from fear and exhaustion, along the banks of the river and ever deeper into the towering forest. And Nina again was astonished as she heard of the strange events that had transformed the fearful girl into a strong and courageous woman.

Vila had been found by the wild people of the woods. They had come across her huddled body as she lay sleeping beneath a wild broken willow. They had taken her with them – along their secret paths and through their mysterious warren of tunnels and underground passageways, until they came to a place where a circle of beech-trees forms a haven for all those who are lost in the forest. In the Mati's garden, Vila had been nursed back to strength.

She had stayed with the old woman for many months, learning from the Mati and the wild wood folk all the ways of the forest. She became a fleet hunter, a tracker, a carver of wood and a gatherer of herbs. The Mati had given Vila much of her knowledge, and then, when the girl seemed strong and brave enough to leave the safety of the clearing, she had sent her down the river to live with the lake people, knowing that they would take her in and treat her kindly.

So Vila had stayed by the lake. But she had never lost her love of the woods. Much of her time was spent with the wild people of the Mati's tribe – strange, free people who could not bear the confines of village life, who lived in the open, who tamed and hunted animals with equal skill, and who would fight with a savage loyalty if any of their number were threatened. But, most of all, Vila loved the old woman who had given her not only the strength, but also the will to survive her fearful past.

Ania fell silent.

'I met Vila in much the same way as you, Nina. I had been wandering in the woods, chased from my village, with Stepan only a few days old.' Ania's eyes were wet as she remembered how Vila had tenderly bent over the red-headed girl and her whimpering baby. 'She rescued me too.' She gazed at Dunya. 'And we must rescue her.'

Dunya breathed deeply. She was summoning in herself all of that strength that she had needed during her life – the strength to raise children, to lose them, to keep a family from falling into conflict and disorder. She raised her head and squared her broad shoulders. Getting up, she began to move from the clearing and back towards the village, where it lay sparkling between the sombre ranks of trees.

'We will stop them. Somehow, we will stop them.'

7   A Road through the Treetops

In the gathering darkness, Masha and Tomilin were walking through the thick woodland that bordered the river near the forest village. They walked quickly, every step of crucial importance, now that they were so near meeting with Nina and Ania. Behind them, in single file, came the other lake-dwellers. Together they made little noise – the ground was soft and their footfalls were silent. Only the occasional crack of a twig gave news to the woods that their secret groves had been invaded.

They had moored the boats in a natural pool of deep water that had been formed over the years by the movements of the river. This pool, overhung by yellow willows, had provided a perfect hiding place for the slim craft, and now they rested there, bobbing gently in the brown water, guarded by Elizabieta and Ilyich. The pool was about half a mile from the village and Masha had decided that, although so close, it would be safe. With a witch in their midst, the villagers would not allow anyone to venture from the safety of their houses.

It had been a hair-raising trip upriver. Even with her new confidence on the water, Masha had been alarmed when Hawk had said that they should navigate the rapids. Fox had agreed – they would lose too much time if they stopped and carried the boats along the path. So they had gone over the white tumbling water and through jagged rocks that towered over the canoe as it pitched and rolled upstream. Masha and Tomilin had both had to help the wild pair as the angry water had threatened to drag them under. Using long paddles, they had pulled the tossing craft through the rapids, thankful to have something to do. Hawk and Fox had shouted instructions, their voices joyful above the roaring of the water, and Masha had marvelled at their reckless courage in the face of such obvious physical danger.

Now the two strange people had disappeared into the dusk. By now Masha was accustomed to looking around and finding them gone; they vanished into the shadow of the woods at the slightest whim, to look for food, follow tracks, or scout for danger – they could never rely on them to be where they expected. Although this could be irritating at times, Masha suspected that they were all considerably safer, thanks to the beast-like vigilance of the two wild people.

'What are we going to do when we get there?'

Tomilin had been deep in thought for many minutes, but now he looked at his sister. His brown eyes were worried, and his face was still flushed from the excitement and challenge of the battle with the rapids. Any fear of the water that he may have felt had soon been overcome, and Tomilin had been thrilled at the sight of the forest gliding gently past, as the long canoe had pushed its way over the green surface of the river. Now, as the excitement wore off, he felt once more an anxiety that was shared by the whole party: what would happen next? It was impossible to lay definite plans until they had found Nina and Ania, and until they had news of what had happened to Vila.

'We must wait and see.' Masha knew that her words sounded absurd. She, too, was deeply worried about what to do. Yet again, the burden of responsibility seemed to be falling upon her, and although she had so much support from her companions, it was still she who knew the forest, she who knew the villagers.

'Where are Hawk and Fox?'

'Oh, they've disappeared again. I don't know where they went.'

'Are we nearly there? I don't recognize this part.'

They were passing through a grove of gnarled oak-trees, their feet swishing through the carpet of amber leaves, and the sound of their voices was muffled by the dense canopy overhead and the soft sea underfoot.

'Yes. Me and Nina sometimes came this far. We'll be there when these trees change to birches – that's how you can tell.'

'I never knew that you and Nina went into the woods.'

'Of course,' Masha replied with a smile. 'We were quite adventurous when we were little. Father used to give me terrible hidings if he found out.'

'Weren't you afraid?'

'Only sometimes. But this was when we were small. We didn't go anywhere once we'd grown up – it didn't matter where we were, we'd just sit and talk.' Masha bit her lip and frowned. 'God, I hope she's all right.'

Boris, the poet, now ran forward to join them, his long face aglow with excitement. He touched Masha's arm and pointed up into the trees on their left. At first Masha could see nothing, but as her eyes accustomed themselves to the waving foliage, she made out, crouched on a lofty branch, the shape of a wildcat, its ears flattened to its skull and its teeth bared in a ferocious snarl, as it spat its anger down upon the intruders.

'Oh . . .' For an instant Masha forgot her worries. This was the first wildcat she had seen alive – how different from the bruised, dead bodies of those that were brought into the village, slung ignominiously upon a pole.

'I will take that as a good omen,' said Boris. 'See how wild and free she is. She gives me courage.'

Masha smiled at him. She, too, would take it as a good omen. What harm could that do?

Just then all three jumped. Before them, grinning with white teeth, stood Hawk and Fox. Hawk, seeing the direction of their eyes, looked up into the tree and saw the cat. She laughed. Then, with her arms over her head, she bared her teeth at the angry creature.

'Shoo! Be off with you, brave one.'

In an instant the cat turned and vanished, springing from the branch and landing gracefully upon the ground beneath. The onlookers laughed in admiration, both at the animal's beauty and at Hawk's wilful bravado.

Masha turned to the grinning woman. 'Are we safe here?' She sensed that Hawk and Fox had been scouting for danger. They seemed to be able to tell if there was any threat, as easily as the forest birds.

'Quite safe,' the wild woman said. 'But we have found the shrine . . . empty . . . your friends have gone.'

'Gone? But we arranged . . .'

Fox broke in: 'They have been there. Have eaten and talked. Now they have gone to the village. But they are still safe. We have spied them. Don't fret.'

'But . . .'

'Wait. We will show you. Come. The shrine is near.'

Fox turned and loped through the trees. Masha looked back at the others who had come up and were waiting.

'Trust them, Masha. They know more than we can.'

It was the yellow-haired Irena who spoke. She and Daria were standing apart from the others, quietly observing the proceedings. Although they were so silent, so withdrawn, Masha had a deep respect for the two women. She had met them many times at the lake village, but had scarcely ever heard them speak. She remembered Ania's words when she had remarked upon this: 'Ah, but when they do speak

'– then one should listen.'

'All right, we'll follow them.' Masha started forward. In the distance she could see the wide furrowed trunks of the oaks begin to give way to slim silver birches. She had come upon Kupala's shrine without even realizing it.

In the deepening dusk, the group of silent travellers made its way through the last of the great oaks and into the silent circle of Kupala's shrine. It was empy, and yet, from the bruised grass and a few plucked flowers, it could be seen that Nina and Ania had indeed been there.

'But why didn't they stay?' asked Masha. 'We arranged to meet here. Something must have happened.'

Again Fox interrupted her. 'We must prepare. There is much to do. We need much wood – great piles of wood. And horses, to carry it. And straw – at least a cartload of straw – all dry.'

'What for? What are you planning?' asked Tomilin.

'For tomorrow. For fire. For fighting,' Hawk replied.

Masha shook her head. All she wanted to know was that her friends were safe. Once they were reunited they could make plans; but Hawk and Fox seemed to be one step ahead of her at every turn.

Hawk looked at her. The wild woman saw her distress and placed a hand on her shoulder.

'Come with us now. We will show you . . . show you how we know what to do.'

So Masha and Tomilin left the little clearing with Hawk and Fox. The others stayed only long enough to arrange who was to gather the wood and the straw, who was to get the horses.

'Zikov and I shall gather wood; because we're the strongest,' said Sonya. 'We'll bring it here – as much as we can.'

'I'll find some straw. There'll be a few sheaves left in the near fields,' said Boris. 'I'll go by boat – skirt round the village and bring it back by river.'

'We'll get the horses,' Irena spoke last. All were aware that this was by far the most perilous mission. She and Daria would have to go right into the village – if they were seen all their plans would be laid waste . . . instead of one, the villagers would have three witches to judge.

'Good luck,' they said to each other, and clasped hands.

'Good luck, and be careful.'

'Goodbye.'

The five shadowy figures disappeared at once into the brown shade of the forest evening. Kupala's shrine was once more deserted.

Masha and Tomilin followed Hawk and Fox through the trees. Night was falling fast, and the two ragged people up ahead moved quickly through the shadows. They went almost to the edge of the trees, where the land had been cleared for building. The two villagers could already see the first lights of their old home sparkling through the gloom.

But then, instead of going into the village, Hawk ducked round to the right and led them back into the trees. After a few minutes she stopped by a tall fir. Then, commanding them to wait at its foot, she quickly scaled the tree, clinging with her hands and feet to the small stumps of wood that protruded from the trunk; even with these tiny footholds it was a feat of tremendous agility. Having climbed for about twenty feet, Hawk disappeared from view. There was a pause, while those on the ground craned their necks to try and catch a glimpse of her. Then, with a cascade of needles and bark, down from above came a small rope-ladder. Laughing, Masha grabbed hold of the bottom rung and began to climb.

As with the Mati's tree, it was a troublesome ascent. Masha found that she was far less sure-footed than she had expected to be. As she reached the top she heard a chuckling laugh: 'Takes practice . . . like most things.' Leaning down, Hawk put her hands beneath Masha's armpits and pulled her up.

They were standing on a slim branch. Masha could make out, nailed and bound to this living wood, a crude kind of bridge, constructed from timber and rope, that went from the tree on which they stood to a neighbouring fir-tree at least thirty feet away. From that tree, on which there was a small platform, another bridge went veering to the left to join a mighty bough of oak; and again, from the oak, disappearing into the distance, was a third bridge.

Hawk did not wait for Fox and Tomilin to join them. Springing away, with the confidence of a squirrel, she ran lightly down the first bridge, rested for a moment on the platform, and then sped over the second and then the third. Masha steeled herself and set a tentative foot on the rough planking of the bridge.

Suddenly she was sick with fear. Her knees turned to water, and she stepped back and clung with feeble, shaking arms to the trunk of the fir-tree, her face cold and wet with terror. 'I can't do it!' She looked down the trunk of the fir to the ground below – it seemed to be swaying, and the motion caused such a feeling of sickness that she sensed the bitter taste of bile in her throat. She leant trembling against the tree. Up ahead, Hawk had turned and was watching her through the darkness. How many times had Masha woken, wet with sweat, from this very nightmare? She could feel now the dreadful, swooping fall . . . down, down . . . and then up . . . into consciousness. In her dreams, she never hit the ground: this time it was no dream, and the earth below would break her like a brittle stick.

She breathed deeply and wiped her hands upon her trousers. She had climbed the Mati's tree, and that had been higher than this. But it had been daylight, and somehow she had been able to overcome her fear. She must do the same now. She must forget the terror, put it to one side, pretend that she was on solid ground. Hawk would not have brought her here were it not safe.

She licked her dry lips. Putting her foot once more upon the narrow bridge, she found that it was firm; it trembled slightly, but did not sway and reel as she had feared. 'I have the courage,' she said to herself, as she placed her other foot on the narrow board. 'I can do it. I have done many things that I thought were impossible. Now I can do this.' She put a hand to either side, where ropes were strung, to help her balance. Forcing herself not to look down, she started gingerly across, her eyes fixed upon the wooden path before her. Up ahead, she saw Hawk beckoning her to come across. 'Come, step along.' she called. 'Such valour we have within us; more than we could ever know.' She turned and swung away over the bridges, from one swaying tree to the next. The sight of the woman's effortless progress gave heart to Masha, and her fear lessened. Swallowing hard, she reached the end of the first bridge, and kept on, determined not to lose sight of the woman up ahead.

The four people travelled in this manner for a good distance. Masha and Tomilin quickly felt more sure of themselves, and almost managed to equal the pace set by Hawk and Fox. Then, as suddenly as she had started, Hawk stopped. She had brought them to the very edge of the trees. Below them glowed the lights of a house. In the distance shone others, and more appeared as they watched; the forest villagers were lighting their lamps, to banish the night from their homes.

Hawk motioned for Masha and Tomilin to be silent, then she pointed down at the house below. On the ground, standing just outside the pool of light cast by the open door, stood a woman. She was a heavy woman, broad and strong, her head covered by an embroidered scarf. In her arms was a basket. She seemed lost in thought as she contemplated the scene before her – the little house, and the light that filtered from the windows, through the snowflake patterns of white lace.

As they watched, the people in the tree saw the woman turn, as if someone had called her name. Then from the deepest shadows stepped a young woman.

'Nina!' breathed Masha in recognition. She craned her neck in an attempt to hear the words of the two women below, but the murmuring of the leaves did not allow the whispered conversation to reach her. The reunion of mother and daughter was thus observed from above by these silent watchers, and Masha felt all the poignancy of the scene she was witnessing from the shelter of her leafy perch. She was weak with relief at seeing Nina and Ania safe, and this reawoke her curiosity. She turned to Hawk, a question on her lips.

Her questions were soon to be answered. As soon as Nina had led her mother away into the forest, Hawk motioned for Masha and Tomilin to follow her. Fox brought up the rear. They went further along the precarious network of bridges and platforms, back into the forest, and then out again to the last of the trees before the open ground. It was now completely dark, and the only light was that from the moon and the stars which filtered through the treetops.

Resting for a moment on one of the crude platforms, Masha and Tomilin began to ask questions. Fox and Hawk answered them indulgently and with humour, reminding them to keep their voices down as they were still so near the village.

'Is this how the Mati knew so much about us?'

'Do the bridges go all over the forest?'

'Who built them? How long have they been here?'

Hawk chuckled and looked about her. 'Oh, they've been here for hundreds of years . . . built by us.'

'By you? How?' Tomilin exclaimed.

'By the wood people . . . by us!' laughed Fox.

'But how far do they go? To the lake?'

'Oh, yes . . . and further.'

'They were the people we saw in the canoes, on the river . . . singing,' mused Masha after a moment. She looked at Hawk in puzzlement. 'How many of you are there?'

'Who knows?' replied the woman. 'Why count?'

Tomilin opened his mouth to ask another question, when all of them froze. From down below came the sound of heavy feet. As they peered through the branches they could discern the shapes of two women and three plump horses. The women were humming a tune beneath their breath, as if to calm the puzzled animals. As Fox scaled down the tree and dropped lightly to the ground beside them, Irena jumped and muttered an oath: 'Hell's teeth, Fox. Do you have to? You might have scared the horses. Why can't you just walk up to us, like most people?'

'Shhh . . . no need to shout. Well done. Hallo, my nags,' Fox caressed the placid animals, but at his touch they shied and whinnied, alarmed by his smell.

'Have you discovered anything?' he asked.

'Yes, we've found out where Vila is – in Alexei's cowshed – under guard.'

'Anything else?'

'The trial's tomorrow . . . not much time.'

Fox bared his teeth in a snarl. 'We'll be ready.' Turning, he shinned back up the tree to join the others.

While the two women continued through the trees, the people in the treetops above made their way even further along the edge of the village, until they had a clear view of the little square where, earlier that day, Vila had been paraded through the market. What Masha saw there turned her blood to ice.

In the centre of the dark, dusty square stood a tall pillar of wood, made from single trunk of a pine tree. Heaped about its base were piles of kindling, freshly cut saplings and great boughs of wood, so recently hacked from the forest that the sap still oozed from them, green and gleaming. Dry straw had been stuffed between the mountains of wood, and in the moonlight the pale gold of it seemed to glow with an unnatural light.

'Oh, my God . . . Oh, no . . . No, it can't be.' Licking her dry lips, Masha turned to Fox in anguish.

'Ah, so they build the fire *before* the trial in your village,' the man said, and he turned to Hawk with a strange look in his glinting eyes.

'Well, Fox, my friend,' the woman replied. 'Shall we give them a blaze then?'

Through the darkness, Masha saw the wild man look at his companion. Slowly . . . deliberately . . . he nodded his head.

8 The Trial

The day of the trial dawned fair and warm, and soon after first light the village was full of activity and whispered excitement. Then men and women went about their morning chores with a nervous haste that seemed to indicate that today was not an ordinary day like any other. As they passed the tall pillar of wood that stood in the square, they glanced at it with awe and admiration – it was so lofty, so domineering – even at this early hour it cast a finger of shadow. The few children who dared to play at its base were soon hurried away by their mothers, as if contact with the dreadful pile of wood and straw could somehow curse or contaminate them.

Vanya was lounging about the corner of the meeting house with his friends. They were enjoying the faint warmth of the sun, enjoying each other's company, enjoying the knowledge that very little work would be done today – today was special, today was . . . .

Vanya had woken early, having slept badly. Although he was glad to be back in his own bed, glad to have once more his mother's cooking, after the meagre and ill-prepared supplies he and Tomilin had shared in the forest; yet he was ill-at-ease. Although he had accomplished all that he had wanted (more by luck than judgement), yet there was still something in the depths of his mind that was taking the edge off his enjoyment. Whenever this unaccustomed feeling threatened to depress him, Vanya would thrust it to the back of his mind, denying its existence, cursing himself for a fool . . . a sentimental fool.

Now, as he leant against the rough wall of the meeting house, he was too busy to brood. His companions were plying him with questions about his exploits, marvelling at the things he had seen, boasting of their own bravery, and laughing lewdly about this strange place from whence came the witch – the place where women dressed as men, or harlots, and could fight like men, could spring through the trees like monkeys, and where they rode upon the water, like their own farmyard ducks.

As they talked and laughed, Voinitsky came from the meeting house where the Council were preparing for the trial. He pushed past Anton and Sergei and stood before Vanya.

'Well,' he said. 'How's the hero?'

'All right,' muttered Vanya, looking at the ground.

'Looking forward to the fun, boys?' asked the pale man, glancing at the young men and licking his lips.

'What's going to happen?' asked Sergei.

'Oh, the usual thing. The interrogation, some witnesses, the verdict . . . then the sentence. It's come at the right time, too. We need to set an example.' Voinitsky's eyes gleamed as he looked towards the market place. 'Yes . . . we have to show them . . .' His voice sank to a whisper and Vanya had to bend his head to hear the words of the pale-eyed man; even so, he caught only a few disconnected phrases: 'They have tormented us too long, the lustful rank girls . . . vomiters of worms . . . filthy, unnatural . . .'

'But who, Voinitsky?' asked Anton. 'Who must we show?'

Voinitsky spun to face the young man. His face was incredulous.

'Who? Who? You stupid fool. Have you never listened to the words of the priest? Do you not know what it says in the Book?' His voice was harsh and cracked as he shouted words that the young men recognized: 'What peace, so long as the whoredoms of thy mother Jezebel and her Witchcrafts are so many?' You know these words – why do you not recall them? Have you been lulled by her sweet words, so that you no longer see the danger? Fools! Fools! Do you care so little for your manhood that you forget the *danger*?'

Voinitsky's face was no longer pale. Instead it was fiery red, though his lips remained white, and his pale eyes sparked with an icy flame. 'Please –' he moaned, passing a hand through his yellow hair, 'will they ever leave me in peace?' He stared wildly at them for an instant, as if he wished to smite them where they stood, then he turned and marched back to the meeting house. As he strode off, he passed Nikolai, who was coming in search of his son.

'By God, he seems in a fury! What have you been saying?' he asked of the young men as they watched the retreating figure.

'I don't know,' stammered Vanya, confused and embarrassed by the wild tirade

'He's mad,' said Sergei contemptuously. He shrugged and turned away.

'Yes,' agreed Anton. 'Who cares what he says, anyway?'

The matter was dropped as a flurry of activity at the entrance of the meeting house caused them all to turn and watch. Alexei, head of Council, had come out and was talking to a group of men who stood beside him. After a brief discussion he raised his voice and shouted: 'Bring forth the witch. The trial shall commence.'

Immediately, people began to hurry from all parts of the village. Dropping tools and leaving horses where they stood, men and women ran towards the meeting house. Jabbering cries rose in the air as people called to their friends, beckoning them to come. Through the hubbub, Alexei signalled to Vanya. 'Come, young man. We shall need you. You are the chief witness.'

Vanya's heart sank. He wanted nothing better than to disappear far from this place – to go and sit by the river, beneath the trees, away from this atmosphere of wild, gleeful anticipation. But he was too deep in it now; there was no way out. It had been he who accused Vila of witchcraft, and now he must stand by his testimony.

He followed the others into the meeting house. It was already full of people. Soon there would be room for no more. All the seats had been taken and Vanya, with relief, began to make his way to the back of the room; perhaps if he hid from view he would not be called. But this was not to be – his father saw him and caught his arm.

'Come on, Vanya. You must be where we can all see you.'

With a heavy heart, Vanya followed Nikolai to the front of the room and stood before the sea of eager faces. There was his mother, small and worried, but looking proud of her big son, as he stood so tall and important before the whole village. There were his friends, Anton and Sergei, sur-rounded by the rest of the young men whom he had always tried to impress. He saw them nudge each other and turn admiring eyes upon him. How could they know that he was feeling as lost and frightened as a little boy? There were the village girls – friends of Masha and Nina – giggling and hiding their faces in their hands, or craning their necks for a better look. Last of all his eyes fell on Voinitsky who, having pushed his way to the front, now stood, arms folded, looking at Vanya with maddened eyes.

'The witch! The witch!' The cry came from all corners of the room as the doors opened and Alexei and Gregor pushed their way through the crowd. Between them was Vila, still bound, her head raised as she came forward to meet her accusers.

There was silence as the two men made their way to the front of the room. But then, as people fell back to let them through, jeers and shouts were heard from the crowd:

'Whore!'

'Sorceress!'

'Murderer!'

'Rusalka!'

'SILENCE!'

The last voice was strange to the ears of the villagers. Everyone turned to see from whence it came. At the back of the room, a tall man was shouldering his way forward. He was dressed in a long dark cloak that fell in folds to the floor; beneath it a blood-red vestment flickered like a flame. Upon his head was the tall black hat of the priesthood, and beneath his arm he carried a large leather-bound Bible. Around the room went the whispered words: 'Look, Atarshchikov . . . the priest.'

The villagers spoke his name with apprehension. They all knew of him, yet few had ever seen him. He lived far down the river, past the two neighbouring villages, alone in a small house by a ruined chapel. He was rarely seen by the people of this village; indeed, the folk who lived close by his little house, and who kept him supplied with food, barely set eyes upon him from one year to the next. And yet everyone knew of him: his name was spoken with awe, his reputation as a man of God was unparalleled.

Alexei came forward. 'Atarshchikov . . . Welcome.' His voice was nervous, and his eyes darted about the room as if searching for some unseen danger. 'We . . . er . . . We are honoured by your presence.'

The tall man ignored Alexei's proffered hand as he strode to the front of the room. He looked about him, his gaze raking the crowd, but all eyes fell before his as, one by one, the villagers fell silent and looked at the floor. As soon as the room was completely silent, Atarshchikov spoke: 'I hear that you have a witch among you.'

Alexei coughed and nodded. 'A party of our hunters found a woman in the woods. We believe that she has spirited away the two girls who fell in the river a month past – also the brother of one of the girls. The elder brother managed to escape.' The big man paused and coughed again. 'Tell me, who . . . er . . . who sent word of the trial?'

Atarshchikov turned and looked at Alexei. His lip curled with scorn, and he raised a bony hand to point to the front of the crowd.

'One among you who wishes to see justice done.'

The villagers followed the direction of the pointing finger and saw Voinitsky come forward. His face, that Vanya had seen so recently flushed with rage, was once again as pale as death. 'It was I,' he said, and he smiled.

Atarshchikov now turned and looked at Vila where she stood by Gregor. At once she was pushed forward.

'Is this the woman?'

Alexei nodded and indicated a rough platform of boxes. Gregor pushed Vila towards it and, giving her a shove, made her mount the boxes so that she stood above the crowd where all could see.

'Has she confessed?' Atarshchikov's words fell like stone into the silence of the room. No one answered.

'No! I have not.'

Vila glanced towards the tall man as she spoke, and the air in the room became charged with violence. As their eyes met, the space between them became thick with hate.

'Why have you neglected to gain a full confession before the trial, pray?' the priest asked. 'Is this to be a charade?' He paused, gathering his sombre cloak about him. 'So be it. I dare say that we shall be able to extract the necessary information without force. If not, then we can resort to . . . sterner measures in due course.'

'We have questioned her fully – but we got no response.

We decided to try her in front of the village,' Alexei answered. His voice now lacked authority – all the power in the room centred on the dark-robed priest.

'I do not like to see the correct procedures ignored. This is to be no mad blood-bath. We do not try witches for fun, you know, but to protect ourselves from the infernal workings of Satan. We have a duty to this poor creature's soul. The fire in *this* world cannot last more than an hour or so, but the torment which Satan has prepared for her in the next is eternal. We have a duty to try and save her from the everlasting anguish of Hell.'

A deep hush followed his words, as the villagers settled down to listen spellbound to what followed. No one dared to move or whisper during the next hour, as the tall priest spoke, questioned, recited from books, and finally called villagers as witnesses. People who thought they had nothing to do with the trial found themselves brought forward to give evidence against the woman. It seemed that every catastrophe that had befallen them in recent times was certainly the work of supernatural forces. The death of a cow, the savaging of geese by a fox, a horse by wolves – these were all, the tall man said, signs of the witch (and other members of her coven downriver) being active in the village: they had been at work for many months before they became brave enough to lure the two poor girls into the rain-swollen river.

Atarshchikov seemed to know of all these unlucky happenings, though no one had told him, and the villagers were astonished and fearful at the depth of his knowledge of their daily thoughts and deeds. Someone had been spying for him, spying with a deadly vigilance; and as they watched the proceedings they gathered – from exchanged glances and subtle inflections – that it could be only one person. The man who had related all their secrets, who had watched their movements so closely, was the same pale-eyed man who had summoned the priest to come and rid their village of evil influence.

Among those called to testify was a sick woman who had lost her baby in the fifth month. There had been no sign of weakness before the day that she had been called to labour, four months too early. This was doubtless due to an enchantment laid upon her by the sorceress. Under oath the woman admitted that, during the early days of her pregnancy, she had been accustomed to taking a stroll along the river; here it must have been that the foul creature had laid a watery finger upon her and cursed her unborn child.

Next, an elderly man was called to the witness stand. His corn had been ravaged by a strange blight while, all about him, his neighbours had been blessed with fine harvests. His alone had browned and died. This, too, was obviously no natural blight, but the act of a malicious and unnatural being.

As the trial progressed, the words ebbed and flowed about Vila like the current of a great river. She did not bother to listen closely to most of what was being said – what was the use of listening? She knew what these people were being led into saying. Each fresh accusation served only to convince her of the tragic simplicity of the truth: that yet again these ordinary people would try to exorcize, through the destruction of a mere human being, the forces of fear at work among them.

While yet more villagers came forward to add to the damning evidence against her, Vila's eyes travelled round the wooden walls of the room. She saw the high windows, the huge barred doors, and the sea of faces below her. But time and again, her eyes were drawn to a small icon that hung above the centre window, at one end of the long room. What was it about this tiny jewelled picture, with its sad, solemn madonna and placid baby, that so stirred her memory? She looked carefully at the golden shards of light that formed the woman's halo, the blade-like folds of her blue mantle, and the look of quiet apology in her dark eyes. What was it? As her eyes once more scanned the crowd below her, she glimpsed a mother holding a baby. As the woman hoisted the infant to a more comfortable position on her hip, she bent her head to give the soft cheek a gentle kiss. Then she turned her attention again to the proceedings of the court.

As Vila watched, she suddenly remembered how, the day that Vila had brought her to the lakeside village, Ania had sat holding Stepan; how mother and baby had each touched the other, as if in reassurance. She had been so fragile and frightened that first day that Vila had thought she would simply fade away from fear, before Vila could give her the anger and the determination to survive. They had sat quietly in Vila's little hut, as evening descended about them, and it had been there, in the darkening hut, that each had resolved that never again would forces – from without or within – ever deprive them of their freedom, or each other.

As Vila's mind rested itself in the comfort of the past, a new feeling of strength was forging itself within her. Whether or not her loved ones managed to free her – and it now seemed too late to hope for that – she knew that they would try; knew it in her bruised and despairing spirit. Even if she perished at the hands of these maddened villagers, she knew once more that she was not alone – she was not the only person in the world who rejected their ill-directed brutality. And she knew that, however many people they killed, they could never kill the fear that these people – that she herself – inspired. One cannot burn a fear away, or drown it, or stone it to death. For the fear is inside the killer, not inside the victim.

A feeling of new freshness and vitality came to her, as she stood on the rough wooden platform. She was no longer alone. As if to convince her of this fact, her eyes met those of a woman at the back of the room. 'Hold on,' the eyes said. 'Have courage. We love you.' It was Dunya, standing silently behind her sons and husband, watching the actions of the court that, in whatever manner it was conducted, had nothing whatsoever to do with justice.

'You have heard the extent of the damning evidence brought against this woman by these good villagers,' Atarshchikov was saying. 'It seems clear to me that there have been evil forces at work among you for many months.' His voice rose smooth and strong, penetrating every corner of the crowded room. The silence was total as he continued: 'We see before us, not a woman, but a most vile spirit – the very embodiment of our enemy; the entire spectre; the whole legion. We have read that woman is more carnal than man, as is clear from her many carnal abominations. And who can doubt it? There she stands. Behold her: vilely clad, a foul mockery of woman. Oh, I had rather dwell with a lion and a dragon than to keep house with a wicked woman . . . all wickedness is but little to the wickedness of a *woman*, for we know – when a woman thinks alone, she thinks evil.'

The tall man paused. For a second he seemed lost in thought; then he ran his bony hands through his hair and turned to face Vila. 'Tell me, woman, how long have you been a witch?'

Vila turned her head slowly to face him; she was pale, but her black eyes glittered. 'I am no witch – but a woman. I have always been a woman. What other answer do you require?'

A slow smile spread across the tall man's face as he nodded. 'Very well. And tell me, how did you become a witch?'

'How does one become what one is not? I have always been as I am – only now I am strong and brave, where once I was weak and fearful.'

'Just so – you will have need of strength. Tell me, now –' Atarshchikov's voice sank to a silky whisper, 'who is the one you chose to be your incubus, your familiar, your devilish lover? What is his name?'

Vila's eyes were full of contempt as she looked about the court and spoke in a clear voice: 'I have none – or many, for all the forest is my lover, and I love everything that is within it.'

Cries of horror greeted her words; the villagers looked at one another, shocked at the witch's brazen depravity. Voinitsky, a sick grin upon his pale face, came forth and pointed at Vanya.

'Ask him,' he cried. 'Question the boy.'

Atarshchikov turned to Vanya. 'Speak, boy. Did you ever see this woman consort with any creature of the woods?'

Vanya, pushed forward by his father, stood before the crowd, his mouth open and his eyes dull with confusion. 'No. I never saw anything. I . . .'

'Did you never hear of any such evil-doing?'

'No.'

'Speak the truth – or burn in the flames of Hell.'

'I . . . she . . . they say she had an owl. And carved many owls out of wood.'

Atarshchikov folded his arms and glanced behind him at the crowded room.

'Very well. Now, woman, tell the court: What was the name of your master among the evil demons?'

At his words, Vila's clear laughter rang through the room. She raked back her hair and looked at the priest. 'Oh, you fool! I have no master.'

Again the room hummed. Vila's laughter hung in the air.

Atarshchikov looked at her. There seemed to be an element of surprise in his impassive features. Then the questions followed thick and fast: 'Where did you consummate your union with your incubus?'

'Nowhere.'

'How was the sabbat banquet arranged?'

'I could not say.'

'What music was played there? And what dances did you dance?'

'Dancing? I'm fond of dancing. But not with devils.'

'What injuries have you caused?'

'None, that weren't warranted.'

'What herbs can you use to cure these injuries?'

'Ah, herbs. Well, I know the uses of most herbs – as do most of the women here.'

A murmur of fear arose in the room at these words, but Atarshchikov raised his hand for silence. 'Who are the children on whom you have cast a spell? And why have you done it?'

Vila paused for an instant before answering, and in the brief silence, a cry came from the back of the room: 'Masha! She stole my girl! And Tomilin, my little boy! And Nina! All lost.' It was Masha's mother, her voice barely rising above the whispers of the crowd.

Now every question was answered, not by Vila, but by wild cries from the crowd.

'What animals have you bewitched to sickness or death?'

'My cows, my best heifers!'

'All my chickens – she came as a fox!'

'Who are your accomplices in evil?'

'The witches – the witches' village. Burn it down!'

'How are you able to fly through the air?'

'I saw her . . . in front of the moon . . . flying!'

'What tempests have you raised, and who helped you to produce them?'

'The storm!' It was Voinitsky's voice, joined by those of Gregor and Nikolai. 'She called up a storm in the witches' clearing. Thunder and lightning. The others vanished. It was sorcery!'

Other voices called out: 'The floods – she brings the floods!'

'Rusalka! She'll kill us . . . burn her! Burn her!'

Above the shouts and screams, Atarshchikov's final question fell on Vila's ears like a deadly blow: 'Has the devil assigned a limit to the duration of your evil-doing?'

Vila looked over the crowd. She looked towards Vanya, towards the young men who stood red-faced at the front of the room, towards the girls who were standing wide-eyed and still behind them. Her words carried clear and strong to the furthest corner of the room: 'No!' she said. 'No! He has not.'

The room erupted in fury and panic. The tension was broken, the inquisition was over. The villagers gasped for the clear air of the outdoors as the atmosphere inside the room reached a level of throbbing terror. There was a crush at the door as they tried to get out. As each villager managed to squeeze through the seething mass, they were followed by the words of the tall man in black robes: 'Confess, woman! Yield to God! Thou art accused by Almighty God, whose statutes thou hast transgressed. Thou art accused by the human race, to whom by thy persuasion thou hast given to drink the poison of death. Why, truculent one, dost thou withstand? Why, rash creature, dost thou refuse?'

Vila looked towards the tall man with the burning eyes and the twitching mouth. He stood before her, with his dark robes flung back to reveal the blood-red vestment beneath. In one hand he held the leather-bound Bible. He opened the heavy book and stabbed at the page with a bony finger. His eyes flamed at her as he screamed the words: 'Do you not care, woman, what it says here? Have you no fear for your immortal soul? Listen! Before you perish in the holy flames, listen! *"For rebellion is as the sin of witchcraft, and stubbornness is an iniquity and idolatry"*. Hear the words – save your immortal soul!'

As Vila beheld him, a strange look passed across her face. No one saw it, but had they done so they may have been surprised by the way that loathing and pity were so oddly mingled in her steady, black eyes.

Alexei and Gregor pushed towards her. They fell back in an instant, as if confused by the potency of the look being

226

exchanged by the tall, wild-eyed priest and the ragged woman on the rough platform. Then Vila broke the tall man's gaze. Turning towards the two men, she smiled, and stepped lightly off the platform. They led her through the entrance and into the crowd outside. The great doors of the meeting house swung shut with a mighty crash, and Atarshchikov was left alone inside with his madness.

9   The Greatest Fire

It was just beginning to get dark when Vila was finally led from the cowshed and out towards the market place. The crowd had been restrained from burning her that afternoon, but only Atarshchikov's final furious command had made them wait for their revenge. She had been put back in the shed; and the crowd had been told to wait for the dusk. Now, the long shadows cast by the evening sun lay deep and cool upon the ground. From the direction of the river came the evening call of a thrush – piercing and endless – as if the bird were indeed learning its tunes from the long, liquid song of the water.

As Vila was led through the streets, she turned her head this way and that, no longer looking for help to come, but rather searching for sights that could make her departure from the world a little less harsh and loveless. And, indeed, everywhere she looked she was surprised to see things that struck her strangely by their beauty – a humble wooden pail standing in a dark pool of shadow; a kitten that turned somersaults as it tried to catch its own tail; the face of a curious child, too young to know the implication of what he saw. Finally, her eyes were riveted by a shaft of sunlight that fell against a rough mud wall. Growing at the base of this wall was a tall solitary foxglove, lit now by the slanting evening sun. Vila stopped dead in her tracks, and for a second, before she was moved roughly on, her vision was washed clear, and it was as if she saw with eyes that were not her own. At that instant she felt, almost tangibly, the presence of the Mati, and in the seconds that followed, as she was pulled along by the crowd, she remembered that time in her life that had been spent in the forest clearing; those long days spent with the old woman, learning about the woods, the lake, people and animals and trees. She remembered her feelings of wonder as her body and mind had strengthened under the Mati's care; the way she had marvelled at each new skill she had learnt, each new problem she had tackled.

Now, in her final moments, she saw that she had paid too little attention to this new way of seeing that the Mati had given her, and which, later, Ania had so readily understood. If only she could be granted the opportunity to live out the rest of her life, she would have made sure of giving praise to this clean, free vision at every moment, and in every action.

The crowd about her called and shrieked. The captors' hands upon her arms could not be shrugged off. As she moved forward, her foot hit something and looking up she saw, towering above her, the slim finger of wood to which she would be bound.

She put a foot upon the first of the crude footholds that had been fashioned into the rough structure surrounding the pyre. Her toe caught in the long cotton shift that the men had put her in – for she had been made to relinquish her clothes. They had stripped her, and put her in an ugly, shapeless gown that chafed her neck and made her feel naked and defenceless, although its great folds covered her like a shroud. But the men had neglected to search the cowshed, and while left alone during the long afternoon, Vila had recovered the slim, sharp knife that she had hidden in the straw; and now she carried it, but it reassured her to think that when they

229

sifted through her ashes, they would find it, twisted and buckled among the cinders.

'Bind her!'

The order came from the outskirts of the crowd, and as people turned to see who had spoken, Atarshchikov came forward. 'Bind her,' he repeated, and he folded his arms across his breast.

A man approached, and Vila saw that it was the pale Voinitsky. He sprang on to the pyre and grabbed Vila's arms. Pulling them back, he tied them behind the stake. Then with a thick rope, he proceeded to bind her round the chest and legs. As he worked he murmured words in her ear, softly so that none but she could hear. Whatever he said, it caused Vila's face to lose its peacefulness and take on an expression of savage disgust.

'Coward!' she spat. 'Where would you be without a mob to commit your cruelties for you?'

Voinitsky laughed and jumped back to the ground. By now the crowd had formed a great circle about the pyre. All eyes were upon Vila, and upon Atarshchikov as he stood looking up at the small figure, who seemed dwarfed by the mighty pine to which she was bound.

'Have you anything to say, woman?' he cried. 'Do you repent of your evil?'

'I repent nothing,' said Vila, and her voice was small but steady.

'Do you still mock the Almighty God, who in his wisdom has told us to purge ourselves of these vile abominations?'

'I mock nothing,' answered Vila. 'But I wonder that you should not see fit to question a God that shows His love for us by setting us against one another, by dividing us, and by asking us to hate and fear each other. Perhaps you should question this mighty sky-god. Or do you fear His tantrums?'

'Vile blasphemer! Do you not fear the flames?'

'Oh, yes.' Vila's voice sank almost to a whisper. 'I fear them.'

'Then ask for forgiveness – it is not too late.'

'I? I already have forgiveness. I carry my Heaven and Hell within me; what have I to fear? But you –' Vila's eyes scanned the crowd. 'You have made this search for forgiveness a terrible yoke about your necks . . .'

'What does she mean?' a man called from the crowd. 'She blasphemes!'

Vila looked towards him. She raised her head and her eyes sought those of the woman who stood at the back of the crowd. 'Do you not remember . . .'

'Remember what?' shouted a young man, shouldering forward. 'Silence the bitch.' But the woman beside him laid a hand upon his arm, and he was quiet. The woman looked up at Vila, and her face was puzzled.

'Do you not remember – how in the days long ago, in order to praise being alive you had only to bend and touch the soil? But now, in these days of an angry sky-god, you must go to a priest who . . .' Her words were drowned out for a second by the ugly roar of the crowd; but here and there a few people raised their faces to the woman on the pyre and seemed to listen.

'. . . a priest who is only an ordinary man. And you must beg for forgiveness, again and again until, perhaps, he will say that you are forgiven. Only there is no forgiveness, not for people with so great a sense of sin.'

'Heretic! Vile heretic! You lie!'

'Start the fire! She speaks the Devil's words!'

Vila's voice rose over the shouts: 'And now – now we are told that the mothering Earth that we come from is merely a toy belonging to this strange, capricious child of a sky-god, and that any woman who speaks against this in her actions, by using the plants of the Earth to heal, or by celebrating Her moods, Her seasons – she is declared a demon, an enemy of the sky-god.'

Vila's gaze moved to the front of the crowd, where the village men stood in rows, each holding an unlit brand of firewood. Their faces were ugly with rage.

'Don't you see how much guilt you feel for having forgotten the Earth. To even be reminded of the old ways makes brave men murderous – oh, how they fear Her, how they fear Her blood and Her clay.'

'You filthy . . .' A man lunged for her with his stick, but he was too far away, and the men beside him dragged him back. 'Lying harlot!' he screamed. 'We'll get you all, you bitches!'

The woman on the pyre looked down upon him. She spoke her words at him, her steady eyes pinning him where he stood. 'But you will not be able to rid yourselves of Her, for She is your food and your life. You may travel far with your murderous guilt, you may make a plaything of the magic moon, you may poison and burn to the very brink . . . but you will not destroy every trace of Her. Her rhythms will prove too strong.'

Vila stopped. It was as if the words she spoke were not her own. As with the glimpse of the sunlit foxglove, it seemed that she saw with another's eyes, spoke with another's tongue.

'Enough!'

Atarshchikov's voice smote the stillness. All eyes turned to him. He raised his arms above his head and cried: 'We have tried to save the woman – but in face of such loathsome heresy, we can do no more. Let her now bandy words with her Maker.'

With one bony hand he gestured towards the pyre. At once a flame was kindled upon a stick. It was Voinitsky who put the first fiery brand deep into the very heart of the pyre. In the shadowy, autumn evening the first crimson flames began to lick at the base of the mountain of wood and straw.

232

As Vila saw Voinitsky lean forward, she suddenly felt the full, dreadful force of her fear, a fear till now so miraculously kept at bay. As grey smoke began to filter through the kindling, she felt a terror so strong that for an instant she was unable to draw breath. Now her eyes scanned the crowd with desperation, while a roaring in her ears drowned out the sound of their cries. The faces below her were like scenes from a nightmare, pale and distorted, shrieking yet soundless. Back and forth, her wild eyes scanned the crowd for the sight of a face that could offer some solace. But every face was masked and implacable.

She looked down at the pyre. By now the fire was gaining a firm hold at its base; already the heat was intense. Once more she raised her eyes imploringly to the crowd, but as she watched, one after another of the villagers turned their heads to look far across the village, in the direction of the little wooden church, where it stood alone at the edge of the forest.

Now hands were pointing and arms were raised; cries were going up from all sides: 'The church! The church is burning!' One by one, people were breaking from the crowd and beginning to run towards the flaming building. Through the sweat that blinded her eyes, Vila could see yet another building burst into flame; then another; then a fourth. In a trice, there were fully five of the deserted village houses ablaze, burning briskly through the dusk.

The crowd below her were in confusion. It seemed to them that the whole world was exploding into flame. But as they tried to run to save their homes, they were brought up short. Out of the shadows stepped many strange figures – wild and ragged, with gleaming teeth and long, dishevelled hair, they quickly formed a circle around the desperate villagers, who stood clustered together as they watched the houses burn. These wild folk, clad in green and yellow rags, were armed with long spears and bows, knives and staves. It was impossible, in the eerie flame-filled evening, to see if they were men or women.

High on her flaming pyre, Vila smiled. Then she laughed. On every side she could see the wild forest people of her girlhood. They stood and grinned, fearless and savage, laughing at the frightened villagers, as if they were the most harmless of foes.

'Vila! Stop laughing.' At the foot of the burning pyre stood Ania, her red hair wild about her small face. Vila felt as if her heart would burst as she saw the woman tear away the burning branches with her bare hands, and begin to climb the flickering crimson mountain. She climbed quickly, ignoring the flames that licked at her feet. When she got to the top, she pulled a knife from her belt, and within seconds Vila was free. Hand in hand, they jumped far away from the towering stake and landed on the ground amid the screaming villagers.

'Quick. Run.' Ania pulled at Vila's hand, her voice urgent.

'Wait, Ania. There is one serpent who must not escape.'

Vila scanned the teeming mass of bewildered people. She saw Atarshchikov standing in the midst of the seething crowd. His arms were raised as he cried for order, commanding the villagers to stand and fight – to capture the witches – and his bony face had become mad with anger as he had seen his victim released. Vila ran through the crowd, and the people fell back as they saw her approach. With a strange look in her eyes, she grabbed a burning branch and holding it aloft she spoke. 'It was not us who declared this war,' she cried. 'The blame for this is yours – the war is in your own minds.'

The people stared at her, amazed. They fell back further, crying with fear, and covering their eyes with their hands. Vila turned to Atarshchikov. 'I lay the blame at your feet, Priest,' she cried, and swinging her arm in a wide arc, she threw the flaming branch towards him. It spun flickering through the air, turned lazily, and fell on the ground before him. As the tall man staggered back, his long dark robe caught on the burning wood. Desperately he tried to kick it away, but the dusty cloth began to flicker about the hem. Uttering a terrified howl, the tall figure was engulfed by a sheet of orange flame. Screaming, he whirled here and there, from one villager to another, his bony fingers stretched towards them, imploring them to help him. But none of them would; they fell back in horror as the flaming figure came near them, fearful of being consumed in the same fire.

'*Run!*' Ania pulled at Vila's hand in desperation. Indeed, the villagers were starting to come towards them – fearful, yet mad with anger.

They broke through the circle of forest folk. Fox and Hawk were right behind them as they sped away towards the river. Hawk was laughing her strange bird-like cry, and Fox barked with delight as he warded off the blows of the villagers with his long stave. Many villagers had run towards the burning houses in a vain attempt to save them; but Alexei's house was now almost completely consumed; Gregor's was flaming, and Voinitsky's was a vast sheet of flickering orange. But still there were many men behind them. The villagers had broken the ring of wild people and were coming after them, pulling knives from their belts.

As they neared the river bank, Vila felt a heavy blow at her shoulder. She fell to the ground, groaning with pain. Hands reached to pull her up, but as she tried to get to her feet, she saw the twisted face of Voinitsky above her. Reckless and murderous, he had flung himself upon her, regardless of the weapons of Hawk and Fox that were poised to put an end to him.

'Filthy witch!' he screamed, his voice crazed and shrill. He raised his fist to smash Vila, but before he was able, the woman tore up the cumbersome shift and ripped a slim knife from her thigh. Voinitsky felt a cool shaft of pain enter his side. He rolled over on to the ground.

Vila leapt up and sprinted across the lush grass towards the river. Before her she could see the broad band of green water, and there, bobbing on its surface, were the boats of her rescuers. Some were the slim boats of the lake; others the long bark canoes of the forest. She saw Irena and Daria in the first craft, their faces anxious. Behind them were Sonia and Zikov. In another crouched Boris, and behind him, with their bows bent, knelt Elizabieta and Ilyich. On the bank stood Nina, smiling. At her side was Masha, and as she saw them, Vila was filled with pride; and as they rushed forward to greet her, she felt the coolness of tears upon her face.

'Hurry! Hurry!' they cried, as they caught hold of the two women and pulled them towards the boat. At its helm sat Tomilin, his face worried, but his mouth curved in a brave smile.

All four women flung themselves into the slender craft, which pitched perilously and threatened to capsize. Tomilin gave a mighty pull with his oar, and immediately the boat was heading for the centre of the river. As they looked behind them, they could see the villagers standing on the bank, their faces full of dread. As they glided away, Vila turned and cried in a loud voice to the men that watched: 'Mark it well, hunters: "And it appears that God hath appointed, for a supernatural sign of the monstrous impiety of witches, that the water shall refuse to receive them in her bosom."' She laughed, and turned to Ania, and her laughter broke into a sob.

Ania stroked the thick, black hair and chuckled: 'Oh, Vila, Vila – what monstrous impiety!' She leant her head against that of her friend. 'Phew! That was close!'

The flotilla of boats was nearing the bend in the river, when a loud cry came to them from the bank. There, wild-eyed and dishevelled, stood Vanya. He was waving his arms in the air, as if to attract their attention.

'Wait! Wait for me!' he cried. 'I don't want to stay!'

Without waiting for an answer, he stepped nearer to the

bank and, with a mighty leap, he threw himself into the water. He sank below the surface and emerged a second later, his arms over his head and a surprised expression on his face.

'Well!' exclaimed Vila. 'What can we do about this?'

Ania turned to her and laughed. Nina joined in, then Masha. Soon the whole boat rocked with their mirth as Vila, tearing the ugly shift over her head, dived from the boat into the river. In no time she was beside Vanya.

'Hold on,' she cried, as his flailing threatened to submerge them both. 'Stay still, for God's sake.'

She grabbed the plunging boy and began to pull him towards the boat.

The laughter in all the boats was heard across the water. The wild folk cried out in triumph, and the lake villagers sang loud songs of victory. Vanya sat quietly, shaking the water from his ears as, one by one, the boats glided round the broad sweep of the wide, slow river.

10 Returning Home

Two weeks later, Vila was sitting on the wooden balcony of the Mati's house. Below her the golden trees swayed and waved, their branches tossed by a wild evening wind. She sat with her legs drawn up, hugging them with her arms, her chin resting upon her knees as she contemplated the forest below her. She had been sitting thus for over an hour, and from time to time she shifted slightly on the hard wooden floor, easing her body and scratching idly at her untidy hair. Beside her, on a creaking branch, sat the owl, its head sunk sleepily into its shoulders, its yellow eyes half-closed.

As Vila sat and watched evening come to the forest, her eyes were drawn here and there to patches of vivid crimson and yellow, and to dancing sprays of brown and coppery leaves among the brave splashes of green. It seemed to her that the wind-tossed forest was putting on a display of beauty for her alone. Sitting there aloft, amid the roaring trees, she felt the same clarity of vision that she had noticed as she had contemplated the dusty foxglove, that had stood so tall and purple in the patch of sunlight, near the dreadful unlit pyre.

It had been like this for two weeks, as if that dreadful day in the forest village, when she had come so close to death, had somehow heightened all her senses — allowed her to listen to the world in all its variety, to smell the sweetness of the autumn forest, and to see the plants and trees with new eyes. It was as if a thin membrane that had long obscured her vision had been torn from her gaze, allowing her to look at the forest afresh.

She shifted once more and sighed – a deep and satisfying sigh from the depths of her quiet, observing self. Then, feeling a chill in the air, she got up slowly from her position on the floor and ducked inside the little house in search of her jacket.

As she moved slowly round the cluttered little room, making a bowl of tea and preparing some food, pausing the while to look critically at a new carving that she had started, her mind went lazily back over the events of the last two weeks.

It had been a triumphant return to the lakeside village. They had been welcomed back by the anxious people with cheers and shouts of victory. The whole day had been given over to feasting and dancing, greeting friends and telling of what had happened. By the time that Vila and Ania had slid away from the crowd and walked back to the little hut, Vila had felt a fatigue so overpowering she thought that she would fall asleep where she stood. Every bone cried out in pain, and her feet felt as if they were made from stone; and the place where Voinitsky's spear had caught her shoulder had become a huge purple bruise that throbbed unceasingly and hampered her movements. She had fallen into bed, but had been unable to sleep until Ania had come and sat beside her, laying a cool hand upon her forehead and speaking softly, until she drove from Vila's whirling mind the images of fire and fear that threatened to haunt her rest.

She had slept for a night and a day, and had woken to find that village life had returned to normal, and that autumn had truly arrived, with day after day of mist and rain. Her shoulder had nearly healed. While she slept, Ania had bathed it with warm water and had pressed leaves of fresh comfrey to the bruise. Vila was upset to find that Ania herself had sustained many burns to her legs and arms, as she had mounted the pyre to rescue her. She had said nothing about them, but had quietly treated and bound them herself.

There had been no other injuries to any of the party. Vanya had swallowed a little water, but not enough to hurt him. Apart from that there was nothing that a few days' rest would not cure. Vila and Ania had spent the next rainy week indoors recuperating, visiting friends and playing with Stepan – who demanded a great deal of attention to make up for having been so abruptly deserted.

Nina and Masha spent much of this time with them. They, too, seemed exhausted by the adventure, drained by the terrible confrontation with their native village. Nina, especially, had been very subdued until, two days after their return, Hawk and Fox had been seen sliding their long canoe across the misty lake and tying it to the wooden jetty. Between them in the boat, there sat a large figure and Nina, rushing over to greet the two wild friends, had given a great cry of joy when she saw who it was.

Dunya had slipped away from the market place as soon as she had seen Voinitsky push the flame into the centre of the pyre. She had been waiting for Vila's rescuers to show themselves, but now, with the fire beginning to smoulder, she could bear to look no longer. She did not know that earlier, before dawn, Nina had crept into the village to see her mother, and tell her to meet them at the river. But she had been unable to get near the house – already men had been out busy with the milking, and there had been no opportunity to see Dunya. Eventually, Masha had come and pulled her away, forced her to go back to Kupala's shrine, saying that they would have to reach Dunya later, when it would be safe.

When Dunya had left the screaming crowd, she had hurried home. The uproar that had greeted the appearance of the wild people she had taken to be the screeching triumph of the mob; she had not looked back. If she had, she would have seen the flaming church and the other burning houses.

She had gathered a few belongings together. She had cut a lock of her long hair – dull gold, shot through with grey – and had laid it upon the table. She had gone to the big bed in the corner and had stood silently at its foot, as she pulled from her finger the ring that her husband had put there thirty years before. Laying it gently upon the pillow, she had turned and left the house. Then she had made her way into the woods.

The next day, as she had stumbled through the trees, wondering how she could possibly reach the village of which she had been told by her daughter, a noise behind her had caused her to turn. It had been one of the strange forest people – a dirty creature of about her own age, but thin and wiry from years amid the trees. He had led her towards the river and had told her to wait. She had trusted him because she had no choice, and, a day later, two more people had arrived in a long boat. It was Hawk and Fox, and they had come to take her back with them.

Only Hawk knew what she had said to induce Dunya finally to set foot in the boat; she had been adamant that she should never venture on to the water. But at last she had been persuaded – and the trip downriver, that had ended with the sight of Nina's happy face, had been something that the woman would cherish for the rest of her life.

The old man who had been caring for Stepan then told the villagers that he wished to give his house to Dunya. He was, he said, bored with living alone; he wished to live with a family. He had so enjoyed being surrounded by children that he now felt he should like to be where there were many of them. Sonia and Zikov, whose large brood loved the old man, said that he would be welcome. They had a big house, and had intended all along to offer him a place within it.

So Dunya set up house by the lake. With her went Nina and Masha, Tomilin and Vanya. There was just enough room for all of them, and they were kept busy in the days that followed, getting it ready, mending the roof, and tending the garden.

Vila smiled at the thought of them all. There had been many compromises made already; as Dunya learnt that Nina was no longer a little girl; as Nina realized that her mother was beginning a new life in her own right; as Masha and her brothers had sparred and argued. There would have to be more compromises. But Vila thought that the people in the crowded house would learn to get along with each other. Nina would spend more and more time in the woods – she would spend time here, in the Mati's clearing, whenever she felt hemmed in by her new family. Masha, too, would be busy elsewhere. She was beginning to spend all her free time drawing and creating designs – working on a huge mural on the side of Irena and Daria's house; and spending whole days with Elizabieta and Ilyich, helping them to fashion new glazes for their pots.

Tomilin had settled down in his new home with astonishing ease. The first night that he spent at the village, he was seen in the midst of a group of children, entertaining them with his flute, laughing and talking with little of his accustomed shyness. If, in the weeks that followed, he had felt homesick, he had never shown it. He had, however, forged a firm and unexpected friendship with Saskia, and he spent long hours in her little house by the cornfield, playing tunes that seemed to give her a strange joy – unthreatened by the presence of this gentle boy, the dark-haired woman began to speak of her fears and uncertainties.

Vanya, as Vila had expected, had had more difficulty in coming to terms with the new way of life. Those first days had been a real trial to him, as he had wrestled with feelings of shame and embarrassment, and an underlying resentment that at times cast a shadow over all who were near him. It had pained them all to see how he suffered, and at last Ania had suggested that he should go out in the woods with Vila, to spend a few days hunting. The villagers had need of meat and hides, with winter on the way.

Vila, although reluctant to leave the comfort of the village so soon after her recent adventure, had seen the wisdom of this, and she had taken the young man on a long and strenuous journey far into the forest. She had listened patiently to his boasts and grumbles, argued strongly with his arrogant assumptions, taught him much that he did not know about the woods and the creatures that lived there. She had even managed to help him overcome his fear of the water, and had taught him to swim, assuring him that no one else would hear of his first clumsy attempts.

Vanya had come to accept what at first had been a grudging and resentful admiration for the woman and her accomplishments. Away from the eyes of his own villagers, he had been able to relax, been able to admit his fears and ignorance. It had warmed Vila's heart to see his eagerness at each new task he managed to achieve, each new obstacle he managed to overcome. It would, she told him, be a long process; but she thought that one day he would earn the respect of the lakeside dwellers – a respect more dearly earned than that of his native villagers.

After a week she had sent him home, back to the lake in a slim boat, having first made sure that the river was completely slow and safe; and then she had come here, to the Mati's clearing.

She had come back for many reasons. She needed solitude. Vanya's presence had been exhausting to her. The lakeside village was her home, and she loved it; but somehow she felt a steady pull within her, calling her to come to this whispering clearing deep in the woods. She had never had time to mourn the old woman who had lived here for so many years, who had loved and supported Vila through all the times of trouble in her life. She had come to say goodbye to the Mati.

But when she had arrived at the circle of ancient beeches, she had felt, not sorrow, but instead a great sense of contentment. And when she had climbed the swaying ladder, and walked into the little room at the top of this mighty tree, she had not felt as if it was empty and deserted, but rather as if the old woman had merely gone out for a few minutes, to gather some herbs or to fetch water from the little brook, or to search for a sound piece of wood with which to start a new carving.

Now, as she moved slowly about the dimly lit room, she still felt the old woman's presence. It was everywhere. It clung to every carving, to every musty clump of fragrant herbs, to the gleaming surfaces of the little bottles and the dusty covers of the old books.

Vila smiled. She carried the bowl of steaming tea outside and set it down on the balcony. Next to it she placed a wooden platter of bread. She settled down to eat, beneath the gaze of the owl, who observed her with lazy, blinking eyes. But then, as if remembering something, Vila rose and went back into the shadowy room. She came back carrying a handful of tools and the large, half-completed carving.

Forgetting her meal, she pushed her hair from her face and began, slowly and patiently, to chip away at the carving before her. The last rays of the evening sun filtered through the golden leaves and fell upon the crude raw wood of the sculpture.

It was of a woman – tall and strong – her hair wet and flattened to her head, her lean features sharp and solemn. Around her legs swirled the tumbling waters of the river from which she had arisen.

As Vila worked, chipping the slivers of wood from the woman's body, smoothing the dust away with her hands, the dark of the forest evening crept slowly over the rustling tree. As the grey dusk enfolded the working woman, the owl opened wide her yellow eyes. Turning her head, she gazed down upon the dark forest. Then, spreading her wings, she swooped from her perch, and with a noise like a passing breeze, she glided swiftly away, across her wide domain.